A chancer and a rogue, Kit Angel is down on his luck. Presenting himself at Rossingley Hall in the dead of night, he begs an audience with the eleventh earl, the most enigmatic nobleman in Regency England.

The visit has purpose. Kit, hungry to ruin the baronet who ruined his sister, believes Rossingley is the only man who can help him.

Lando Duchamps-Avery, Eleventh Earl of Rossingley, doesn't trust the sinfully handsome stranger one bit. He does not care for the tales he spins, his hot temper, or his thick, ebony curls. And, most definitely, he is not in thrall to the delicious golden hoop dangling from Kit Angel's left ear. Lando has his own motivations to ruin the same lord, and the two men form an uneasy alliance.

As the dangerous plot they hatch unfurls, the suspicious earl and the shady scoundrel are increasingly thrown together. Whilst the wily earl gradually surrenders to his growing attraction, Kit can't make up his mind if he wants to swive him, declare undying love for him, or throttle him.

Bit by bit, as mutual desire swells between them, Kit wins over the earl's body, his passion, and his trust.

But in order to win the earl's elusive heart? The scoundrel must risk losing everything.

This first book in the new Rossingley Regency romance series introduces Lando Duchamps-Avery, nineteenth-century predecessor to Dr Lucian Avery of the contemporary Rossingley romance series. With Lando's story, we return to southern England and the Rossingley estate. This book can be read as a standalone.

TO TEMPT A

TROUBLED EARL

REGENCY ROSSINGLEY, BOOK ONE

FEARNE HILL

A NineStar Press Publication

www.ninestarpress.com

To Tempt a Troubled Earl

First Edition, March 2025

ISBN: 978-1-64890-846-0

Also available in eBook, ISBN: 978-1-64890-845-3

CONTENT WARNING:

This book contains sexually explicit content, which may only be suitable for mature readers. Depictions of a MC grieving for a lost love, and discussion of past trauma and sexual assault (briefly recounted, off page, not a MC).

To Victor Lustig, who, in 1925, successfully convinced a group of wealthy industrialists that he was selling the Eiffel Tower for scrap metal.

Chapter One

ROSSINGLEY ESTATE
Summer, 1821

"YOU HAVE VISITORS, my lord."

Inglis floated across the eleventh Earl of Rossingley's sleepy eyeline, looking peevish. Lando swore the man had silken castors in place of feet. With white-gloved hands clasped together in front of his vexed frame, his head butler awaited his response.

"And you have chosen to disturb me about this because..." Lando tilted his balloon of brandy this way and that, playing the flickering candlelight against the delicately engraved crystal. That the evening was late was an irrelevance. He and his butler were of the same accord; visitors at any time of day were unusual, unwarranted, and unwelcome.

"A Mr Christopher Angel, my lord. And his sister, Miss

Anne. The young man says it's important."

One of a pair, the balloon glass had been a gift from dear Charles. "I know of no one named Angel. Begging the question 'important for whom'?"

"He didn't make that distinction, my lord," admitted Inglis. "But he gave the impression the matter is somewhat urgent."

Lando took a warming sip of brandy. The drink of the damned. He didn't especially care for it, but he fancied it lent him a louche, philosophic air. "What is urgent is seldom important, Inglis," he deemed, pleased with his wisdom. Rousseau himself might make a similar pronouncement. "If it's alms he's after, toss him a half-crown, some cold meats, and send him on his way."

The gloved hands wrung together. "I did try that, my lord. But he's...ah...more insistent than our usual callers, and neither is he a pauper. And..." Inglis paused. Never let it be said the butler couldn't milk a drama. "He...he mentioned one of his close relations. His uncle. One...ah...a former cavalry officer sadly no longer with us, God rest his soul."

As Inglis made the sign of the cross, Lando took another, more contemplative sip. So many good men had fallen during the wars in France, and a chap struggled to keep up. "Oh, yes?"

Inglis cleared his throat. "Yes. A...ah...Captain Charles Prosser, my lord."

Like rancid vinegar, the fine liquor soured on the earl's tongue. He fought to swallow it down. Perhaps he should have stuck to port after dinner. Maybe it would have better softened the dull ache now swelling behind his rib cage. *Captain Prosser.* His dearest Charles, his lover. His heart.

Lando didn't make his older lover's acquaintance until after the wars, from which Charles returned hale and hearty. But where French bayonets and the battlefields of Waterloo had failed, the insidious wasting disease prevailed. An annoying tickle became a cough, a cough tinged with blood. Slowly, inexorably, his lover faded away, their time together, in all of its perfection, too brief. A life only half lived; a conversation forever unfinished. Lando, not daring to be at Charles's bedside at the end, heard the news of his passing from a mutual friend some two weeks after his lover had been buried beneath Kentish loamy earth.

Three long years ago. Yet even now, at unprepared moments such as this — and was there ever such a thing as a prepared one? — that name still had a powerful hold upon the eleventh earl. If Inglis hadn't broken the crushing silence, it might have persisted well into the night.

"I have taken the liberty of passing the young man's sister over to Mrs Sugden, my lord. The girl is in a state of great distress. And I have shown her brother to the small parlour. He's…ah…not fit for the library."

Inglis's waspish voice sounded as if coming from an awfully long way away. "My lord might wish to be more suitably attired before receiving him?"

Tipping back his fair head, Lando forced another swallow of fiery amber liquid. For a second or two, it threatened to reappear, then he pulled himself together. Ridiculous. Three years gone and one mention of Charles turned him into a limp dishrag. Well, it was high time it didn't. Time to make a clean breast of things. Time to stop bloody moping. Charles would have hated him squandering his salad days drinking alone and brooding in front of a dying fire.

He cast his gaze down his spare frame. Fussy Inglis might wish him more suitably attired, but Lando gave not a fig. As purportedly one of the richest men in England, Lando could host a ball clad in only his underclothes, and the *ton* would declare it the latest fashion in Paris. He pinned Inglis to the spot with his pale eyes.

"I'm decent. Uninvited callers find me as I am, or not at all. As you damned well know."

*

"MR CHRISTOPHER ANGEL, my lord," announced Inglis before closing the parlour door with a flourish.

If the visitor was flummoxed by the earl's grey silk banyan, of a thinner fabric than most and leaving very little to the imagination, he hid it well. He held his hands neatly behind his back as if enjoying discourse with a chum over a flagon of ale, not begging his way into a wealthy nobleman's home at such an ungodly hour.

Skirting the fringes of the gentry, Lando wagered, he'd travelled here from town. Perhaps a secretary or a senior clerk. A man sufficiently versed in the eccentricities of nobility, at any rate. His dark frock, though of decent quality, showed wear, and his bearing was tall, broad, and strong. Added to ebony hair, unfashionably long and messily tied back with a black velvet ribbon, a straight nose and sulky mouth—all in all, the youth cut a striking figure. Even the jaded, lovelorn earl recognised him as tolerably handsome, and he didn't seem in obvious distress until one's gaze settled upon his eyes. Strained yet defiant, they were the same rich brown as the cognac warming in the earl's palm.

Angel executed a low bow, his words fighting one another

in their haste to escape his lips. "My lord, please accept my humblest apologies for this intrusion into your home. I beg your forgiveness for the imposition on your time, but I fear I have been left with nowhere else to turn."

"Then you must be in exceedingly dire straits indeed," Lando drawled. Not known for his effusive welcome, even his friends described him as chilly. "If you hadn't claimed Captain Prosser as your uncle, my footmen would have shown you the door." Taking his time, Lando arranged himself on the chaise, wrapping his banyan tightly about him.

"Are you?" he enquired, fixing his cool gaze on the man. A single gold hoop glinted in his left ear, an affectation Lando found oddly distracting. "In dire straits?"

The man shook his head. "My lord, I am not, and I do not beseech for myself. I come on behalf of my dearest sister, Anne, whom my uncle, Captain Prosser, cared for most deeply. Indeed, he treated her like the daughter he was never gifted."

'Never gifted' for intimate reasons Lando thoroughly understood. He wasn't a medical man, was vaguely squeamish, in fact, but even he was aware a man could never beget a daughter if he had never bedded a woman.

He granted Mr Angel a small nod of concession. "I heard him speak of his niece in favourable terms."

In his infinite kindness, his beloved Charles had, indeed, told of the girl many times. If Lando's memory served correct, he'd found her a position as a lady's companion, and by all accounts, she was sweet and harmless. With no interest in the doings of the fairer sex, Lando might not have paid the topic much notice. He had, however, given the topic of the brother his full attention and had a clear recollection of his lover describing his nephew as a person of good morals and determination. Though, Lando found it rarely served to reveal one's hand to a stranger.

"He did not mention she had a brother," he lied.

As the young man girded his loins for what would undoubtedly be a convoluted petition for funds, Lando regretted not having taken up a pose against the mantel if only to prevent Mr Angel from dizzily pacing to and fro in front of it.

"Being older when our father perished, I was never Captain Prosser's ward, though we were on excellent terms. Since his passing, I have lived and worked in London and sent money to Anne so that her circumstances were less straitened. Three days ago, however, I learned that my sister's situation had become rather…compromised. Naively, may I add, and through no fault of her own." He clenched his jaw, unable to hide his anger. "In a word, my lord, her hitherto good name and the good name of Captain Prosser, by association, has been besmirched."

If the man would stand still, Lando would be able to get a jolly good look at him. Instead, he persisted in wearing out the earl's favourite Aubusson rug. And he continued to toss his beloved Charles's name high into the ether with scant regard for how perilously close each mention chipped away at the façade of disinterest Lando was working so hard to preserve.

"Your concern for your sister's position is a credit to you, Mr…Angel," Lando observed. "But whilst you have my sympathies, I'm at a loss as to how her misfortune is a matter of mine." He adjusted the delicate lace trim at the cuffs of his banyan. "Is there anything else?"

For most, simply being granted an audience with the

indifferent earl in his opulent surroundings sufficed to cow them. Indeed, Lando frequently used this to his advantage, never more than when the dull spinsters from the church came calling. He had already surmised his visitor was nothing but a variation on that, albeit a more visually pleasing one. Add in the earl's daring state of *déshabiller*, and Captain Prosser's nephew should have been blushing like a new bride and shuffling from the room.

Alas, he showed no sign. If anything, the man was but launching into his impassioned stride. "As he weakened, my uncle assured me that if ever Anne had a pressing need, I should present myself to you without haste. And appeal to your better nature."

Lando's lips curled into the smallest of smiles. "Do let me know when you've located it, Mr Angel."

His guest bowed his head. "Forgive me, my lord, but he also advised that might be your response."

The earl's heart seized. Of course he had; his Charles had known him as well as he'd known his own self. *My darling Lando, why must you insist on cloaking your true nature? Everyone thinks you're a beast when I and your bedpost both know you're nothing but a pussycat.*

Gadzooks, Lando needed to remove this youth from his house.

"He spoke of you often, my lord," Mr Angel pressed.

"We had a friendship," Lando acknowledged.

"He inferred that…" Angel gave a tiny cough. "…the two of you were very…close."

Close. The word hung heavy in the air. Like pipe smoke puffed out on a sultry, late summer afternoon. One of those lazy afternoons, all too rare, both stretching forever yet ending too soon. The kind of afternoon upon which one laid down cherished, joyful memories of one's illicit, passionate lover. The hazy sort of afternoon one hadn't recognised as the very last, precious gasp of summer until it was far too late.

"Were you, my lord?" Angel's knowing dark eyes dragged over the earl's banyan as Lando's grief fought to betray him. The man's low voice was soft as silk. "*Close?*"

Close. As if that brief, disposable word could ever encompass the depth of the earl's and Charles's love. Three years on, and still, the taste of his lover lingered on his tongue. His sweet scent still engulfed him; his tender, murmurings of love still whispered in his head.

And this damned vagabond youth had come to sully it.

With all traces of lazy-limbed languor gone, Henry Orlando Fitzwilliam Albert Duchamps-Avery, Eleventh Earl of Rossingley, rose from the chaise and stalked to the door.

"Get out," he barked, flinging it open. "At once. Before I have you thrown out. Inglis!"

Chapter Two

AT TESTING TIMES like this, Mr Christopher Angel picked himself up from the ground, plucking grit from his skinned palms, and reminded himself that even the most majestic and glorious of swans must have failed at their first attempt to take wing. Though the earl's burly footmen hadn't needed to be quite so heavy-handed.

To add insult to injury, not only had Kit failed to enlist the earl's help, but night had fallen in the interim, black as pitch. Collecting his hired nag from the earl's stables was out of the question, so thus began a slow limp away from the house, Kit's every pained step tracked by two of the earl's suspicious henchmen until he was out of sight. The village inn, where he'd left his meagre belongings in a bare closet laughingly described as a guestroom, felt an awfully long distance away.

Anne was now safe, at least. He trusted that she was safe

from the earl's advances, of course, but also from the male members of his lordship's household if their loyalty could be measured by the magnitude of the bruise blossoming on his kneecap. Anne had been in no fit state to ride with him back to London, and even if she was, his lodgings on Sindell Street were hardly suitable. Whilst not quite the worst address in London, some of the goings-on in the narrow alleys bookending it would make a bawd blush.

So Rossingley it was, where the fierce housekeeper had helped Anne into a chair, her stern gaze falling kindly on his poor sister.

As Kit fumbled and cursed his way towards a sup of ale and bed, he reflected his petition for the earl's assistance might have garnered a more positive outcome if he'd approached it from a different angle. Though, in Kit's defence, Uncle Charles hadn't forewarned him that his noble *amour* was carved from a block of ice. *That* bloodless creature had been the love of Charles's life? Kit obviously hadn't known his uncle as well as he'd thought. Uncle Charles had been gregarious and warm, a man who found joy in the first daffodils of spring, in art and poetry. A man radiating bonhomie. The earl's *froideur* risked melting stone.

He was singularly beautiful though. His uncle hadn't warned him of that either. Even if it was beauty of a wintry sort, savage even. Vacant and statuesque, dripping with ennui. One looked but didn't dare touch.

Nevertheless, the earl was not entirely void of sentiment. At mention of Charles, two angry points of red had settled on the crest of those haughty cheekbones; a flash of fury had burned in those silvery-blue eyes. Even so, Kit couldn't picture the man warming anyone's bed, man or woman. Fires of passion burning bright? More like tupping a snow-covered rock.

With the inn in sight, Kit vowed if he never clapped eyes on the disagreeable earl again it would be a day too soon. Alas, he'd have to return to Rossingley tomorrow to retrieve his horse, enquire after his sister's wellbeing, and beg that confounded iceberg for his assistance in the matter. Again.

That grey silk slip of a thing he was wearing though. So at odds with its bearer. Outside of a molly house, Kit had never seen such a flimsy garment. It seemed almost as if another person had chosen it; the whim of someone fey and light of heart, a frippery intended to please a lover. The way it clung to the earl's every lean sinew and draped across his shoulders, softly kissed the jut of his hip bones — Kit would forfeit an egg on his other kneecap just to catch a glimpse of the earl dressed in that again. Not that he'd ever admit it, not even at knife point.

Chapter Three

IT WAS A truth widely known that Rossingley estate's smooth running rested on the vagaries of its housekeeper's humour. Acknowledged even by the earl himself. Thus, next morning, Lando allowed his valet, Pritchard, to dress him in muted tones before approaching Mrs Sugden's below-stairs domain. Whilst confident the woman would approve of his attire, he could do nothing about the dark circles shrouding his tired eyes. Lando had slept fitfully after Angel's unspoken threat and his subsequent ejection. The sister, Pritchard informed him sniffily, had been housed in a distant wing of the draughty manor Lando never found reason to visit. As far as the earl was concerned, her brother could have spent the damp night in a thick hawthorn hedge.

Lando's beloved Charles had been a reliable judge of character, and a cursory glance at the nervous young woman perched on one of Mrs Sugden's uncomfortable upright chairs lent credence to both his own fears and to Mr Angel's tale. Timid as a snowdrop and twice as plain, poor Miss Angel was as puritanical-looking as the hard chair in which she was seated.

"Miss Angel." Lando approached her in as unthreatening a manner as possible. No easy task when his own noble blood was all too evident in his strong lean proportions, in every turn of his white-blond head, in every expression settling on his fine features — even sympathy.

Nonetheless, he endeavoured to try. "Until you are quite well, my dear, you will be safe here at Rossingley as my guest. I trust Mrs Sugden to ensure that. And if there is anything you require, such as the assistance of a physician, then she will see that it is done."

The girl shrank away from him, trembling in the chair. A less likely temptress he'd yet to meet. A hearty bowl of soup would topple her, never mind a male taking liberties not his to take. "I thank you, my lord," she managed, her eyes filling with tears.

Lando arched a shapely eyebrow in the direction of his housekeeper, a fearsome woman, and knowing her, no doubt of the opinion that Miss Angel should have sought solace elsewhere rather than disrupt the well-oiled machine of her establishment. On more than one occasion she'd scolded Lando for being softer than underbelly of her late husband's favourite terrier.

"If I might have a word, my lord," Mrs Sugden murmured, jerking her chin towards the door.

"Please don't tell me what I think you're about to," said Lando grimly when they were alone. Unless Miss Anne had travelled by foot for days, he only had one near neighbour. "The girl has come from the Gartside estate, hasn't she?"

"Yes, my lord." Mrs Sugden folded her arms across her ample bosom. "And I'm afraid her tale is that which you would expect."

The knowledge his suspicion proved correct gave Lando no pleasure whatsoever.

"The girl has been serving as companion to the dowager Lady Gartside," reported Mrs Sugden. "The dowager usually keeps to a quiet life in Sussex, but for the last month or more, she has resided at the Gartside estate, visiting her son. I shall spare you the intimate details, my lord, but on several occasions, Sir Ambrose...pressed his affections on Miss Angel—affections neither sought nor desired."

Lando could have written the damned script himself. "And did he..." he enquired delicately.

"No, thank heavens. Not quite. Regardless, her reputation is ruined. A housemaid came upon them and reported straight to the dowager, who favoured her favourite, eldest son's version of events and dismissed Miss Angel on the spot. She'll recover, but the damage is done." Mrs Sugden shook her head. "And to think her a niece of our lovely Captain Prosser; he'll be rolling in his grave."

"Quite," said Lando crisply. "Any sign of the brother?"

"Not yet. Though I daresay he'll show up again. Very affected by it, he is. Baying for blood."

"How did they arrive?"

"On horseback, according to the head groom. One horse."

The last part was accompanied by a grimace. Mrs Sugden had a healthy fear of horses, stemming from her firm belief they were as likely to step on your foot as look at you.

Lando turned to leave before she could begin enlisting the perils. "If and when he does, send him to me."

*

MR ANGEL REAPPEARED as Lando was sitting down to a light lunch, improving neither his mood nor the taste. From the moment Lando had heard the name of the poor girl's attacker, his small appetite had deserted him, though he kept Angel cooling his heels in the library. Sadly, Charles's poor niece's tale was not the first of its kind to spring from Gartside Manor in recent years. Ambrose Gartside, Eighth Baronet of Airdrie, was nothing more than a leery drunken oaf, hellbent on destroying his estate and his family's reputation. Those facts, though unsavoury, were as clear as daylight. What wasn't clear was why Angel felt the need to embroil Lando further. And make an enemy of him, too, by hinting as to the nature of his friendship with Charles. Lando had done his duty by providing a safe haven for the girl; as soon as she was mended, he would wash his hands of the whole nasty business.

"His lordship," announced Inglis as Lando eventually swept into the library. Ever suspicious, his butler had not left Mr Angel alone. With a gracious nod, Lando dismissed him along with Jasper, the same footman who'd tossed the man out not twenty-four hours earlier. And from the glimmer in his single eye, Jasper looked eager for an opportunity to do so again.

No sooner had the door closed than Lando fixed Mr Angel with an arctic stare, determined to get the wretched business over and done with. "You will regret tussling with me, sir," he said coolly. "Consider this a warning. My patience with your prettily dressed-up words is wearing thin."

"I have no desire to tussle with you, my lord. I've come asking for your assistance, not to rake up trouble. My uncle's memory is too dear to my sister and me. Though I live in London, I visited him in Kent as often as time would allow."

"What is your business in London?"

"I…I strive to earn enough to send money to Anne and to keep a roof over my head. I cannot see the relevance, my lord."

Seldom had Lando encountered a more evasive response. He gave the glowing embers an unnecessarily vicious poke before adopting a commanding position in front of *his* mantel. His visitor was dressed in the same plain coat as the night before. At best, it was clean.

"Very well. Tell your tale, Mr Angel. My staff have relayed your sister's version; I want to hear yours. Explain why you chose my doorstep. If it's with the intent to extort money from me, under the misapprehension I'm harbouring shameful secrets, then you are wasting your time. If not, you have three minutes."

The man seized his chance. "My sister sent word to me in London, via a housemaid, that all was not well, and I rode to Gartside Manor with all haste. Given the nature of her distress, I was for breaking the door down, but the place is well attended. After two days, another message reached me, and I found my poor sister, Anne, wandering the Allenmouth road alone with nothing but a handful of coin and the clothes she stood up in. You were the nearest refuge, my lord. My sister has been…well, I have just paid her a visit. And I can assure you she is in no fit condition to travel further at this present time."

As if the library were his own, Angel took up from where he left off the night before and paced the length of it, his coat swishing like a cat's tail on each agitated turn. A lock of hair had fallen across his forehead. Roughly, he pushed it back while his other hand tugged at his loosely tied cravat, a gesture reminiscent of his uncle when under duress, and despite himself, the earl's hibernating heart softened a fraction.

"Give thanks to the lord above that she'll be safe here, Mr Angel. My housekeeper, Mrs Sugden, is both capable and discreet to a fault. I can assure you."

Mr Angel's hands balled into tight fists. "You expect me to thank the lord for *that*? Well, I don't! Because someone who thinks he can lord it over everyone else is the damned reason she's in this mess in the first place. Sir Ambrose Gartside has defiled my sister irrevocably, and rumour has it, she is not the first."

"No," the earl conceded. "Regrettably, the rumours are true."

"Bastard." Raw anger glittered in Angel's exquisite dark eyes. "Forgive me for my uncouth language, Lord Rossingley, but I have a mind to break down his door and murder him with my bare hands."

"I…ah…don't advise it." Lando threw him a cold smile. "You swinging from a gibbet will be of no conceivable benefit to your sister."

Lando's pulse took up a steady drum beat at his temples. So far, the man hadn't seemed inclined to further his insinuations. If he was here to merely vent his spleen, he could jolly well go and do it somewhere else. Preferably a long way from Lando's library.

"Your sister has my condolences, Mr Angel," he said calmly. "And, as I've stated, she may stay here until she is quite well."

Angel rounded on him. "Forgive my impertinence, my lord.

But what good are your condolences when this fiend is getting away with whatever he chooses? They're no more use than an offer to…to rearrange my furniture whilst my house is burning down!"

Angel's wretched pacing came to a halt, his dark eyes flashed, and his flared nostrils breathed fire not six inches from Lando's face. The man's balled fists seemed itching to connect with something, and for a second, Lando wondered whether that something might be him.

No one discomfited the eleventh earl in the seclusion of his own library.

"Why don't you position yourself nearer the door, Mr Angel?" Lando suggested, summoning all his noble astringency. "That way, you'll have less far to travel when I kick you out again." Turning his attention back to the fire, he delivered another sharp poke. "It would serve you well to remember that your sister is a guest under my roof. That situation could change very easily."

"You wouldn't." Mr Angel's furious gaze fixed onto Lando's.

"Try me."

Danger lurked in those dark, dark eyes. Gadzooks, this man tested Lando's patience. If the poor innocent girl hadn't already been treated so poorly by a member of the upper echelons, Lando would have had a mind to carry out his threat.

The pacing resumed. "Anne was Captain Prosser's ward, my lord. And that was a responsibility he took very seriously, so much that she took his good name to gain employment."

"He held her dear," Lando replied testily. "What of it?"

"I was with him in his final days before he passed. We spoke of you often."

Wrath's chilly fingers seeped into Lando's veins. Angel's true purpose was about to reveal itself, and it was precisely as he'd surmised.

"You were worth a great deal to him," continued the man. "Which is why I am confident of your assistance. What was he worth to you if you disregard all that he held dear?"

"Ah." Lando's tone was quiet and smooth. Careless even. If Mr Angel had known the earl better, he'd have recognised it signalled white-hot rage. "Finally. And I was just thinking you'd forgotten."

"Forgotten what?"

"The part of the story where you attempt to frighten me, of course. Do carry on, I'm all ears."

"I mean to do no such thing," Angel protested. "You have my word."

"Forgive me if I take your word with a pinch of salt."

Angel, his brow furrowed, squinted at Lando. "For reasons that are frankly inexplicable, my uncle cared very, very much for you. He was…not to put too fine a point on it, dammit…he was in love with you."

A crashing silence followed in which Lando resisted placing his hands around the impudent young man's neck. His pulse slid from his temples to set up a white-hot hammering in his throat. "How dare you come into my house and say such things!"

"If I may be so bold, I will say a deal more. Because it is so very clear to me, from how your eyes mist over and your hand trembles at my every mention of his name, that you were so very much in love with him too. And therefore, you know even better than I that your condolences are not enough. Whether you join me or not, I have vowed to avenge my sister until that scoundrel Gartside falls to his knees begging my forgiveness. And I know I speak from my fine uncle's heart when I say that having you beside me is everything Charles, your dear friend *and lover*, would have wanted."

Inglis and the second footman were already yanking open the door as Lando shoved the man through it. It had taken every ounce of Lando's breeding not to send him on his way with a smashed jaw. Slamming the door shut behind him, he staggered back into the chaise's rich upholstery, Angel's words pounding in his ears. *Love*. Charles's precious love and Lando's most carefully guarded secret had been turned into a weapon against him.

Enveloped by a sudden and dreadful bone-crushing weariness, he dragged in a breath. Lando's staff knew his inclinations, of course, how could they not? But now this hot-headed young man did too. He had been there at the end, at Charles's bedside, where Lando should have been. And instead of kindness, he was twisting his knowledge to… Lando was unsure, but doubtless, it would involve money. All that romantic flummery was nothing but a thinly veiled prelude to extortion. Angel was on the cusp of exposing his and Charles's love to the world if Lando didn't cooperate; he didn't care for his uncle's deep affection for his sister or for Lando; Angel cared for money.

Lando could pay the fellow off, he supposed, with enough blunt to set him and his sister up so he never bothered the earl again. Or, less charitably, he could fight fire with fire, threaten Angel with something untoward, make a subtle suggestion to a friendly magistrate. An earl's word against unknown Mr Angel's.

How could Angel retaliate? The chap didn't have any proof. He and Charles had always been too careful. There were no trinkets, no treasured locks of hair curled behind dull cameo brooches, no damned sonnets secreted between the pages of a dusty, earnest book. All that remained of his short years with Charles were mountains of happy memories now increasingly tarnished by this damned avenging *Angel* with every passing moment. It was as if he was ripping love letters from the earl's heart and reading them out loud, one by one.

Nobody had so much as whispered the name Charles Prosser between the walls of Rossingley these last three years. Lando had grieved silently and alone. His every word, every gesture, and every social invitation turned down had been nothing but another frosty layer concealing the cold white stone buried deep in his chest.

And now, this handsome young man with his gold earring, his brash fury, and his impudence scattered those layers like rose petals, dancing through Lando's armour like it wasn't even there.

Chapter Four

TO BE THROWN out of an earl's house once was careless. Twice, and a pattern was developing that Kit's sore knees would rather didn't persist. At least this time, it was in broad daylight, though the one-eyed footman was even uglier in the afternoon sunshine. Wisely, Kit refrained from telling him so.

After attending to his horse, Kit returned to his cell at the inn, where he nursed his knees and his grievances with a bottle of gin and concentrated his efforts on devising a plan to bring down Sir Ambrose Gartside without the aid of the Earl of Rossingley. Needless to say, with very little money, no status, and no family or friends in possession of either, Kit's options were few.

He could kill him and be done with it, as simple as that. But Kit was no murderer, and as Rossingley had so plainly pointed out, murder came with its own set of unique risks. And how could Kit's own death ever advantage his sister?

For the same pragmatic reasons, he crossed duelling off his list. Like all these feckless gentlemen of the *ton* with too much time on their hands, Gartside was no doubt a decent shot and an adequate swordsman. Kit was neither.

Reporting the crime to a magistrate? That was out of the question too. Not only was it Anne's humble words against a baronet, but a well-connected one such as Gartside could extricate himself from the criminal justice system as swiftly as a snake through grass.

Which left...trickery. Trickery on a grand scale. Set a thief to catch a thief. Set a lord to catch a baronet. A lord with a grievance himself, a lord of high moral standing, wealth, and time. A lord with a secret he would prefer remained concealed. Kit had tried softly-softly, appealing to the earl's better nature, and it had been an unmitigated disaster. It had left him with no choice but to increase the pressure and make bolder insinuations, no matter how much threatening to expose Uncle Charles's deviancy pained him. The earl never needed to know Kit wouldn't go through with it. Kit didn't want money from Rossingley, simply his cooperation, his sharp mind, and the doors his involvement would open so that Kit could crush Gartside once and forever.

Chapter Five

WILLIAM BLANDFORD, THE earl's longstanding man of business, accompanied Lando on his daily ride across the estate. On this cool crisp morn, Blandford was unusually quiet. Perhaps he recognised his employer's reflective mood and adjusted his own accordingly. Prepared for a lengthy hack, he expressed mild surprise when Lando drew Twilight to a standstill at the eastern boundary separating his well-maintained properties and land from his scruffy Gartside neighbour.

"I need the scuttlebutt, Will. Speak freely." With a critical eye, Lando surveyed the overgrown fields and the ruins of a roofless cottage in the distance. "How fare Gartside's tenants these days?"

Gentlemen of the earl's class were sniffy about tittle-tattle, claiming to be above it while fearful of being the subject. Lando, however, was quite partial; that gossip was a double-edged pastime bothered him not. On the contrary, knowing his retreat from society was a topic of clueless, sweet speculation around the *ton* was one of life's few pleasures. In his absence, stories of his eccentricity had run riot.

The question, therefore, did not seem to perturb Will. "Badly, my lord. And much worse since his lordship's father passed and Sir Ambrose took his place. Corn and barley yields have been down these past two years on account of the late rains, yet rents have gone up. I'll wager at least one tenant farmer will be in the workhouse by Christmas. My wife's cousins, prudent folk, tell us they fear for the winter too."

Lando cursed. Gartside had the emotional integrity of an automaton. "I see," he said, then pointed with his slender riding crop. "That tumbledown cottage yonder. Are there others like it?"

The Rossingley estate boasted 60,000 rich and profitable acres. With a more modest 35,000, Gartside was still home to an entire village, made up of a chapel, an inn, farmland, and umpteen tied cottages.

"I believe there are, my lord. Inglis's brother has suffered terribly with his chest these past two winters and blames it squarely on damp and dry rot. His father succumbed from the same two months ago. The doctor is in firm agreement and has raised the matter with Sir Ambrose on several occasions, to no avail."

"Is that so." Lando grimaced.

"My wife's cousin says the baronet doesn't know the first thing about managing farmland. At their family seat on the Scottish borders, his sister's husband does all the work and with great success, by all accounts."

"Such a shame Gartside prefers this one," Lando commented.

"Indeed, my lord. The proximity to London society may have something to do with it." Blandford cleared his throat. "I hear Sir Ambrose finds the Scottish borders quite dull. And cold."

"Succeeding in such a harsh environment requires perseverance and intelligence. Ambrose Gartside, I fear, is distinctly lacking in both."

With a click of his heels, Lando turned from the boundary and back towards his own lush, rolling pastures. Not immune to poor weather, Rossingley crop yields were down, too, the difference being his tenant farmers' rents had fallen along with it. Lando had made up the shortfall with a wise investment in a Manchester cotton mill. Like his father before him, he had never shied away from plunging forward with new ventures. Not of the moneymaking sort anyhow. Moving on from his grief was another matter entirely. At moments such as this, he yearned for Charles's sensible advice to guide him.

"I'll ride alone from here, Blandford." Lando's man of business's broad posterior was much happier behind his walnut desk than precariously balanced on a coarse leather saddle. "But I would be obliged if you could make some enquiries of your wife's cousins. And Inglis's brother. Hearsay is all well and good, but I'd like some proof and figures to go along with it. And ensure they are remunerated for their efforts along with anyone else who cares to assist. But not so handsomely questions are asked, you understand."

"That I do, my lord."

Dismissing him with a nod, Lando cantered away. Astride

Twilight and eating up the hard ground, he filled his lungs with pure Rossingley air. His favourite stallion was hungry to run, and cantering cured most evils, Lando found.

However, no matter how fast he urged the beast onwards now, he couldn't outride his hammering thoughts. On reaching stonier ground around the lake, Lando slowed to a trot and let them wash over him instead, pondering the conundrums of Mr Angel, his poor sister, and his dastardly neighbour.

Emotions he wasn't yet ready to examine nagged at the edges of Lando's conscience. Who would defend the next serving girl and the one after that? Where would Gartside's tenants go when their roofs caved in? When the crops failed? When every last penny was gone?

Lando's dislike of Ambrose Gartside stemmed from boyhood; he'd been a nasty sort of child, one who drowned kittens and stamped on spiders. That such an unattractive, unpleasant boy had grown into a contemptible rake, ruining innocent young women for pleasure and ignoring the responsibilities of his land, did not surprise Lando one bit. It vexed him though. Gartside was heaping shame on his hitherto good family name and ignoring his duty as custodian of the estate and the hardworking folk whose lives depended on it. Moreover, as Mr Angel so shrewdly observed, the world offered its condolences while comfortably spectating from the sidelines.

The young man had called for revenge, with his strong fists clenched and chin held high. A nourishing emotion, it outlasted most others unless attended to. If Lando's beloved cavalry officer were still alive, his fighting spirit would have wholeheartedly approved. And despite grabbing Angel by the hair and booting him through the door—twice—his heart was telling him Charles would have expected Lando to assist his nephew in any way he saw fit.

With a sigh, Lando tugged on the reins, patted Twilight's sleek withers, and turned the beast north.

His destination, the largest of his impeccably maintained tenant farms, sat high on a hill, commanding some of the finest views of the Rossingley estate. If he couldn't seek Charles's advice, then the opinion of the occupier of this property was the next best thing.

As Lando slipped from the horse and adjusted the sweep of his full riding coat, his troubled soul stilled. A sense of home and tranquillity stole over him. He could be himself here; he was amongst friends.

No doubt warned of his lordship's arrival by one of several inquisitive small children, Robert Langford, whose extensive family of Langford's had farmed Rossingley land since time immemorial, waited to greet him. After Lando handed the reins and thruppence to one of Robert's eager brood, the two men embraced in the shadow of the sturdy farmhouse. As the two fair heads, resting on similarly angular shoulders, warmly bent to each other, an observer might be forgiven for mistaking them as brothers. And they wouldn't be far wrong. Lando's father had a few illegitimate offspring scattered around the estate, though he'd always seen their mothers and their issue well cared for, unlike Lando's neighbour. Childhood friends, Lando and Robert had played side by side in the nursery and even schooled together until Lando had been sent away.

"I'm only stopping if your dear Mrs Langford has made a batch of her seed cakes with ginger sugar," Lando announced.

"I'm famished, hot, and desperately in need of your sound advice."

Robert grinned, a grin not far removed from the rare, quick smile returned by the eleventh earl. "I've never met a problem yet that a slice of her seed cake couldn't fix."

Children scattered as he ushered Lando into his modest parlour. By a minor miracle, Lando was a father himself — — and an indulgent one at that. Nevertheless, his lack of enthusiasm for other people's progeny knew no bounds. A quarter-hour bathed in inconsequential pleasantries passed by until Mrs Langford departed, leaving the men alone save for the seed cake and a fresh pot of tea.

"To what do we owe the honour?" questioned Robert with a twinkle in his eye. "I'd have taken a bath if I'd known you were intending to visit."

Smiling, Lando nibbled at a moist corner. "I have come with a proposition for you, Robert." He wiped a crumb from his upper lip and sucked on his finger. Even his own cook failed to make ginger sugar as well as Mrs Langford. "It will involve travelling to town and skulking around. Chatting to some old chums. You may take one of the gigs, of course, and lodge at the town house. Do you think they could soldier on here without you for a few days?"

He posed the question because it was the polite thing to do; he had no expectation of Robert declining. It wouldn't be the first errand he'd trusted to his loyal tenant and half-brother, and neither would it be the last. Garrulous and venturesome, Robert relished a trip into town and an opportunity to refresh old acquaintances. Privately, Lando believed he'd be much better suited to the earldom than himself.

"Our neighbour, Gartside, has been making several unwise decisions of late."

"Nothing new there," observed Robert. "That estate will be ruined if he doesn't start paying it more attention. I had a look at his Chevalier barley in the north fields over the summer. All the leaf tips were yellow." He shook his head. "Riddled with aphids. And if he'd planted Spratt like I said, then he wouldn't now have bollworm running roughshod down to the lake either."

At this point, Lando returned the full weight of his attentions to his cake. As much as he adored Robert, his brother sorely overestimated Lando's interest in barley varieties.

"There has been a new development," he cut in after a sip of tea and a lengthy discourse on maize. "And because of it, I'm wondering if the time has come to take Gartside in hand. I have become privy to a disturbing tale suggestive that Gartside's poor form extends beyond crop husbandry and neglected thatching."

Robert nodded at him over his china teacup with an expression Lando interpreted as disappointed but not surprised. It mirrored his own.

"May I ask why you would choose to involve yourself?"

A pertinent question and one which had troubled Lando long after he'd retired to his bedchamber last night.

"Because it is the right thing to do."

He met Robert's steady gaze. While Lando's proclivities were a secret well hidden from the *ton,* his long-serving loyal staff and half-brother were another matter entirely.

"And because…Charles would have wanted it."

They ate in peaceful silence until the heavy rock of Lando's grief settled once more. Robert Langford was the only person alive who comprehended the weight of it.

"So dig around, would you?" said Lando once he was able to speak again. "Starting with the high *ton* and working your way down. Visit a couple of gambling hells too. Find out which are Gartside's favourites. Whether he has bills mounting with his tailor and so forth. He has deep pockets, but they won't be bottomless. Speak to your pals on the door at White's."

Robert's keen eyes lit up at the task — by a similar degree as Lando's, who, by now, had tossed decorum out of the window, circling his plate with a wet finger and then lapping at the ginger sugar with his tongue as if they were back in the nursery.

"You have not mentioned Charles for over a year," Robert observed in his usual blunt fashion. "May I enquire as to what has changed?"

"His niece has become Gartside's latest toy." Lando dabbed at his lips. "And as much as I'd prefer to do nothing, I don't think I can sit by and let him get away with defiling another innocent girl. God knows our own father had a generous appetite, as did Gartside's, but at least their conquests were willing spinsters. Or widowed, like your own mother. Not..." Anne Angel's pale, haunted face flashed before his eyes. "Not naive and ruined."

Robert chewed as he ruminated. "So it's not simply about the estate."

"No, although I'd rather his tenants didn't suffer any more than they already have. I have an inkling he's running short of ready blunt, but I need to be sure before I act."

"You have something in mind, don't you?" Over the rim of his teacup, Robert's clear eyes regarded his half-brother.

"Yes. Possibly. But I need to be sure of my facts first. And I need time to think."

"It will do you good," ventured Robert. "Having a project. You know, Lando, you can't spend the rest of your…"

"Yes. Precisely."

The exact moment that Lando's profound grief merged with ennui had passed unnoticed. But admitting, even to Robert, that his days smelled of boredom and he craved distraction from it was tantamount to acknowledging that a part of himself buried along with his lover was stirring again. And putting that into words felt like an enormous leap. So, he stayed quiet and took another mouthful of cake whilst pretending he had nothing else to add, and Robert went along with it.

"While you are at it, Robert," he added carelessly, as if it mattered not, leading Robert to understand it must matter a great deal. "See if you can unearth anything about a young man going by the name of Mr Christopher Angel. He hails from London; he purports to be Charles's nephew. I don't trust him."

"Describe him."

Hungry. Determined. Roguish.

"Tall." Lando demonstrated with his hands. "Around this much taller than me, and broad. Muscular even. Perhaps twenty-two or twenty-three. A gentleman, perhaps once upon a time, but down at heel. And of dark complexion, with hair reaching his shoulders. In his left ear, he sports a ridiculous gold earring, like a pirate. Clean shaven, and he has unblemished skin."

Robert's lips twitched. "Unblemished skin, eh?"

"And what of it?" Lando glared. "As opposed to pock-marked or scarred."

An image of his handsome visitor as he squared up to Lando

filled his mind. "I had the misfortune to study it at unexpectedly close quarters."

"And his eyes? I don't suppose you remembered the colour of those?"

"Hazel. Autumnal."

Robert chuckled. "Autumnal? How poetic. Autumnal eyes and unblemished skin. Dark, broad. Why, it sounds almost as..."

"You did ask. I'm very observant, as you know."

A smile replaced the sceptical raised eyebrow. "Just remind me which of my children led Twilight to the stables?"

Gadzooks. "Your young Jack," hazarded Lando. Didn't every country family have a Jack amongst its brood?

Robert laughed. "Harriet. But good try. Lando, it's about time I pointed out to you that admiring a living person is not the same as stamping on precious memories of a dead one."

"I have no idea what you mean."

"You know exactly what I mean."

"The man is Charles's nephew. He...he suggested that he knew him well." His appetite for cake suddenly diminished, Lando flopped back in the chair. "I...I am nervous of... I have questions for him, Robert. So many questions. He knew Charles well! He saw him during his final illness when I could not. I had to pretend the man was nothing but a moderate friend when he was my...he was my everything."

Was. Now, Lando's everything was the seamless running of his estate, meeting his man of business, discussing barley, having tea with Robert. And raking over old memories, shuffling through them like a deck of playing cards, the faces fading with every fresh hand.

"And yet you don't trust him."

Pure anguish pierced Lando's soul. "No. I don't. I'm fearful he's going to try to use that knowledge against me if I don't assist him in bringing down Gartside."

"You are above reproach, Lando. And if he tries, then he'll bring down his own name too. And that of his sister."

"Hers, I fear, is lost already."

Robert examined the teacup in his rough farmer's hand. "Of course, you could always join him. Keep thy enemies close and all that. You never know — you might have an adventure along the way."

"I'm no adventurer. You know that. I've barely left the estate these past three years."

"Then maybe this is just the prompt you need."

Lando sighed. For several months now, Robert had been coaxing him to take up a new pastime or return to society. Perhaps the hour had come. Perhaps he should pit his time and his money and sharp wits against someone as odious as Gartside.

"You're still young, Lando. A father too, with the responsibilities that entails. You have a future. Perhaps you could even find love again if you…"

"Please." Tears, hot and unexpected burned behind Lando's eyes. "I…I am not ready to say it. But…"

"You think it?" Robert supplied, and Lando turned his face away from his brother and towards the window. "That's no crime."

"Perhaps," he admitted. "I'm…yes. A project may do me good."

Robert sat back, a tiny, satisfied smile pulling at his lips.

"Why don't I go to London and discover what I can. And you do some digging of your own by further acquainting yourself with the mysterious Mr Angel."

Chapter Six

KIT'S PREFERRED COMPANY over the next few days became the old mare he'd hired, for the principal reason she had no interest in waxing lyrical over the bloody eleventh Earl of Rossingley. Unlike every other inhabitant of the small village. He even wondered whether the cold fish he'd the pleasure of aggravating was an imposter because the real earl, according to everyone he met, was a veritable saint. A true paragon of virtue, sprinkling charity like rain drops, lowering rents when times were tough. A lord who hosted cricket matches on his lawns every summer, hoisted the maypole himself come spring, and tucked all the villagers up into feathered beds with mugs of steaming chocolate every night throughout winter.

Kit might have embellished the last part, though, from the way the stout innkeeper drivelled on, nothing would surprise him anymore. If it weren't for the necessity of Anne's safety and good health, he'd have galloped away from this mythical El Dorado after the second time he'd picked himself up from the Rossingley rose beds and not looked back.

As Kit brushed down the horse, who had received far more attention from this temporary owner than she'd ever known in her hardworking life, he acknowledged that even if he could leave Rossingley, he didn't have anywhere to go. He had his London lodgings, of course, as rudimentary as they were, but then he risked confronting the delicate issue of…Clark, a Bow Street runner. When the earl had queried Kit's employ in London, it was with very good reason Kit had been vague about it. He could kiss goodbye to any assistance from the earl if he knew Kit was nothing but a common thief.

Persistence personified, Clark had finally unearthed Kit's address. Twice, the Bow Street runner had come close to capturing him, and on each occasion, Kit only narrowly escaped by virtue of knowing the streets and alleyways of the stews better than his pursuer. As dreadful as Anne's predicament was, it couldn't have come at a better time for Kit to leave London. Indeed, now he thought about it, the earl's rose beds were probably the lesser of two evils.

A stable boy sidled in, his expert eye giving Kit's nag a look drenched in disdain. "Mr Angel?"

"Who's asking?" Never admit to anything was Kit's motto. Being chased by a dogged Bow Street runner had taught him that.

"His lordship. And I know it's you 'cos you're the only stranger 'ere. An' they said up at the big 'ouse that you had a shit 'orse."

Kit gave the old girl a pat. "Not up to Rossingley high

standards, is she?"

"Not likely." From the look in the boy's eye, Kit had a feeling he wasn't making the grade either. "His lordship's waiting for you outside if you wanna see a proper 'un."

Kit turned back to his very ordinary mount. "Tell his lordship I'm not sure my knees are up to a third pummelling."

"He doesn't like to be kept waiting."

"No," mused Kit with a lick of irritation. "Of course he doesn't."

Naturally, the earl was astride a horse as noble and untouchable as himself. A full seventeen hands of sleek ebony muscle and taut sinew, the stallion's bearing was as erect and poised as that of the frosty creature sat atop him. In fact, in profile and with the late afternoon sunlight disappearing behind the inn's stable block, it was difficult for Kit, from his lowly position on the ground, to see where the majestic beast ended and the earl, clad in an immaculate black riding cape, began. Not habitually prone to self-doubt, Kit became acutely aware of his untidy coat, hair, cravat...everything.

Fortunately, Rossingley didn't notice, given that he stared rigidly ahead.

"Mr Angel," he stated, then stopped, pursing his lips.

"Lord Rossingley," said Kit, puzzled. "Do you come with news of my sister?"

"No, to my knowledge she remains well."

"So this is a social call."

"Hmm." His eyes slid sideways and down to Kit with an expression suggesting the earl didn't pay social calls to men such as himself. "I rather assumed you might have left Rossingley by now. I happened to be simply passing on my route back to the house."

Something from his rigid posture told Kit that wasn't strictly true. "I'm not leaving Rossingley until I have Anne well enough to join me," he answered. "You have my apologies if that disappoints you, my lord."

The earl produced another little harrumphing noise, though made no attempt to ride on. Not often having the chance to admire such beautiful horseflesh, Kit stepped closer to the animal's head and reached out a hand.

"Twilight does not care for petting," Rossingley snapped. As if to demonstrate, the horse tossed back its mane and pawed the ground.

Kit grinned. "Temperamental beast, is he? Why aren't I surprised?"

The earl shot him another cool glance, taking in Kit's dishevelled appearance before his attention returned to a row of beech trees lining the road, already shedding colour. He swallowed as if it pained him to say any more.

"Mr Angel. You...you said you had been at Captain Prosser's deathbed. So, tell me this; was it...was it quick? In the end?"

Ye gods, how on earth did one answer that? With a lie or the truth? The wasting disease was a punishing master; Kit wished it on no one. His uncle's death had been slow, painful, and absolute. In his final hours, the pitiful captain had died drowning in his own juices, like every other poor sod. Surely this earl must have realised that?

"Peaceful," he pronounced with as much conviction as he

could muster. Even this cold fish did not deserve the truth. "He did not suffer. Captain Prosser slipped away peacefully in his sleep with Anne tending to him at his bedside."

"I don't believe you." The pale hands gripped the reins tighter. "I believe you to be a liar, Mr Angel."

"And I believe you're scared to face the world without him. That you hide from it, here in your private kingdom, untouchable."

Kit regretted the words as soon as they flew out of his mouth. He was supposed to be winning the man's support, not riling him further. But there was something about this immaculate earl's cold-bloodedness that made him want to...heat him up a little.

A pulse ticked in the earl's jaw. After a drawn-out silence during which the stallion remained as still as his master and sweat broke out across Kit's brow, Rossingley spoke in a voice made of daggers.

"You tread on thin ice, Angel. Men have been called out and killed for less."

"But you will not," declared Kit with much more conviction than he felt. "Granted, I am a thorn in your side, but I am also the blood of your beloved. And hear this; I cared for my uncle very much. As did Anne."

The earl's eyes held a coldness Kit felt right to his core. "I don't think you had as much affection for Captain Prosser or care that he died as much as you pretend. I think you have come to Rossingley with the preposterous idea you can frighten me into exchanging money for your silence by throwing around outlandish accusations regarding the nature of my friendship with the late captain. And I'm here to tell you that you can't."

Kit clenched his fists. A vein in his forehead throbbed as red-hot anger swept through him. "Shall I take it that you prefer, my lord, to hear of the messy, cruel indignities, the endless coughing, the bloodied, soiled sheets? Or shall I speak of the consummate terror in his eyes when your lover realised his battle was lost? Even our greatest war heroes are cowards at the end. If that is your desire, then I am more than happy to fill in the…"

Rossingley dismounted with such speed and grace Kit didn't have time to finish. Before he knew it, one of those slim, pale hands only a second ago gripping the reins now twisted around his cravat. With the element of surprise, the earl's strong lean body propelled him backwards.

"Call that man a coward again, and you'll be sorry you ever heard the word Rossingley, Mr Angel. Let alone set foot on my land." The earl's pale, silvery eyes flashed with frozen fury. "And if you utter one more whisper regarding my *close* friendship with Captain Prosser, then you'll be begging for a messy cruel death yourself."

A hot burst of agony exploded in Kit's head as his skull smacked against the stable wall. With Kit momentarily stunned, the earl wedged his thigh in between Kit's, pinning him between his firm body and unforgiving brick. Teeth bared, Rossingley twisted Kit's cravat higher. A meteor shower of stars flashed before Kit's eyes as fresh beads of sweat broke out on his brow. Kit had been in scrapes before, but none like this, none against an opponent so untouchable and so fuelled by rage. As the linen tightened, a panicked gasp escaped his lips.

"Now let's see who's cowardly," spat the earl with a

bloodless snarl.

The metallic tang of Kit's own blood seeped warmly from the gash on his head into his mouth. The hard length of the nobleman's torso squeezed up against Kit, and with it, an overwhelming rush of clean, citrus cologne and fresh male sweat. Dizzily, his mind spiralled between fear and lust, and with a vicious thrust, the earl pressed home his advantage. For a second, they were as one, eye to eye, chest to chest, hip to hip...groin to groin. Kit let out a cry of...something...as his body reacted to the searing heat in the only way it knew how.

Rossingley relented, but only for a second. He shot Kit a bloodless, thin-lipped smile, then tilted his head closer so that his hot breath puffed across Kit's cheek. With a roll of his hips, he thrust again.

"Like the feel of that, do you?" Once more, he ground into Kit, his lips brushing Kit's ear. "Enjoy the feel of an invert like me up against you, do you?"

Without warning, the earl licked a savage stripe across Kit's earring. Sharp teeth tugged on the gold hoop causing a piercing jolt of pain. A hand snaked between them, and the earl cupped Kit's balls in a strong grip. Kit gasped, bracing for a sharp knee or a brutal twist that never came. Instead, his attacker's touch gentled; with a lover's tenderness, he cradled them in his warm fist.

"You want me, don't you, my pretty?" Rossingley crooned in a chilling tone. "You can't help yourself." His mouth grazed Kit's jaw, and as the pointed edge of his teeth teased the skin, Kit's breath caught in his throat. With a low chuckle, the earl rubbed one of Kit's balls between finger and thumb, and despite himself, Kit let out a low moan. His member pulsed; he was horribly close to humiliating himself.

"You may have to reconsider those blackmail plans of yours, Mr Angel. You might need to—" He gave Kit's ball a threatening squeeze. " — tweak them a little."

With that, the earl shoved him aside, and Kit toppled to the ground in an untidy heap. Above him, Lando straightened his cuffs. "You've bitten off more than you can chew, Mr Angel, wouldn't you agree?"

"Quite possibly," gasped Kit.

"Stay at the inn until I send for you."

As he gathered himself to his feet for the third time in as many days, Kit reflected it might have simply been easier to ask the earl nicely.

Chapter Seven

BY THE TIME Robert returned from London, Lando had sufficiently calmed to extend him a cordial greeting. He'd spent the
two days since his altercation with Mr Christopher Angel end-
lessly pacing the library. Fury vied for prominence in his thoughts
with something indefinable; Lando's frustration sharpened its
teeth on it. Like a starving fox blundering into a henhouse, his visitor had demanded Lando's assistance in as crude a way imagina-
ble, ruffling every single one of his feathers in the process. And
yet, the young buck's swagger, his boldness, his *newness*, stirred
up emotions in Lando he'd resigned himself to as all but lost.

"I'm hoping you have come to inform me that Mr Christopher Angel is a crook and a scoundrel and wanted in three coun-
ties for treason and gross crimes against our dear king himself,"
said Lando, as soon as they were alone. "Because otherwise, I
may have... um... taken liberties against his person unbefitting

of an earl."

Now was not the moment for Robert to unveil Mr Angel as a duke's undersecretary or trusted emissary of the King of Spain. Not after Lando had threatened to kill him, then rubbed himself up against him. In broad daylight. Gadzooks, he'd licked the man's ear too.

"Ah." Robert winced. "I have good news and bad news in that regard."

With maddening slowness, he poured himself tea from the fresh pot. "Turns out he's quite an interesting fellow. Your Mr Angel is indeed a crook. But only a petty thief—a pickpocket—and currently sought after by a keen Bow Street runner by the name of Clark. He's wanted for a whole host of small crimes against the careless well-shod, a couple of whom insist the devil be brought to heel."

Robert examined the rim of his teacup. "Unknown to them, Mr Angel nudges around the edges of society. He slips his light fingers into coat pockets and reticules when their masters and mistresses are otherwise occupied. Brooches, silk pocket squares, buttons, and the like. Sells bits forward. When Angel's not engaged in that, he counts cards. And he's damned good at it. He hasn't worked any establishments the *ton* visits. Not yet, anyhow. Earns enough blunt to keep a roof over his head. He's been at it for two or three years."

Since Charles passed, Lando thought. No wonder the youth had been imprecise as to how he supported his sister. "Good heavens," he exclaimed, not sure whether to be impressed or dismayed. "Should I be locking away the Rossingley diamonds?"

Robert cocked his head. "On balance, I think not. Whilst he

is sought after by this Clark fellow, it is my understanding the magistrates only have a woolly idea of his identity. Stealing from you would expose him and his sister, too, about whom he cares a great deal."

"So she is his sister? That part isn't a lie?"

"'Fraid not. The Angels are from a moderately genteel family, hailing from Kent. Following the untimely demise of their parents, they fell on hard times. Their mother died from an unspecified illness many years ago. Their father returned early from the war, much weakened, and never regained full strength. Their uncle, Captain Charles Prosser" — at this Robert's eyes flicked up to Lando's — "did indeed act as a conscientious ward for his sister."

"Not a liar, then," confirmed Lando with a touch of relief. "I don't know whether to be pleased or otherwise. You haven't made mention of women. He's not a…a rake either?"

With a huff of laughter, Robert shook his head. "No. I couldn't confirm — my acquaintances don't run in those circles — but I am of the opinion your Mr Angel is very discreet regarding his intimacies."

Lando's mind flashed back to their altercation at the stable, to the sensation of Mr Angel's taut body straining under his own. To an unexpected look of something in the man's eyes he'd interpreted many times as only a man of his proclivities could. And, though Lando had hidden it, he'd been most shocked.

He took a delicate bite of iced fancy, meeting with his stomach's approval. "This Clark fellow, the runner. Is he actively seeking him?"

Robert considered it. "Yes. He's a tenacious sort and will be paid well for his efforts. Though the trail has run cold, they're keeping a weather eye open, that's for sure." He grinned. "If you're worried that they'll track him here and arrest you for collusion, don't be. He's not that important."

Lando had no desire to unearth how Robert came by all his information. All he knew was that his brother cultivated mysterious friends in a host of peculiar places. Singling him out to his government pals, the late tenth Earl of Rossingley had his illegitimate son off to war for a few years. Reluctant to ever divulge precisely where and in what role he'd participated in the effort, Robert had returned home to take up a quiet farming life, marry, and impregnate his wife many times over. Lando deduced it had been Important And Classified Government Business; he was awfully proud of him.

"And Gartside," prompted Lando. "Does your reach extend to news of his vile doings?"

Robert grimaced. "I regret to inform his lordship that one's reach doesn't have to be very long at all to discover those. The man is currently staying in town and is a cad of the highest order. In the last month, he has discomfited Lord Cobham's daughter most disgracefully by calling off their engagement, snubbed the Marquis of Didlington's wife more times than I care to mention, and if he doesn't change his ways, will lose his substantial inheritance hand over fist at cards. Any one of those reasons would be enough to call him out."

"I believe his estate next to mine is not entailed," said Lando thoughtfully.

"No," agreed Robert. "His grandfather won it in a duel, if I recall. The entailed family seat borders Scotland; Sir Ambrose rarely visits. By the skin of his teeth, he still has the town house, though minimal staff. Recently, his finances have become sketchy on account of his determination to own a bigger stable than the Duke of Ashington."

"Horseflesh is an awfully expensive hobby," remarked Lando. "And Benedict Fitzsimmons, the new Duke of Ashington, has very deep pockets."

Ambrose Gartside had been hopeless at cards as far back as their Oxford days. He'd a fondness for horseflesh too. But as for the rest... Lando could only deduce that the death of his father and the taking up of the heirdom must have gone to his head.

He frowned as a thought struck him. "You mention that he has slighted Lord Cobham's daughter? Isn't Cobham dead?"

"A fit of apoplexy, which he survived," corrected Robert. "Though he's not well. I'll wager he'll have another one any day now, especially after Gartside's interference. In the limited time remaining to him, Cobham's out for his blood. You really haven't been keeping up much, have you?"

No, agreed Lando silently. Grief had left precious little room in his head for anything else. "Perhaps I should make more of an effort."

Robert gave him a fond look. "You should. It might do you some good. When did you last entertain?"

"I'm hugely entertaining," replied Lando, affronted.

Robert laughed easily. "You could always make a start with Mr Angel. What better way to reaccustom yourself to conversing with other gentlemen than practising with one over a few glasses of wine in the comfort of your own home?"

Lando examined his neat, polished nails. "That sounds such a bore, Robert."

"And you have a ready topic of conversation," Robert pressed, ignoring Lando's feigned apathy. "Your mutual axe to grind regarding Gartside and his nefarious activities."

"Yes," Lando acknowledged with a sigh. "I suppose we do have that." He continued to muse, chewing ruminatively on a second iced fancy. "Gartside always had something of the weasel about him."

"I'm inclined to agree with you. The man needs taking down a peg or two." Robert scratched his head. "If only I knew a person smart enough and connected enough to do it. Someone with time and money. Someone respected, dignified. And so above reproach, yet so *idle* that no one would ever suspect them capable of planning anything more sophisticated than an evening soirée." He finished by winking at Lando rather audaciously for a tenant farmer.

"I object to idle," protested Lando, biting back a smile. "I prefer *brooding*." He stroked a contemplative hand across his smooth chin. "Or even mysterious, at a push. A man possessed of depths ordinary men fear to plummet."

Still chuckling, Robert stood, no doubt eager to return to his bonny wife and litter of children. Whilst Lando knew he very much enjoyed his noble half-brother's errands — that they reminded him of his past adventures — Robert also enjoyed running his farm.

Stepping closer, he swiped a finger down Lando's cheek. "But most importantly, the mastermind behind Gartside's downfall should be someone not afraid to have icing around his mouth and a dribble of tea on his lace ruff. It makes him so much more approachable." He performed a careless bow. "Finding one of those should be no trouble at all. And on that note, I bid you farewell, my lord, and look forward to tales of your exploits."

*

MR PRITCHARD HAD served as trusted valet to the eleventh Earl of Rossingley for as many years as Inglis had served as head butler. And neither of them approved of their lordship's dubious dinner guest. In Inglis's opinion, a man sporting an earring didn't warrant unboxing and damp dusting the deceased tenth countess's sixteen-piece dinner service. And in Mr Pritchard's, Angel's lowly status didn't warrant his lordship's turquoise crushed silk waistcoat with the silver brocade. Nor the matching nacre sleeve buttons, which were a devil to take out afterwards.

Lando himself wasn't sure why he had invited Mr Angel to dine with him, nor why he was going to such effort. Except that Lando had behaved, on an irate impulse, in a manner unbecoming of a person of his station. Truth be told, he was ashamed he'd let his temper get the better of him, no matter how much the other had goaded him.

Whilst Lando had occupied himself in the stable yard, clarifying his position to Mr Angel, rather effectively, his man of business, Will Blandford, had been putting the finishing touches to a bleak account of the state of disrepair of the Gartside estate. In summary, if no one put a stop to the rot now, three of Gartside's tenants would be in the workhouse come Christmas and several children would be fatherless on account of poor health, poor prospects, and poor accommodation.

What with Robert's startling news about Mr Angel's dubious occupation, and the unavoidable truth regarding the Gartside estate, Lando could be forgiven for availing himself of a fortifying sherry in his bedchamber whilst shedding his widow's weeds.

"How has my house guest been faring?" he enquired as Mr Pritchard shaved him, sweeping the blade across his jawline.

"I hear Miss Angel is much rested," the valet replied. "Cook's chicken broth is a better restorative than anything that quack in the village has to offer."

Given that a sharp implement hovered dangerously close to his upper lip, Lando stifled his tiny smile.

Pritchard's bushy brows pinched into a single long one as the blade hovered over the contours of Lando's left cheek. "She'll be good as new within the week, excepting cuts and bruises. She's lucky nothing was broken."

Along with the remainder of the household, save for Inglis and Mrs Sugden, Pritchard was under the misapprehension Rossingley's unexpected visitors had suffered a carriage mishap.

"Mr Inglis has directed Jasper, the second footman, to put himself at Mr Angel's disposal before he presents himself at dinner," continued Pritchard, dipping the soapy blade into a pitcher of warm water. "As the gentleman has nothing suitable, Jasper is to lend him something from your late father's wardrobe until his own belongings are located."

He and Lando exchanged a look of dismay. Latterly, the tenth earl had tended to portliness, and, thanks to Napoleon's efforts to run roughshod over the British Empire, Jasper was missing an eye.

"Mind you," Pritchard remarked, "that young man could wear a hessian sack and be the Pink of the *ton*. Despite the earring."

"Could he?" answered Lando distractedly. "I daresay I hadn't noticed his looks at all."

Pritchard wiped the blade with a flourish. "Yes, my lord," he murmured. "And pigs fly, so they tell me. However, he is still not worth nacre buttons."

"Jasper's brother is also a footman, isn't he?" questioned Lando, with a swift change of subject.

"Was," corrected Pritchard. "For old Sir Horace Gartside. Not anymore, not since he passed. He's gardening for that squire out on the Allenmouth road now. Couldn't stand for the new baronet. Didn't like the way he took liberties with the young housemaids, begging your pardon, my lord."

Lando waved him away. Yet another nail in Gartside's coffin and all the more reason to agree to assist Angel in whatever scheme he'd devised to bring the vile creature down. Assuming he had a scheme. Or maybe Lando was simply using the whole Gartside saga as an excuse to see Christopher Angel one more time. The flush on the man's face, the way his eyes had widened when he realised what Lando was about, the gasp from those sulky lips as Lando's hands confirmed what the man's squirming sought to hide had not been…unpleasant.

Buggeration. As Lando topped up his sherry, he grudgingly acknowledged he *was* using the whole scheme to see Mr Angel again. He was only glad Robert wasn't around to tell him so. Pritchard's knowing look had been enough.

*

CONSIDERING THE BURGUNDY velvet full-skirted coat he presently wore hadn't been sighted in public since the fag end of the previous century, Mr Christopher Angel cut a rather roguish figure. It was too big around the middle, of course, and unreasonably stretched across the young man's broad shoulders, but notwithstanding, the man was considerably tidier than yesterday evening and a damned sight more collected. In fact, Lando would go so far as to say he had an air of defiance about him. As if he had lost the battle but won the war.

A now familiar black velvet ribbon tamed his thick dark waves, one end of it left tantalisingly long, giving Lando a curious desire to tug it. He had always leaned towards sultry, dangerous-looking men and tried to recall the last time he'd ever had the pleasure of being alone in the company of such a handsome one. While his all-encompassing grief for Charles was…all encompassing, Lando wasn't *quite* dead below the waistline of his French silk drawers. Charm and flirtatiousness, however, had thoroughly deserted him.

"Why the devil are you standing over there, next to the door?"

"Good evening, my lord." Angel issued a graceful, sweeping bow that did peculiar things to Lando's insides, and he took a gulp of claret. "And may I thank you again for your kind hospitality. I am pleased to report that my sister is in much better spirits."

"Answer the question?"

Angel responded with a polite smile. "I'm saving both your servants and myself the bother of crossing the room when you decide you've had enough of my company, my lord." His eyes flicked down to his shortened, outmoded breeches and back up again. "But I'd appreciate some forewarning if you intend on manhandling me again this evening. Parts of my anatomy are…"

"Claret for Mr Angel," barked Lando.

For once, he was discombobulated. Repartee he handled with ease, but repartee combined with the suggestiveness dancing in Mr Angel's fine hazel eyes, of a hue rarely seen on a man, was another matter altogether. "Come into the room properly."

"I will. But first I must apologise profusely. In the midst of my anger, I spoke some unkind and untrue words regarding my uncle. Captain Prosser fought a hard battle against the wasting disease and died in pain but with dignity and great courage. He was an example to us all, and I should not have spoken ill of him."

"We have both behaved in a fashion of which to be ashamed," admitted Lando in as close to an apology as he could manage. "One's mood should never dictate one's manners. But come, let us dine, I have other things to discuss."

"Why did Charles rarely mention you?" he began after taking his seat at the head of the table.

Under the instruction of the first footman, his guest made himself comfortable at the other end, rendering him as near as dammit in the next county. The sixteen empty chairs betwixt them were impervious to Lando's directness. Angel, however, allowed his rather generous mouth to curve into another polite smile.

"When our father passed, our uncle took it upon himself to take responsibility for my sister — she had barely turned fourteen — allowing me to concentrate my attentions on making my way."

He lifted a spoonful of beef consommé to his lips. Lando tried to ignore the bob of his Adam's apple by taking a (much daintier) spoonful himself. "And," continued Angel, "two years ago, I found her a position suitable for both her modest station and her retiring temperament as a companion for the dowager Lady Gartside." Consternation drew a line between his brows. If anything, it added to his jagged handsomeness. "So, I wholly blame myself for her current predicament and am at a loss as how to proceed further."

Having already devised a simple solution for Miss Angel's future, namely as a second governess for his sister's hellish devil spawn, Lando was not to be sidetracked. He put down his spoon, abandoning his consommé, preferring to save what little space his flat belly accommodated for pudding.

"How did you support her?" he questioned in his most imperious tone.

"Oh, by various means." Angel's enigmatic smile began with a slight twitch of his top lip before engaging the bottom one, then stretched wide to reveal even, healthy teeth. Two delicious dimples rounded it off.

No, reflected Lando, he was not dead at all underneath the white linen tablecloth. Far from it.

"Expand on those various means," he demanded.

"Initially, I was a secretary in the employ of Sir Brandon Gower. An elderly gentleman of the Kentish Gowers and, sadly, no longer with us."

"I did not have the fortune of making his acquaintance." Lando filed the name away for Robert to check.

"He preferred the company of his bees and his walled garden to society, rarely leaving Kent."

"And then?"

His companion's eyes cast down to his soup bowl. "I'd

rather not say, my lord. Not all my endeavours befit a gentleman. Especially a gentleman requesting the assistance of a member of the nobility."

Lando pursued his lips. "Which is precisely why you should own up to them. Or were you planning on lying in addition to blackmail?" He sipped at the last of his claret, then indicated his empty goblet to the first footman, who leaped forward. "Or, perhaps after dinner, you plan to fleece me at cards. Or pilfer my sleeve buttons. Though, as Mr Pritchard, my valet, will attest, they are the devil's work to take off." Another sip. "And I never allow myself heavy losses at the card table."

"You know of my crimes," said Angel, flatly.

"I do," acknowledged Lando. "Very little escapes me."

Fewer things were more satisfying than being underestimated. Perhaps this would be the last time Angel made that mistake. He hoped so because Angel's shady past served Lando's purposes remarkably. In fact, as he applauded himself with another swallow of claret, Lando couldn't recall the last time he'd felt so alive. He smiled prettily.

"You haven't finished your consommé, my dear Mr Angel. Is my cook's recipe not to your liking?"

"It's…it's… The soup is excellent, my lord."

"Then I shall pass your compliments to her. Now, where were we?" Lando dabbed at his mouth. "Ah, yes. You were regaling me with your various endeavours. Specifically, your endeavours to be economical with the truth."

"I can't deny it," admitted the other, finding his voice at last. "Though our impromptu, intimate rendezvous at the inn's stables should have reminded me of the futility of it."

At mention of the episode, Lando's thoughts took wing on a scandalous flight of fancy. "Are you good at what you do? Are you...skilled with your hands?"

"Yes." Angel's eyes were modestly downcast. "Regrettably, I am. I've had a good deal of practice."

Lando acknowledged that with an incline of his head. "And?"

"And I find myself in the invidious position of admitting to my own nefarious doings whilst expecting you to help me exact revenge on a person committing his own manner of sins."

Lando toyed with his bread, determinedly averting his gaze from Angel's remarkably well-shaped hands and absolutely not imagining them roaming anywhere on his person. "Rest assured, I do not lump your misdeeds and Gartside's in the same bracket. Do you use your...skilled hands to impose your person on ladies unable to defend themselves and brag about it afterwards?"

"No, of course not!"

"Are you robbing the poor and giving to the rich?"

Angel spluttered into his glass. "Hardly. I am the poor!"

"Are you blackmailing the Duke of Ashington? Are you tupping the Duke of Norfolk's wife? Are you the cause of the Duke of Denbigh's perennial ill humour?"

"No! I do not move in ducal circles, far less the circles of their wives."

"Are you a murdering fiend with an insatiable blood lust? Do you seize the necks of your innocent victims as they sleep in their warm beds and sink your fangs into their softly yielding flesh as they beg you for mercy? Which you then cruelly deny?"

It was possible during his prolonged period of mourning

that Lando had read far too many penny dreadfuls. And already imbibed a few cups more claret than he was accustomed.

Greatly amused, Angel threw back his head and laughed. "Yes, alas, my sins have been found out. I have jars steeped in royal blood closeted about my person. Indeed" — holding aloft his glass, he dropped his voice to a stage whisper — "I have cunningly swapped out your claret."

"So, which is it?" Lando cried, now thoroughly enjoying himself. He motioned to the first footman to replenish his wine. "Is your petty thieving nothing but cover for a murderer, a black-mailer, or a rake?"

The dashing dimpled smile reappeared, fuelling a fullness in Lando's drawers that two spoonsful of soup and half a bread roll could not account for.

"Alas, nothing as remotely sinister, I'm afraid." Angel's eyes lit up as a further footman piled his plate high with venison. "Your omniscience has uncovered all my secrets."

"Yes." Lando stared at Angel, prying him open with his eyes. The young man's cheeks coloured an attractive dark hue. "Added to our encounter at the stables, I do believe it has."

Too late, Lando realised that three full glasses of rich claret on top of two thimbles of sherry made his head spin. The last time he suffered from overindulgence, Pritchard wisely observed that if he ate more, it would dilute the effect of the wine. But some-times, ignoring sound advice was fun. And, God knew, fun had been sorely missing from Lando's life for far too long.

"Come closer, my dear Angel. We have things to discuss."

With a wave of his hand, a footman scuttled over, and a sec-ond later, it was done. Angel's seat was now at kitty-corner to his own, albeit two settings away for the sake of decorum.

"Much better," he remarked approvingly. "Now I don't have to strain my voice." *And can inspect you more closely.*

Angel's own mellifluous voice and latent, leonine poise were even finer at close quarters. His hazel eyes, gold-flecked this close, sparkled with the vigour of youth. Lando found himself quite unable to tear his own away.

Though he would have enjoyed flirting with Mr Angel throughout dinner and beyond, at least as far as the library and perhaps even up the sweeping staircase and into his bedchamber, the tiny morsels of rich venison Lando permitted to pass his lips performed their duty of soaking up some of the wine. Thus, his sharp mind took over the reins, and conversation ambled between further complimenting the cook and denouncing the fresher weather.

"Whilst unhappily assisting me into this *divine* waistcoat" — Angel's amused eyes flicked down to the mud-coloured garment, seemingly comprised of horsehair, then up to meet Lando's — "your charming footman, Jasper, mentioned your sons, my lord. I was...surprised."

"Naturally, I have sired sons," answered Lando with a degree of hauteur. That he had begat children, given his natural leanings, was amongst his proudest achievements. Not his happiest, mind; the effort had been humiliating and draining. Even now, he winced at the memory, very much an unsuitable topic for the dining table. "Surely you are not questioning my commitment to my obligations or my...my virility, Mr Angel?"

His virility wasn't a suitable topic for the dining table either, he concluded, a little too late.

"Goodness, no," replied his guest in his pleasant, light tenor. "I wouldn't dream of it, my lord. Merely, I hadn't been aware you were married."

"I'm not." Lando pushed his plate away, deciding three mouthfuls of venison were ample. He reached again for the wine. "I was once; I married at twenty-one—a union arranged and agreed upon by our fathers. My poor dear wife, Lady Rossingley, died during childbirth. Our twin boys survived."

For a moment, sorrow washed over Lando. Any young woman's death was tragic, and Elizabeth had been a kind and understanding wife. Given that her own passions had also lain elsewhere, she'd tolerated Lando's needs, or distinct lack of them, without fuss and paid for doing her duty with her life. Elizabeth would have made an excellent, devoted mother. For all of that, she held a very special place in his heart.

"I'm so terribly sorry," said the other. "Forgive me for bringing it up."

"It was a long time ago now." Tossing his head back, Lando emptied his wine glass and permitted himself a watery smile. "My sons are schooled at Eton and just turned thirteen. Rascals, the pair of them. It isn't the done thing to brag of one's assets, nor to admit to caring deeply for one's offspring, but I...I miss them terribly."

He pressed his lips shut after that admission and would have liked to have done the same with his eyes as sudden hot tears welled behind them. It was a funny old thing, loneliness. Caught one unawares when one was least expecting it.

With a degree of sensitivity Lando was unused to since the death of his beloved Charles, Angel reached for the decanter, leaned across him, half out of his seat, and refilled Lando's glass. His mother would have been aghast at the lapse in decorum, but strangely enough, Lando wasn't at all. As Mr Angel's loose and, frankly, hideous velvet sleeve brushed against his own, Lando experienced a strange urge to turn into the man, to rest his head against his solid chest, allow the other to wrap his arms around Lando's shoulders, and let him take the weight of everything.

He did no such thing, of course. Instead, uncharacteristically flustered, Lando expressed his desire for the venison to be whisked away and replaced by the pudding course. Pudding being his entire raison d'être for owning a dining room.

Despite a preference for savouring his desserts in silence, Lando's manners were sufficient that he continued to engage his guest in conversation while simultaneously devouring an enormous helping of cook's incomparable lemon syllabub. Having only touched briefly upon Mr Angel's vengeful desires, now seemed a suitable window of opportunity in which to raise the subject properly. From prior experience, Lando knew that his mind didn't always function at its keenest after syllabub. Already, he concentrated quite hard on stringing coherent sentences together. Syllabub, an excess of claret, and a handsome man were as much excitement as he'd faced in years.

"You mentioned revenge," he prompted in between spoonsful. "A noble sentiment, in my humble opinion, although don't tell the vicar I said so."

Angel's sunny countenance clouded over.

"Yes, I did. Two days ago, I had a mind to break down Gartside's door and kill him with my bare hands." He examined his large square hands as if still toying with the notion. "But on reflection, my lord, and your sage counsel against it, I have concluded that murder is too good for him. Instead, I want his life to be a long and painful one, overflowing with suffering. I want to see him banished from society, scorned by his friends, and fleeing with his tail between his legs from everything and everyone he knows. Humbled, mocked, and outcast."

"I beg you, sir," Lando drawled. "Don't hold back on my account. Pray make your desires clear."

Mr Angel huffed an apologetic laugh. "Forgive me, but such is the bitter strength of my hatred for the man."

His fist clenched around the fragile stem of his wine glass, his tanned cheeks flooded with colour. Truly, the man was a vision in burgundy velvet.

"But I require your assistance," Angel continued. Those gold-flecked eyes blazed with righteous fury. Lando blinked, his own feeling rather claret-hazed.

"I have approached you badly." Angel pursed his lips. "I realise that now. But if you would still be so gracious to give the matter your consideration, I would be your ever faithful servant." As he awaited Lando's response, the anger in his eyes faded. Amusement danced in its place. "But do give the syllabub your full appreciation first."

He treated Lando to the dimples again, a wholly unfair means of persuasion. "And if I may be so bold, my lord," he added with an audacious wink. "I can't help noticing that your gold fob watch has been half-inched by the invisible dinner guest sitting to your right."

*

TOO SOZZLED BY half, Lando didn't remember sojourning to the library. Nor how a nip of his finest French brandy found itself clasped in his hand. After gulping down half of it, something he'd most certainly regret in the morning, he recalled that the sloe-eyed devil currently leaning against his own mantel had performed a rather fantabulous sleight of hand. Lando felt faintly dizzy.

"Bravo, sir," he said weakly from his favourite bergère. "I shall ask Inglis to count the silver spoons very thoroughly on the morrow."

His guest gave a low chuckle. "That won't be necessary, my lord."

The man could at least have had the decency to look sheepish. Instead, his solid elbow rested on Lando's mantel as if the wretched thing had been constructed for that very purpose. And his lips still had that plump, ripe air about them, as if tempting someone to take a nibble. Studying his brandy glass, Lando endeavoured to marshal his tipsy thoughts.

"You amuse me, Mr Angel," he said eventually. "You have shown dogged persistence and clearly care very much for your sister. And, I believe —" He swallowed, and his eyes darted to the fireplace. " — you cared for Captain Prosser. As he did for the both of you. Gartside is a rake and a bounder and should not be allowed to continue in his current form. So, I am going to assist you."

Angel didn't answer directly. He gazed into the fire for a minute or two first, swirling his brandy in his glass before lifting it to his lips. With the tip of his thumb, he wiped a drop from the corner of his mouth before licking the thumb thoughtfully as if choosing his words with great care. At last, he levelled that dark gaze on Lando.

"You are a good man, my lord. Kind and moral. Everything, in fact, that Gartside is not."

"I'm not impervious to flattery, Mr Angel, but one doesn't take the law into one's own hands simply because a person's morals do not match one's own. Society would come to a crashing halt. And yet, I have been moved to action not simply because of Captain Prosser's love for his poor niece or sympathy for Gartside's scattered by-blows. In addition to that, the man is not fit to run an estate, and his family's reputation and his people are suffering."

"Ruination of a man such as Gartside is a tall order."

"Yes. It is. I have the beginnings of a plan, but it will require a degree of cunning. And is not without risk."

"May I ask as to the nature of that plan?"

With effort, Lando cocked his brow at him. A rush of tiredness accompanied the rich brandy. Sparring with Mr Angel, as pleasant as it was, had exhausted him. His bed was calling. But Lando could leave his guest with one last surprise.

"I'll give you a flavour if it," he replied sleepily. "Whilst you are adept at petty thievery, Mr Angel, I'm going to raise the stakes with some thievery of my own." Lando paused a beat, his vision now hazier still. "On a grand scale."

He'd eaten too sparingly at dinner, been plied with claret, flattered, and charmed. Yet, his stupendous idea had been bursting to be shared ever since he'd had his epiphany, whilst idling in his bed that morning. His lonely bed.

Lando threw Mr Angel a glittering stare. "I'm going to steal his estate."

Mr Angel's scoffing wasn't quite the effect he'd been after. "His estate?" He scoffed some more. "Estates aren't like fob watches, my lord. One cannot distract Gartside with…with pretty words and topping up a drink while pinching his property from under his nose."

Ah, so that was when it had happened. "I'm fully aware."

"So, how on earth do you plan to do it?" demanded Angel impatiently.

Truth be told, Lando could hardly remember anymore. He couldn't think clearly at all. He was too foxed on brandy. The drink of the damned. And his bergère was so terribly comfortable, he could curl up on it and sleep for a week. With a sigh, not too far removed from a yawn, Lando's pale blue eyes fluttered closed.

"Ah…all in good time, Mr Angel. All in good time."

With a little *chink,* Lando felt his fob watch drop into his waistcoat pocket. Sweet-scented breath gusted across his ear, like the ghost of a faded summer afternoon. Cool fingers loitered on his jaw, followed by the press of soft lips. In welcome, Lando's own parted, and his mind wandered back in time, back to that summer of a thousand July's when his lover's kiss had stolen his heart.

When soft lips pressed against his a second time, Lando's eyes flew open to be met by a pair of dazzling autumnal ones.

"Charles fretted about you, my lord." Angel's mouth caressed Lando's. "As he lay dying. He was fearful you would grieve his loss in silence. And I promised that if ever our paths were to cross, I was to pass on his sorrow that you were not able to be by his side at the end."

"And is bewitching me how he requested you do it?"

Mr Angel chuckled, low in his throat. A rather glorious sound. "I daresay not."

Lando sought his mouth again, chasing that chuckle. "I am damned," he whispered as he lost himself to the kiss.

"Then we shall be damned together," returned a voice like warm silk.

Chapter Eight

THE ELEVENTH EARL of Rossingley woke late, still spreadeagled in the same awkward position in which he'd crashed across his bed at some godforsaken hour last night. His mouth felt like a repository for crushed dead flies, and when he attempted to extract his head from its wedged position between his mattress and his Louis XV chevet, his neck creaked alarmingly.

"Good afternoon, my lord," said a breezy voice approximating his valet's. It was distressingly grating. "Tea and a coddled egg? Or would you prefer to remove last night's attire and bathe first?"

Lando's swift reply was most unnoble. He lay, mewling, as Pritchard fussed around him, each brush of cloth, each trickle of water, each pad of softly shod foot on thick Aubusson ringing in his head as if a screech owl was nesting on his shoulder.

"I may have overcooked things last night, Pritchard," he croaked after the pitiful whimpering failed to achieve the desired level of concern. "And my neck hurts."

Bravely, Lando stretched it, this way and that, tempted to ask Pritchard to give it a rub but fearful the man's touch might prove too vigorous for his fragile brain. Perhaps hanging himself over the side of the bed would help iron it out.

"I imagine, for a couple of seconds, those ancient torture rack thingies feel incredible, don't you, Pritchard?" Lando prodded at his knobbly upper back.

"If only they didn't leave a man too dead to appreciate it," answered Pritchard, his tone dry as sand. He was used to Lando's flights of fancy. "It's their only fault, really."

Lando groaned, wondering if death might be more pleasant than his current state of woe. But then he looked blearily down at his rumpled, ruined shirt from the evening before and suddenly remembered that kiss (or a misty, foxed version of it, anyhow). And what a kiss!

A giddy smile spread across his waxy features, and all thoughts of death vanished. Mr Angel had stolen his fob watch and then kissed him! What a delicious sleight of mouth, sleight of tongue, sleight of mind! Once more, his insides turned molten, nothing to do with the mound of syllabub and strong liquor marinating there but everything to do with that wonderful, extraordinary, heart-stopping kiss. Mixed with a not inconsiderable cool draught of relief that Mr Angel was, incredibly, of the lavender persuasion too. So, not a blackmailer after all, which would have been a terrible bore.

"Actually, an egg might be just the ticket." Lando beamed at

Pritchard as he scrambled to sit up against his pillows. "And then I fancy I shall spend the day here, resting." *Daydreaming* of ebony hair and velvet ribbons and hazel eyes and…

A constipated look crossed Pritchard's face. "That won't be possible, my lord. Mr Robert Langford awaits you in the library. He is keen to hear how you fared at dinner with your young guest. A dreadfully tedious evening, I take it?"

"So tedious," agreed Lando, careful not to catch his valet's eye. "No wonder I availed myself of an uncommon amount of brandy. The only way one could endure it."

"I can only imagine, my lord." Tutting, Pritchard held up Lando's ruined waistcoat. "An entire evening alone with a young man as singularly unattractive as Mr Angel."

"My thoughts exactly. Send Robert up! And pass me my banyan. The rose silk one. I'll conduct our meeting from here."

Another pained expression. "He…ah…he thought you might say that and asked me to pass on his apologies. He said, and I quote, 'inform his lordship that until he is sober and dressed in a fashion fit for a peer of the realm, his cake will be awaiting him in the library. And might be all gone if he isn't smart about it.'"

Lando pouted. "Buggeration."

*

STILL POUTING, LANDO, dressed in shirt sleeves and a ravishing aquamarine waistcoat paired with a peacock-patterned cravat swept into the library. Robert Langford, dressed in his plain grey riding coat, lounged in Lando's favourite armchair, picking through a plate of iced fancies. If Robert selected Lando's favourite of those, he might have a conniption. The coddled egg had defeated his tender stomach, so sugared almonds might be exactly what the doctor ordered.

"Why did you insist I meet you here, Robert? I should be abed." He clutched his head as if it might fall off. "I have a terrible pounding at my temples. It must be the change in the weather."

"Then you have my sympathies." Robert smiled sweetly, reminiscent of Lando's own, when he was in the mood for smiling. "Inglis informs me you were drunk as a wheelbarrow last night. Do you think the two things could possibly be connected in any way?"

As Lando collapsed into his comfy rosewood daybed, one arm flung across his brow, Robert took pity on him by placing a cup of tea in his other outstretched hand.

"Your visitor is perhaps a little more used to strong liquor than you." Robert drank deeply.

Lando peeled open a bleary eye. "Have you come to gloat?"

"No. How was it?"

"It was…" Lando sighed. He might as well tell Robert everything. He'd prise it out of him eventually anyhow; he always did. "We can put our blackmail concerns to bed. Mr Christopher Angel has rather shown his hand in that direction."

Robert raised a questioning eyebrow.

"He kissed me," said Lando flatly. "I was…quite foxed."

Robert snorted. "And he was quite brave."

"Yes. He is brave. He…he doesn't seem to be fooled by my…my exterior. In much the same way as it didn't fool Charles." Lando closed his eyes again. "Or you."

"So you like him."

"Possibly." He paused. "I like his mouth, anyhow. Isn't that enough for now? A man's heart and his…his physical needs are not one and the same, Robert. One is quite capable of placating the latter without involving the former. As long as one retains the upper hand. Surely, you know that."

Robert let out a guffaw and helped himself to another iced fancy. "It's too soon in the morning to be hearing about your needs. Let me dampen them for you."

He pulled out a piece of paper. "I have Will Blandford's summary of his enquiries into the goings on at Gartside, in addition to my own. At the last count, Gartside has three by-blows roaming feral, sleeping in barns, and relying on the goodness of the village ladies."

Robert could have been describing his own fate if his and Lando's father had been such a man as Gartside.

"The rest of it is outlined here. Cottages requiring work with a description of repairs and the costs needed for each. Wages, crops, the deplorable state of the schoolhouse." Robert stood to depart. "I can't stay, I'm afraid. I have fields to plough."

Handing the list to Lando, his eyes flashed with anger. "Take it. Fuel your plan with it. Whatever assistance you need, I'll be only too happy to provide. And as for the by-blows, come the winter months and they need good food and beds, you know where I am."

*

LANDO'S CONFIDENCE IN his ability to retain the upper hand with Mr Angel lasted for the length of time it took for his handsome guest to arrange himself in a chair in Lando's majestic library, thank Lando for his generous hospitality — again — then fix that warm, honeyed gaze on his host. There was a strength in it, Lando decided, feeling decidedly weak by comparison, a penetrating intensity. Added to a lethal concoction of boyish charm and self-possession. And Lando admitted he was quite flayed open by it.

"I trust your sister is on the mend," he opened, grateful for the barrier of his solid mahogany desk.

"Very much so," agreed Angel. "Thus, we should not trespass on your hospitality any further. Already, you have done so much."

Lando waved him away. "I have only done what your uncle would have wished. I believe, via a… um… circuitous route, we have established that."

He swallowed, struck by a pang of guilt for referring to his beloved whilst entertaining lustful fancies for his nephew. Somehow, this dimpled, perplexing youth, with his whispered messages and his lush mouth, made any desires Lando held in that direction feel less like a betrayal of Charles's memory and more a natural fork in the road dividing the past and the future.

"And to that end, I have a proposal for Anne," Lando continued. "My dearest sister over at Horton is seeking a governess for her three daughters. Her husband, Sir Angus, is a kindly man, and a Member of Parliament. He rarely entertains in the country. In fact, he is rarely in the country himself. The family join him in London once in a blue moon, so you can be assured your sister will not be plagued by unwanted male attention. I take it she reads and writes adequately?"

"More than," answered Angel promptly. "Her nose is

forever in a book. She is also uncommonly skilled at the pianoforte and has a smattering of French." His shoulders dropped with relief. "All she has ever wanted is a simple country life. She would be most grateful, my lord. As am I. I don't know how I could ever adequately thank you."

Lando could enumerate several ways, a few of them encompassing the sturdy desk currently separating his newfound unseemly desires from his grateful guest. Nobly, however, he stayed quiet, as befitted his station.

"Then that's settled. I'll have one of my chambermaids accompany her on the trip and stay with her for a time until Anne is totally at ease. I'm confident she will find my sister's scholarly household to her liking."

Angel rose to his feet. "Thus, my lord. I shall also beg to take your leave. My family must not trouble your generosity any longer."

Gadzooks, no. "I...ah...I haven't quite finished with you yet." Heat rose up Lando's neck; that sentence hadn't come out the way he'd intended. "What I mean to say is that you and I have unfinished business."

He wasn't convinced that was any better, but at least Angel sat back down again. A curious smile played on his lips.

There was a pause whilst Lando formulated his next few sentences. The plan that had been assembling at the fringes of his consciousness had now, since his discussion with Robert, taken full bloom. It was a plan so bold he could hardly believe his underemployed, overindulged mind had conjured it.

"If I was a bit vague last night, it is because I have been thinking long and hard about what to do about Gartside," Lando began with a nervous glance up at his guest. *And nothing to do with too much brandy.* "I have also been making discreet enquiries."

He pursed his lips. "In my possession is written proof that your poor sister is not the only girl of whom the baronet has taken advantage. Furthermore, he is an appalling landlord, and loyal Gartside tenants are suffering — matters which I can also demonstrate. He has gambling debts and several examples of poor form around the *ton*. And if he is not taken in hand, there will be nothing left to show for his esteemed father's efforts. Sir Horace Gartside, a dear friend of my father's, was a good, honest man."

"So I gather. The dowager Lady Gartside was also kind, if oblivious to her son's behaviour. Anne had a fondness for her."

Lando inhaled deeply. "In summary, we will not stand by and watch innocent women and poor countryfolk suffer while he racks up debts. I have devised a scheme to teach him a lesson he will never forget."

Angel would be forgiven for wondering where his languid, playful earl had disappeared; this one had fire in his belly and a gimlet eye. "You mentioned stealing the estate, my lord. Ah... how do you propose we do that?"

"By sleight of hand, Mr Angel, by sleight of hand. Gartside is desperate for blunt. He's in damned low water, and so we're going to trick him into believing there is a simple way of restoring his fortunes. We'll create an illusion, and he will cling to it. And shame him in the process, so that he never sets foot in the *ton* again. Or indeed, as I hinted last night, on the Gartside estate."

As each pronouncement dropped from Lando's lips, Angel's fine eyebrows travelled higher and higher up his forehead. "Stealing an estate using trickery sounds like a very tall order, my lord."

"Perhaps. But I have devised a plan that I believe is worth a shot. At first light on Tuesday, you and I travel to London."

"We will?" Angel appeared momentarily stunned.

"We will," Lando echoed. "There is much to accomplish if one is scheming to steal an estate."

Angel shook his head in disbelief. "I am astounded. You—"

Lando took pity on him. "Your dear uncle was very…precious to me. And as a wise man recently pointed out, it is only that which he would have expected. That there are so many other reasons to ensure Gartside's downfall only serves to strengthen my resolve."

"Yes, but…that…someone…someone like you would come up with—"

"'Someone like me'? An eccentric dandy, you mean?" Lando permitted himself a small smile. "Dandyism is a species not to be underestimated. It is a species of genius, haven't you heard?"

Lando doubted his companion was familiar with the works of one of England's finest eighteenth-century essayists, but then Angel strived to keep a roof over his head, whereas Lando spent most of his days lolling with his feet up, making his way through his extensive library.

"I'm beginning to think it might be," Angel answered slowly. He permitted himself a small smile. "A species, if allowed, my lord, I would like to examine a little more closely. But forgive me, what I had actually been going to say was that my astonishment stems from admiration that a man such as yourself, who takes such pride in running his estates and affairs has the mental capacity and fortitude to also focus his attentions on someone so lowly as myself."

If Lando had a fan to hand, he would have made coquettish use of it. "Your flattery is most welcome, sir." Demurely, he dropped his gaze. He was being played like a fiddle but thoroughly enjoying the experience. In truth, he felt a touch giddy, as if standing on the precipice of something and preparing to jump. "You have my permission to offer it freely."

"Then I shall. I shall flatter you as often as time allows," answered Angel, dimpling wickedly. He tapped on the heavy slab of wood in front of him. "Starting by complimenting your choice of furnishings. I imagine one could put a sturdy desk like this to very good use, don't you?"

*

INGLIS MATERIALISED AFTER Mr Angel's departure to find his lordship flapping a hand across his blushing face. "Inglis," Lando said in a weak voice. "Mr Angel is an awfully nice chap, don't you think?"

"I take it your meeting was a success, my lord."

"A great success. I feel quite…invigorated."

"Very good, sir."

Mr Angel. Christopher Angel. Even his name intoxicated. Lando inhaled deeply, suddenly aware of his blood thrumming through his veins, vibrant with the essence of his own existence. A raffish adventure was around the corner; he could feel it. Even perhaps, an adventure of an altogether more intimate sort, with Mr Christopher Angel.

Be that as it may, Lando had a baronet to bring down. He sat up straighter, aware of Inglis awaiting orders.

"Now, if you will, we have things to do, Inglis. Starting with a suggestion that you invite Pritchard to warm your bed tonight, as it will be the last opportunity for quite some weeks. The day after tomorrow, Mr Angel and I will be departing for London. Pritchard will accompany me, of course, whilst you will maintain a steady ship here. And, though Angel is not yet convinced of it, we shall not return until I have the keys to the Gartside estate clasped in my hand."

Chapter Nine

"SIZE MATTERS TREMENDOUSLY, Mr Angel," breezed Lando in response to his companion's enquiry as to why a solitary person required such a large carriage. "No one enjoys a small glass of port, do they? I'm an earl! I have the *ton*'s expectations to uphold! Not to mention my trunks and my…um…all my other trunks, and my Mr Pritchard, and my books and…and you."

"You overlooked my single valise," added Angel, eyes twinkling. He studied the assembled luggage, most of which would be trundled behind them in a second, equally fine carriage, under the watchful eye of Pritchard. "Have you secreted that delightful desk in one of them?"

Gadzooks. An obscene image filled Lando's head. "No, sadly."

"Pity," replied Angel, still twinkling.

"Though I do have one remarkably similar at the

townhouse," remembered Lando. And a rosy heat climbed his cheeks.

Considering the generous dimensions of Lando's carriage, he was at a loss to understand how Angel's knee bumped his with increasing regularity. Since their meeting in the library, Angel had run a few errands, according to Inglis. One of them had been the acquisition of some more clothing for his sister from the modest tailor in Allenmouth. The man needed some himself if he was to accompany Lando in town, though his dark travelling coat suited him very well indeed. As did the midnight-blue ribbon — velvet again — holding his thick tresses in place. Until he'd made the acquaintance of Christopher Angel, Lando hadn't previously appreciated a fondness for ribbons. Discreetly, he adjusted his lap rug.

"Anne left safely for Horton this morning," Angel informed him. "I'm pleased to report she was in good spirits and looking forward to the trip."

"Good." Lando dragged his eyes away from the ribbon. "My own sister, in one of her endless pieces of correspondence, will no doubt keep me updated on her progress in unnecessary depth."

The next occasion his companion's knee brushed Lando's, it remained there, the length of Angel's firm thigh snugly pressed against his own.

"Warm enough, my lord?" Angel enquired, sharing his dimples with Lando for at least the fourth time since they'd left Rossingley, not that he was keeping score. With an innocent expression, Angel glanced down at the rug before turning his attention back to the countryside. "Thank heavens for thick woollen rugs."

"Thank heavens indeed," agreed Lando.

"Though, we are fortunate with the weather this morning,"

observed Angel. "The last time I travelled by carriage to London, I was caught in a devil of a storm not far from—"

"You kissed me," blurted Lando hotly. "After dinner. You plied me with strong liquor, then kissed me. I…I did not…request it."

It may have been his imagination or merely a pothole, but Lando could have sworn Angel's thigh nudged even closer.

"Neither did you object," Angel pointed out in a mild tone. With a curious smile, he turned away from the carriage window, his gaze latching onto Lando's. "Elms are so majestic at this time of year, don't you think?"

"If you are trifling with me in order to convince me to assist you in bringing ruin upon Sir Ambrose, you need bother no more. I made my intentions in that regard quite clear."

Lando nodded to himself. For his plans regarding Gartside to unfold without hiccups, it was necessary to clear the air; now they could both breathe more easily.

"Understood," came the reply. "The trifling will cease."

Relieved to have unburdened himself, Lando couldn't help a twinge of disappointment. "That's not quite what I meant," he elucidated. "Your trifling is most satisfactory." The hazy parts he could recall, anyhow.

Lando turned to his own window, and the carriage fell quiet, save for the clattering of the wheels and the squeak of leather. And if Angel's thigh still happened to be squashed up against his own, then Lando would pretend to ignore it and—

"I'm trifling with you for reasons much more basic than that, I'm afraid, my lord," Angel said in the same careless murmur he'd used to comment on the elms. His mouth darted closer to Lando's shapely ear. "I want to get inside your drawers."

In the shocked silence, Angel's hand dropped to the rug and slid under it, his palm closing around Lando's slim thigh. When he squeezed softly, all the breath left Lando's throat. He fancied his heart stopped beating, too, and for a long, long second, Lando could only stare at Angel while the young man stared back, undressing him with his eyes.

"You…want to…" Lando trailed off.

"I do, yes. Terribly basic, I admit."

Angel's sinfully dark eyes dropped to Lando's lips. The air in the carriage hung hot and heavy, as if the sun itself had descended upon them. The hand on his thigh moved a fraction higher as Angel's calf rubbed up against his own.

"Coincidentally, I have…uh…some basic needs myself," Lando managed and then lunged with a greedy surge, closing his lips around Angel's. He kissed him, hard and hungrily, while Angel thoroughly, urgently, kissed him back. The blunt edges of his fingernails tangled in Lando's hair, the hand on his thigh massaged his warm flesh. When the heel of Angel's palm found the growing firmness at the front of Lando's breeches, he let out a pained, choking sound.

"I confirm that you are, indeed, skilled with your hands," he gasped.

As he pulled Lando closer, a low growl vibrated through Angel's chest. "You have no idea."

White bliss licked up Lando's shaft. He thrust his hips upwards into Angel's punishing touch in a manner not unlike how Angel's tongue thrust into Lando's mouth. On each upward stroke, Angel's thumb circled the head of his prick through the fabric of his breeches. Lando whimpered, a sound that only spurred Angel on. A hot tingling at the base of his spine signalled the inevitable, and if the carriage hadn't slowed, if the ear-splitting hooves of a fast-approaching stage hadn't jolted Lando back to his senses, he might very well have spilled into his drawers, then and there. Which would have been hellishly embarrassing to explain to Pritchard later. But in the nick of time, as the stage thundered towards them, he jerked away, dishevelled, debauched, and a damned sight less composed than at the outset of the journey.

"Gadzooks." Panting, Lando arranged his clothing as best he could, then let his head drop back against the carriage seat.

A mischievous smile spread across Angel's face. "Any objections to my trifling now?"

"Gosh, no," breathed Lando. "Trifle away. I adore a trifle. As long as you don't frighten the horses."

"Good." Angel smoothed down his frock coat. "I'm glad you approve. I've had a dreadful need to kiss you since I first clapped eyes on you. Since you interviewed me in your parlour, dressed in that frivolous little grey silk robe."

Two splashes of colour rose high on Lando's cheekbones. He felt rather hot and out of puff. Yet again, this man had set his agile mind fumbling. "I…ah…yes. My staff are used to my little foibles. I apologise if it…offended you."

Angel laughed loudly while his heavy-lidded eyes roamed Lando's face as if undecided about which part to take a bite out of first. Under the scrutiny, Lando blushed even harder; as far as he was concerned, the man could take his pick.

"On the contrary, my lord," Angel murmured, his eyes now

tracing a line down to Lando's throat. "The garment…intrigued me. So much so that I may need to examine it more closely." He jerked his chin towards the rear of the carriage. "If it is not in one of those stupidly heavy trunks you insisted needed to travel with us, then your groom can jolly well turn this carriage around, and we'll return to Rossingley to fetch it."

The stage rattled past, stilling further conversation. Braving the elements and riding high above them, a footman and the groom relished a heated debate regarding the extraordinary discovery of a terribly distant place called Antarctica. Hidden inside the carriage, Mr Angel once more addressed his attentions to Lando. Cupping his smooth chin with a firm hand, he brought Lando's soft mouth to precisely where he wanted it. As his tongue leisurely explored every warm crevice and his clever fingers toyed with Lando's, Lando decided Mr Angel was far more intoxicating than any amount of claret and fine brandy. And kissing a handsome rogue for no other reason than to assuage his basic needs was a damned fine way to occupy oneself during a long and dull carriage journey.

Chapter Ten

THOUGH KIT WOULD have enjoyed nothing more than to continue kissing the earl well into the night and probably into the following morning, the opportunity didn't arise. The earl excused himself on their arrival at his Grosvenor Street residence with a wish to attend to some pressing business. No sooner had he set foot in his residence, his lordship exchanged the ostentatious carriage for his nimble curricle and signalled to an unimpressed Pritchard to join him. He then flamed his way out again, only to turn on his heel and pop back in to issue instructions for Kit to visit his Jermyn Street tailor and allow himself to be exquisitely clothed at the earl's expense. Before Kit could protest, he'd disappeared.

Whilst not at all what he had planned, it afforded Kit plenty of time to ponder his increasingly lustful attraction to his eccentric new acquaintance.

Kit's acknowledgement of a preference for his own sex was a story he'd rather not dissect, having made an uneasy truce with it several years ago. For appearances' sake, he'd courted a couple of chaste local girls in the small Kentish town where he'd been raised, interspersed with some delightful but amateur grappling with one of the farmer's boys. On moving to London after the death of his father, Kit had sought comfort when needs must, rarely with the same person twice.

The earl was a different kettle of fish altogether. Once he'd fully sampled those delights, Kit had a feeling he'd be loath to dine anywhere else.

To his dismay, he soon discovered that those delights came with a hefty side serving of footman of the beefy, one-eyed variety, whose *foot* had already made acquaintance with Kit's rear. Twice. Seems the second carriage had contained more than the earl's extensive collection of silk peignoirs.

"I thought I'd left you behind at Rossingley," Kit grumbled, as the man—Jasper, he recalled—took the reins of yet another of the earl's carriages. This one was a rather sleek phaeton pulled by a pair of equally sleek greys.

"And I thought I'd left you picking rose thorns out of your arse," retorted Jasper as they set off at a brisk trot. Brisker than Kit would have liked, they hurtled around the first corner almost as if the man was purposefully making the short journey painful.

"Do footmen even drive carriages?" Kit clutched the rail as they swung around another corner. "I'm perfectly capable of driving myself to the tailor's, you know. Or walking."

"Following instructions," said the man mournfully. "I'm to be your valet and groom for as long as his lordship requires it."

"Val — I don't need a valet! Nor do I need a trip to the blasted tailors! This coat is perfectly adequate for all my needs."

"His lordship says it's not. Coats, breeches, boots, shirts, cravats, waistcoats, evening wear. I have a list."

"A...a list? I'm not a bloody...a bloody doll to be dressed up and played with!"

Jasper regarded him sidelong. The carriage swerved alarmingly. "No. You're not."

Kit cursed. If they hadn't been travelling at such breakneck speed, he'd have half a mind to leap out. The earl and his tailor be damned. "Well, I'm telling you now, after this ridiculous trip to the tailors, I'll be heading back to my lodgings."

"Which have relocated to Grosvenor Street until further notice." The footman/groom and now erstwhile valet nodded with relish. "Until I am ordered to kick you out again."

"Damnation," muttered Kit. He'd managed perfectly well without both the earl and a valet for three and twenty years.

"Couldn't have put it better myself, sir," his travelling companion agreed. "I'd rather be facing the Frenchies than pandering to you. And they took my eye."

Which left Kit in no doubt as to where he stood. This short carriage trip was turning out to be far less pleasurable than the previous one. "Does the earl often temporarily house young men of his acquaintance?"

"No. And if you upset him again, you'll be the last."

"I have no intention of it. I spied rosebushes either side of the front door here too."

The remainder of the uncomfortable journey passed in silence. As Kit reflected on his strange few days, his thoughts inevitably drifted in an earl-ward direction. A *bossy* earl. And his new accomplice and lover, or would-be lover, at any rate. He'd made his desires perfectly plain, though if he was honest with himself, *basic needs* were already a poor description of his feelings for his lordship. How could anything related to him be basic, when the man himself was so complex? Which parts of his character were real? The aloof nobleman astride his ill-tempered stallion, the shrewd assessor of Gartside's failings, or the fey dandy dissolving in his arms, with lips softer than the silk around his neck?

Kit was damned if he knew. Which wasn't the same as not wanting to find out.

Thankfully, whilst Kit tolerated two hours of manhandling at the tailors, Jasper made himself scarce. A waspish little man, the tailor also seemed unable to find a bad word to say about the earl. He spent the first half of Kit's fitting proclaiming the earl's figure and style to be amongst the finest in the *ton* and the second lamenting how little he saw of him these days. This left very little time for him to ascertain Kit's identity and background, which was just as well as Kit hadn't a suitable answer, given that Rossingley hadn't yet filled him in on *the plan*.

When he finally emerged, it was with the intention of sending Jasper, the carriage, and his purchases back to Grosvenor Street, then hailing a hackney to his lodgings. Having left in haste to rescue his sister, he was keen to collect a few belongings and, more importantly, some pilfered trinkets waiting to be sold. Being the earl's guest was all well and good, but a man still needed to feel he had a little blunt of his own in his pocket. If his circumstances were to suddenly change, Kit needed to be damned ready.

No such luck. Jasper's expression turned murderous the second Kit broached the idea of taking a trip to the stews without him. Thus, Kit had no alternative but to pull up outside the shabby boarding house in the earl's fine phaeton, its showy crest emblazoned on the side advertising his return as boldly as a trumpet fanfare. Though, the look of absolute disgust on Jasper's face as he peered at his surroundings made it almost worthwhile. Kit had a good mind to half inch the man's purse just for the hell of it.

"Wait here. I'll be five minutes," he instructed Jasper.

"I have no intention of going anywhere, sir. Wouldn't return to any wheels on the carriage if I did. Nor horses."

"It's not that bad. You've spent too long living in Rossingley splendour. Not all of us gentlemen are blessed with estates and inheritances as grand as the earl's. Some of us have had to work for a living."

"His lordship works," said Jasper mulishly.

"At what?" Kit's voice was full of scorn. "Maintaining his golden locks? Counting his money? Booting men out of his house? Or, let me guess, does he roll up his sleeves and plough the fields during harvest?"

"Keeping a whole village happy. Even when he's not."

Kit jumped down and threw a coin to the pitiful pile of bones begging outside his lodging. "One day, I'm going to find someone with something bad to say about him."

Jasper chuffed. "Let me know when you do."

Kit's custom was to approach his abode via a circuitous route to be sure he wasn't spotted. A murky covered alley ran down the side of the boarding house, hiding a side entrance leading into it. Kit found approaching from the rear and entering that way more to his liking than advertising his presence at the front door. Regularity was what got people caught. Who knew how much time and effort a frustrated Clark had been expending trying to find him?

Today, he crossed his fingers in the hope that Clark had taken his dogged efforts elsewhere.

Kit's lodgings were cheap, which was about the kindest thing he could say about them. What little money he'd inherited on his father's death, combined with his secretarial work for Sir Brandon, had covered the doctor's arrears and a roof to go over Anne's head until Uncle Charles took pity on her. Sir Brandon's untimely death from a sudden attack of septic quinsy left Kit without decent written references, hence he'd resorted to card sharping and petty theft. Which were all well and good but did not provide a regular income.

Kit's heart sank as he opened the door. All his fears that Clark, the Bow Street runner, might know his name and address were confirmed. He hadn't realised he possessed enough belongings to cover the floor of his humble room, but apparently, he had. Underclothes, cravats, books, and papers had been tossed over every available inch of space. And not too carefully either. A cushion ripped apart and a jagged split down the centre of his thin mattress told their own tale.

The pilfered trinkets were nowhere to be seen.

Kit sagged against the doorframe, a young man without honest employment and prospects. And now penniless too.

At that moment, the earl and his lavish homes, his deadly flirtatiousness, and Kit's new clothes seemed very far away. Even his ire against Gartside paled. And yet somehow, in a few minutes, he'd have to compose himself, gather what little he had left into a carpet bag, and saunter back to that stylishly upholstered carriage and its suspicious driver as if his world couldn't be pleasanter.

If the earl knew about his shady dealings, or, heaven forbid, Clark discovered his association with the earl, it would ruin everything.

Chapter Eleven

UNSAVOURY DARKNESS LURKED in all corners of Drury Lane, but never more so than during the lull before a matinee performance. The *ton* would be appalled if they unearthed Lando's destination at such a God-fearing time of day. Add in the threat of fire, robbery, and the infamous attempted shooting of one of the players several years earlier, and it was no wonder Pritchard was reluctant to venture within a mile of the place. Thus, he was hugely put out when Lando dragged him along to guard the curricle whilst he went inside.

"I'm your indispensable valet, my lord," he squawked as two urchins immediately closed in on the smart carriage. "I'm hardly going to beat off these ruffians with a pocket square and my clothes brush, am I?"

"Half a crown should do it, though," answered Lando with a grin. A grin which had hardly left his face since his wonderful journey with Mr Angel. "And tell them there's another one if they prevent that enormous rat hiding over there from crawling up the rear axle and scurrying across your feet."

With Pritchard's squeals ringing in his ears, Lando disappeared through an unobtrusive side door and into the murky depths of the theatre.

Locating his quarry by sound alone, Lando picked his way through a series of dust-sheeted rooms, drawing closer to the source of the godawful racket otherwise known as Tommy Squire's singing voice. His final obstacle course, a mountain of costumes, hats, props, and other theatrical accoutrements, made up the clutter in the actor's dressing room.

Applying face paint whilst belting out a bawdy tune, Tommy Squire peered into a gilt mirror perilously balanced on even more colourful garments. A dozen thick candles dotted haphazardly around the room assisted him in his delicate task. The faint odour of greasepaint wafted under Lando's nose. Goodness knew how the magistrates had never ascertained a cause for the great Drury Lane fire of 1809; the likely reason was staring Lando in the face.

"From a little spark may burst a flame," he murmured so as not to startle his old friend and set the whole place alight. Sweeping the room with a glance, which was about as close as it would ever come to being tidied up, he braced for Tommy's reaction. "A quote from Dante Alighieri, darling, circa early fourteenth century, in case you were wondering. Although I don't believe he meant it literally. More allegoric, really."

"You're back! His lordship's back!"

Tommy leaped across the room, and Lando found himself

crushed against a makeshift clothes horse and a wriggling, de-lighted…Dick Turpin, judging from the jaunty tricorn hat atop Tommy's head. "The gods be damned! His lordy's bloody back!"

With a second set of male arms wrapping about his person in as many hours, Lando felt his chest expanding, his heart soaring, his soul singing. He felt *alive*.

"Yes, I…I do believe I am," he answered with a little laugh. "And this time, Tommy, I'm…I'm quite recovered. Unless you persist in squeezing the living daylights from me."

"God, it's been too long!" Tommy finally put Lando down to look at him properly. "Yes, you are recovered! You look in fine fettle, my lord."

"Thank you." Lando had a ridiculous urge to give a little twirl. "So do you. Thespian life must suit you."

Tommy still drank Lando in. "Yes, but not for much longer. Got my eye on another gaming room. The first one's started turning more than a few bob." He tapped his nose mysteriously. "And the betting stands are multiplying. This is my last run treading the boards, I reckon."

"If anyone could do it, I knew it would be you, Tommy." Lando beamed with delight.

From the time his path had crossed Lando's more than fifteen years ago, Tommy had dreamed of owning and running gambling hells. But unlike most folk with big dreams, Tommy also had a strategy, buckets of determination, and a miserly attitude. And, as Lando teased, friends he viewed more as opportunistic acquaintances.

"We'll be running in the same circles soon, lordy. You mark my words."

"I don't doubt it."

Tommy's keen gaze raked over Lando's beautifully cut travelling attire, his foxy features turning lascivious. "You look good enough to eat."

A fortnight earlier, Lando would have been sorely tempted. "At risk of disappointing you, on this occasion you may have to…ah…dine elsewhere. I am here with a very different sort of proposition, I'm afraid. Your purse will approve, even if—" He flicked his eyes down to Tommy's nether regions. "—other parts of you are chagrined."

Tommy grinned, uncaring. He was never short on bedfellows. "So you've finally taken Robert's advice and found something to occupy your time?"

"Yes."

"Good. I've been worried about you, lordy. You've been so lonely."

Lonely? How inadequate that one word always sounded. As if Lando didn't know his own bed.

"Yes, I have."

"Is the new project a fella? It is, isn't it?" Tommy's eyes gleamed. "The lucky bugger. That's what's got you looking so well."

Black curls escaping from a velvet ribbon danced before Lando's eyes. Curls smelling of country air and sweet caramel. Lando shook the image away. A basic bodily need, that was all Mr Angel was filling. "No, although I have found myself a temporary distraction."

A language Tommy understood very well.

"More importantly," Lando continued, "I have a job for you,

Tommy. One I think you're going to enjoy very much, and I'll pay you handsomely. Ah...how's your American accent?"

Affecting a slouch, Tommy slapped his thigh and then pulled at the kerchief loosely tied around his neck. "Pretty darned good, Lord Rossingley," he boomed in the tones of a man thrice his size. Despite the buckle heels, the tricorn, and one cheek thick with rouge and the other as pale as nature intended, the transformation was uncanny. "Pretty darned good."

*

"I TRUST OUR houseguest is being well looked after by Jasper?"

"They haven't descended to fisticuffs yet, if that's what you mean," answered Pritchard drily.

Seated at his dressing table in the grey banyan so admired by Angel, Lando examined his reflection and found it satisfactory. Fine fettle indeed. Over by the chest, Pritchard laid out his attire for the evening.

"And what does Jasper have to report?" Lando asked.

"That Mr Angel looks very fetching in his new wool tailcoat," answered Pritchard. "He assures me it will be to your liking. As will the peach figured silk waistcoat."

"You know that's not what I mean, though I'm thrilled to hear it." Idly, Lando riffled through a box of cravat pins. "They were gone for five hours, and Mr Angel is perfectly proportioned. My efficient tailor would have completed the job in under three."

"They ran another errand afterwards," admitted Pritchard. "But Jasper didn't want you to worry yourself, my lord. Not now you are quite well."

Through the mirror, Lando gave him a look of disdain. "I'm

a thirty-four-year-old earl, Pritchard. I do not need coddling."
Sometimes, Lando wondered whether he was actually in charge
of anything. "Has it not occurred to Jasper that Mr Angel's wellbeing might contribute to my own current state of health? What
is this terrible thing he thought he might need to hide from me?"

"Mr Angel's abode," said Pritchard shortly. "It's not the
most salubrious."

"Silly me. I'd been assuming he resided in a palace. Where
is it?"

"Sindell Street, my lord. But a stone toss from St Giles."
Pritchard's tone suggested a cave might have been better. Throwing Lando a dark look and pausing for dramatic effect, he lowered
his voice. "But there's more."

"Out with it then, man. Don't worry. I shan't have a fit of the
vapours."

"A boy is watching his lodgings. He's in the pay of a Bow
Street runner to report when Mr Angel is back in town. Jasper wa-
gers there's a beggar in the runner's employ too."

"And may I enquire how Jasper extracted that information
from the boy?"

"Painfully, I believe. But, alas, not enough to scare him off.
The boy is being rewarded too well. Jasper is of the belief he will
continue to report Mr Angel's comings and goings."

And could so easily be replaced by another, thought Lando.
Regarding his own reflection once more, he fingered the heavy set
of pearls draped across his dressing table. They belonged to his
late mother, and his hands often strayed to them when he was
deep in thought. This Clark fellow clearly hadn't given up; the
dogged Bow Street runner could derail Lando's scheme in a

heartbeat if he located Angel. Even worse, once the scheme was underway, he could unwittingly expose Lando as the orchestrator of it. As he rolled one of the cool pearls between his finger and thumb, Lando's uneasiness expanded further; he didn't care for the image of Mr Angel — his *temporary distraction* — behind bars.

"Jasper must not let Angel out of his sight," Lando instructed. "When he ventures *beyond* Grosvenor Street, obviously." Within, Lando hoped to have him to himself. Lando's London bedchamber held few melancholic memories; Charles had rarely visited the earl's townhouse. Their love affair had been much simpler conducted at Rossingley, away from prying eyes.

"And inform Hargreaves that our guest will be best served if his belongings are moved into the rose room. I've always found it one of the most comfortable of this house's bedchambers, don't you think?"

"Certainly, my lord," agreed Pritchard as he fussed with the earl's powder-blue cravat. It was Lando's favourite. His Mama had once commented that it brought out the colour of his eyes. Given that she rarely commended anything or anybody, he deduced it must be true. "And the door connecting it to your own bedchamber will be an asset, what with all the important business you have to discuss."

"Exactly my thoughts, Pritchard."

Having one's valet so in tune with oneself was a boon. "And as I'm still so weary after such a dreadfully long journey yesterday —" Lando gave a theatrical yawn that wouldn't have fooled a frightened rabbit and certainly didn't fool Pritchard. " — I would prefer not to be disturbed in the mornings. It might prove to be the sort of weariness that drags on for days."

"I expect Mr Angel will also be struck by it," observed Pritchard. "After all the travelling."

"Precisely."

Chapter Twelve

ONE TENDED NOT to decline a supper invite from the elusive eleventh Earl of Rossingley, if only to placate one's wife waiting at home, impatient to discover which of the multiplying stories about the former dandy were true. Such an opportunity would allow her to be the first amongst her pals with the news confirming he'd become a delinquent, deformed, a drunkard, or a dolt.

As they met in the drawing room prior to the guests gathering, the earl filled Kit in on the fellows fortunate enough to receive an invitation. The flustered coquette with whom Kit had *trifled* in the carriage had vanished, replaced by a cool, commanding peer of the realm. The teasing snips of information Rossingley casually offered Kit whilst still giving very little away regarding the blasted *plan*, made him all the more intriguing.

"Lord Cobham loathes Gartside." All business, Rossingley began ticking his guests off, one by one. "The man broke off an engagement to his only daughter in a very public, very distressing manner."

"Why am I not surprised," Kit answered.

"Which is why I have arranged to have them sat side by side," Rossingley added with a hint of mischief. "Sir Richard also loathes him, though his reasons are of no concern to you."

"And the other guest?" Kit prompted. The table had been laid for six.

"He is a mystery to all." Rossingley's pale eyes glittered. "I daresay everyone will find him fascinating and irritating in equal measure." He adjusted his impeccable cuffs. "Which is precisely why I have invited him."

Surveying the earl's guests as they took their seats, Kit would be hard-pressed to find a more peculiar gathering in the whole of the *ton*. There was a paucity of ladies for a start, but then the earl had never fostered a reputation as a ladies' man, despite the efforts of many a flirtatious debutante and their scheming mamas.

With his lilac embroidered waistcoat, ramrod frame, and sweep of shockingly white-blond hair, the earl cut a striking figure. Kit mused how Lord Cobham might report back to a disappointed Lady Cobham that Rossingley didn't appear to have succumbed to any afflictions whatsoever; on the contrary, that fine country air must suit him. And then he might further suggest when this darned thing was all over, they might also retreat to the country, taking their wretched daughter with them. A suggestion that would not land well with his verbose lady.

Sir Richard Hinton, taking up a seat opposite Kit and abstaining from all offers of beverage except for water, wouldn't report back to anyone at all. Introducing himself as a bachelor, the unprepossessing baronet spoke little whilst observing plenty.

The third of the earl's guests, a Mr Arthur Hamilton, not only puzzled Kit but, as Rossingley had forewarned, became a source of increasing annoyance. Over the entrées, Kit mostly ignored him, deciding the flamboyant young American was nothing more than a bothersome social butterfly. Over the excellent venison, however, Kit revised that opinion; the man was a street rat masquerading as a bothersome social butterfly. By dessert, he concluded the man was both. He also deduced that Mr Arthur Hamilton was a fellow sodomite and one with clear designs on pinching the earl from under Kit's nose. Which simply would not do.

And then there was the final guest. Sir Ambrose Gartside himself. The less said about him the better, but prematurely balding, self-important, and weaselly summed him up perfectly. One of those folks whose only path to making their own candle shine brighter was to blow out someone else's, using whatever means they had at their disposal to do it. That Kit maintained a veneer of civility was neither tactic nor sentiment but a clear instruction issued by the earl prior to his guest's arrival. *Trust me,* his lordship had ordered, impaling him on those silvery-blue eyes. *Remember, Angel, I have a plan.*

Gartside had no idea who Kit was, of course. And having been introduced by the earl in rather vague terms as 'a man of business visiting from the provinces', he'd immediately dismissed him, with a barely disguised sneer, as unimportant. *Trust me.* Fortunately, the earl's warning still rang in his ears because the alternative to Kit's cordiality was chaos, and Kit didn't think his exquisitely mannered earl would be too thrilled if his dinner party dissolved into a common brawl. He comforted himself with the reminder that if the mysterious plan failed and he still wanted to kill Gartside, he'd lead him to a quiet spot and strangle him.

Therefore, despite occupying the seat adjacent to the earl and consuming the most tender, succulent mouthfuls of meat, Kit was out of sorts. Not only was he forced to curb his anger while making polite discourse within six feet of his sister's attacker, but he was also contending with Mr Hamilton's determined efforts to render his charming host helpless with laughter. Which he did far too frequently. Adding to his woes, Kit also prayed that Lord Cobham didn't examine him too closely. Whilst one plethoric iron-haired gentleman in evening dress looked very much like another, Kit had a niggling suspicion that around six months ago, he'd relieved Lord Cobham of a silver snuff box.

But what truly soured his wine was that he simply couldn't fathom why his earl had gathered such an odd group at all. Yes, Cobham had a daughter in a similar predicament as Kit's own poor sister. But why invite him to dine with Gartside? Sir Richard, Kit had been apprised, had neither wife, sister, or daughter, and neither did he have a country estate or a fondness for card games. So, what was his objection to Gartside?

As for Mr Hamilton, Kit wouldn't have the man within ten miles of his own dining table if ever he had sufficient funds to purchase such a piece of furniture. And he would gladly banish him to another continent if he continued batting his lashes at the delectable earl.

And then there was Gartside. Unless one could add being a sodomite to Sir Ambrose's list of crimes, which Kit hugely doubted, Kit was totally befuddled as to why the earl would ever invite such a thorough bastard into his house to sit alongside Cobham and the rest of them in the first place.

Kit had to patiently drum his fingers until the dessert course came to an end to find out. He had a feeling he wasn't alone in his musings, as by the time the earl's guests retired to the sumptuous drawing room, Grosvenor Street's well of mannerly conversation had run dry. A restlessness settled amongst them or perhaps a re-alisation that this was no ordinary supper gathering. When the earl's townhouse butler, Hargreaves, finally withdrew, Lord Cobham—no stranger to his host's port already this evening—pounced.

"What the deuces is going on, Rossingley? You behave like a recluse for three years, then pop out of the woodwork and de-mand my presence at dinner with—" he threw his lofty gaze in the direction of Gartside, Mr Hamilton, and Kit, himself, before adding, "these gentlemen." He said *gentlemen* in the tone one used after mistakenly stepping in horse muck. "Are you so out of touch?"

The earl responded with a beatific smile. "Believe it or not, my good sir, we all of us have much in common." Adopting the master of the house's rightful position of warming his backside against the fireplace, he eyed his attentive guests thoughtfully. "A great deal in common, in fact."

"Is it that when we take our last breath, we all go to the same place?" suggested Mr Hamilton in an affected drawl. He flicked an imaginary speck of dust from his coat as he treated Lord Cobham to a weary look. "Because I'm at a loss to see how I could possibly have an association with anyone who finds Palmerston's

views on the General Maritime Treaty in any way worthy of a fif-
teen-minute monologue." Lord Cobham frowned while Kit suppressed a smirk. "And if I ever find myself in that unfortunate
position, then could my last breath be sooner rather than later?"

"I'll see what I can do," answered the earl.

A slow, seductive smile eased across Hamilton's face in the
direction of their host. At the same time, a look of annoyance
spread across Kit's as jealousy ripped through him, like the slice
of a paper cut. He hadn't anticipated competition for the earl's affections.

"I must say, this is frightfully cloak and dagger, Rossingley
old chap," huffed Gartside. "I do wish you'd get on with it."

"D-did w-we all at-t-tend Eton?" hazarded Sir Richard, then
cringed as four sets of eyes turned to him.

Some of these nobles, thought Kit irritably, really had no
idea an entire world of misery existed beyond Mayfair.

"'Fraid not, old chap," replied Mr Hamilton in a remarkable
imitation of Lord Cobham. "It's a dreadful thing to admit, but I'm
an old Harrovian through and through."

Kit nearly guffawed, astounded the American strumpet had
even heard of that revered educational establishment, let alone
the nerve to claim to be a former pupil. Sprawled across the
chaise, his every move and every gesture were designed to better
display his wares to the earl. The man was an utter enigma, one
Kit had already decided much earlier in the evening that he didn't
care for. If anyone was going to tup the earl tonight, it would be
him, and him alone.

"I can't imagine Mr Hamilton and I have anything in common whatsoever," stated Gartside with an air of finality. "He's

done nothing but agitate. Why he's here defeats me."

"To improve the scenery," quipped Hamilton. "Which is distinctly lacking. My lordship excepted, of course." He gave the earl one of those smiles, again, of the type setting Kit's teeth on edge.

The earl returned it with a mildly disapproving look, suggesting now was not the time. As far as Kit was concerned, the time would be never. "Mr Hamilton is here at my behest," the earl said. "For reasons which will soon become clear."

Cobham dabbed at his damp forehead. "Well, do get on with it, Rossingley. I have my mistress to call upon within the hour."

"That lady is truly blessed," murmured Mr Hamilton.

Inevitably feeling the warmth, Rossingley moved away from the fire and perched his neat, small behind on his solid desk. He'd deliberately intended to keep them all waiting, Kit was sure of it. Though it was entirely feasible, given his sweet tooth, Rossingley had become distracted by the Bakewell pudding.

"Some of you may be aware that, a year ago, I acquired a large cotton mill in the small northern town of Runcorn, situated on the outskirts of Manchester. Like others who have gone before me, and as Sir Richard can no doubt attest, it is proving to be an extraordinarily decent investment. I have purchased the most sophisticated carding and spinning machines available, meaning that instead of piecemeal cotton cloth production, all the stages of assembly now take place under one roof. Added to the recent installation of powered looms, my factory is the most highly productive mill in the north of England."

Whereas Sir Richard showed a very keen interest, Gartside's eyes glazed over. He sighed heavily.

"I was hoping we were here to play a few hands of piquet, Rossingley. Not receive a potted history of cotton manufacture." According to Rossingley, Gartside's enthusiasm for business matters extended to calculating race odds and no more, much to the vexation of his deceased father.

"Have some patience, my good fellow," countered Rossingley briskly. "I'm just coming to the interesting part. What you may not be aware of is that I also acquired a parcel of land adjacent to my mill. This extends it to eight hectares and plenty large enough for the construction of four more profitable mills. And they can all share the same power supply, thus making my process even more economical."

"Runcorn is l-l-linked to t-the Bridgewater C-C-Canal," observed Sir Richard knowledgeably.

"Indeed." Rossingley shot him a grateful smile. "Which brings me around to Mr Hamilton and Mr Angel. Mr Hamilton's family owns a large cotton plantation in South Carolina; his raw cotton is transported to England via Liverpool and provides for my mill." He inclined his head towards Mr Hamilton, who beamed back. "May I take this opportunity to point out that Mr Hamilton's family does not use enslaved labour?"

Kit had the impression neither Cobham nor Gartside cared one way or another how the Hamiltons procured their raw cotton, but the observation won an approving nod from the more enlightened Sir Richard. The earl continued.

"The construction of four more mills will establish me as the Hamilton plantation's most important overseas business partner. Indeed, I will become the biggest single buyer of raw cotton in England."

"My word, you have been busy," spluttered Cobham. "And there was the *ton* believing you had intractable gout or an exhausting young filly keeping you chained to the bedchamber."

"'Fraid to disappoint," answered Lando with a tiny smile. "I have simply been ensuring that when I throw in my dinner pail, my eldest son inherits a healthy earldom."

At this, he gave a pointed look in Gartside's direction, not that the man picked up on it.

"Now, if I may." The earl gestured with his glass. "The time has come to properly introduce Mr Angel here. Or, if I may be so bold as to use his full title — Master Collector of Customs at the Northern Board of Customs and Chief Inspector of the River. As the most senior government officer at Liverpool Docks, Mr Angel oversees His Majesty's customs in the region in their entirety. He reports to, and has the ear of, the foreign secretary himself."

For a second, Kit wondered if he was still in possession of his own ears, never mind someone else's. He...*he what?...he was who*? Four sets of eyes swivelled in his direction.

Rooted to the spot, it took all of his poker skills honed from two years fleecing his fellow man at the card tables not to gasp out loud. He was *what*? A Master something...something Collector of the *River*? The most senior government official? Buggeration. Kit didn't have the first clue about the cotton industry, let alone the shipping one. What the blazes was the earl up to?

While all present sized him up, Kit became acutely aware of two things. One, he was now the centre of attention and not entirely happy about it, and two, he understood why the earl had ensured he was clothed in his tailor's finery. Very snug, very hot finery. *Trust me*, he'd said. And Kit had until he'd pulled this rabbit from the hat. The lord was as bold as brass!

"Monthly meetings with Castlereagh, I understand?" reiterated the earl, his steely pale gaze boring into Kit's.

Trust me. At that moment, Kit felt more of an urge to kill him. "Absolutely," he agreed with a lot more swagger than he felt. "We dine together the third Wednesday of every month."

Adopting a severe expression, praying it chimed with acting the part of Viscount bloody Castlereagh's most revered member of the Northern Board of Customs and Trout Collecting or whatever it was—did such an establishment actually exist?—Kit stroked his chin thoughtfully.

"If you brought us here to brag, Rossingley, then you could have saved yourself the bother," chuntered Gartside. "As fascinating as you clearly believe this cotton stuff is, I have a table and three chums awaiting my sharp wits at White's, and—"

"He hasn't b-b-brought us here to b-b-brag, have you?" Sir Richard's eyes narrowed. "He needs s-something."

"Quite right," agreed Rossingley warmly. "I knew you'd understand." He took a minute swallow of port. "In principle, Mr Angel here—and thereby the British government—has approved an enhanced trade agreement with Mr Hamilton's family and the building of four more cotton mills adjacent to my existing one. All that remains, in order for my enterprise to become the biggest producer of cotton cloth in the whole of England, is to expand the trade route via the Bridgewater Canal and then build the blasted things."

"But even you can't do that on your own," chimed in Cobham, Sir Richard's obvious interest stirring his own. "Can you, Rossingley?"

The earl tilted his head thoughtfully. "More that I am of the opinion one should never put one's eggs all in the same basket, should one not?" His tone was solemn. "As tempted as I am to keep this potential goldmine to myself, even I am reluctant to fund the building of four mills *and* sponsor widening the trade route through Liverpool Docks all by myself. The project is costly as well as complicated and necessitates more than one sound mind to oversee it. Working at *very* close quarters with Mr Angel, of course."

Before Kit could divine whether that last comment was quite as innocuous as it seemed, Rossingley sucked in a breath.

"Mr Angel assures me that, in partnership with a shrewd fellow investor, the project is viable and will become the biggest of its kind in England." He hooked Kit in his glittery gaze. "Isn't that right, Mr Angel?"

Kit swore he was going to kill him. All that remained was the method. "Y-yes," he replied weakly. "Absolutely."

"Maybe in the world," interrupted Mr Hamilton in his southern drawl. "England already produces half of the world's cotton cloth. Rossingley's empire would sure be as big as anything we have back home."

"Indeed, Mr Hamilton." The earl gave him an appreciative nod. "So I have been informed." He turned his regard back to the others. "You have been invited here tonight as I view you all as possible partners in this venture. It goes without saying that you all have reputations as honest businessmen of great wealth and excellent standing."

The words hung there as the gentlemen examined one another. To his left, Kit became aware of Cobham leaning forward, brow furrowed in concentration, his full glass of port and his waiting mistress forgotten. Sir Richard's eyes were closed; his fingers twitched as if performing sums in his head. Gartside's oily gaze was so fixated on the earl it was a surprise he didn't recoil from the putrid heat of it. Meanwhile, Mr Hamilton simply crossed one well-shod foot over the other and examined his well-kept fingernails as if the earl was discussing a rout at Gentleman Jack's or his favourite snuff box. Kit found himself in the same position as Gartside, unable to tear his eyes away from the immaculate slender figure in lilac, commanding the attention of every man in the room.

"Developing such a swathe of land will be controversial and likely spark some unrest," Rossingley continued smoothly. "There has been a recent outbreak of smallpox at a mill in Bury, and a growing number of workers are petitioning Parliament about working conditions. There's a call to put a halt to expansion. Which means that we must tread lightly. It is imperative that my proposal not be spoken about in public until everything is signed and sealed. So, as gentleman, I trust you will be as silent as clams until I choose a suitable investment partner, and the deal is done."

"Only one p-p-partner?" queried Sir Richard.

"Only one," confirmed Rossingley. "Given the project is of such magnitude and national import, Angel here will be charged with selecting the right chap on my behalf. And…" At this point, he slowed to capture the eye of every man in the room. "…as I have already made clear, I would like that person to be one of the fine gentlemen here in this room."

Kit stared at Rossingley intently as he topped up everyone's port except his own. His guests stared at one another. Trickery was afoot, of course. Of that much Kit was certain. Trickery on a vast scale. *I'm going to steal his estate.* Kit had thought that wild assertion had been simply an excess of brandy talking. Now, with the man spinning a tale so outlandish, he wasn't so sure.

A sliver of excitement curled in the pit of his belly. Rossingley's foppish exterior was nothing but an affection. The man was cunning as a snake. The whole thing was an elaborate lie, or huge tracts of it, built on nothing but the earl's title, wealth, and good standing.

But for the life of him, Kit couldn't pinpoint what Rossingley was up to. How did he know so much about the cotton trade? And why these particular guests? Presumably because they were as wealthy as he purported. No doubt Cobham had deep pockets, Sir Richard too. And he'd have to take the earl's word regarding Hamilton, the odd American. But why Gartside, when both he and Rossingley knew the man had begun accruing unpaid debts all over the *ton*? He still had some funds at his disposable, according to the earl, but they were slipping through his fingers as fast as he could shuffle cards.

"One thing, Rossingley," queried Lord Cobham, the first to formulate his thoughts. "The investment sounds promising—I will need my man of business to look into the finer details, of course. But if this thing is to be done so quietly, why the devil have you not simply approached us one at a time in a more discreet manner?"

The earl smiled broadly. "Oh, the answer to that is quite simple. Mr Hamilton here has already made me an excellent offer to be my business partner, one he doesn't believe I can refuse. Essentially, it is with the aim of supplying his own American cotton to

English mills in which he would have a half share. And, I admit, I was sorely tempted. But—forgive me, Mr Hamilton, for being so indelicate, though I have already expressed this opinion to you." He threw Hamilton an apologetic smile before readdressing the others. "One simply cannot trust foreigners, can one? As much as I'd enjoy Mr Hamilton's blunt, I don't care for it. And nor does the Northern Board of Customs as Mr Angel can vouch. If American cotton supplies take a downturn—and simply one poor summer will suffice—we would revert to Indian trade routes, yet be stuck with an American owning half of all my mills."

"As you can imagine, gentlemen," answered Hamilton, with the first hint of displeasure Kit had heard from him all evening. "I have reassured Rossingley on numerous occasions that my plantation thrives regardless of inclement weather. I can provide all his needs." His dark gaze flicked to Rossingley. "Every single one of them."

"And I have reassured you," Rossingley countered with a sweet smile, "That whilst your offer is much appreciated, I prefer to deal with old friends and families who have been in the ken of my own family for nigh on a hundred years. One cannot ignore the weight of history, my dear Hamilton, even if one hails from a country so thrillingly grand and progressive as America."

"You are m-m-mitigating risk," got out Sir Richard.

"Exactly," said the earl, pleased. "Like every astute businessman should. So, if you are interested in pursuing this venture, over the coming days, you will have ample opportunity to study the finer details with Mr Angel, who will be delighted to share them with you. After that, if you feel you have the heart for it, place a bid! Join me! And if your offer comes close to the amount that Mr Hamilton and his family are prepared to put on the table, then I daresay I will have found myself an excellent business partner. What say you, chaps?"

Chapter Thirteen

LANDO'S HEART SUSTAINED a wild and erratic beating long after his guests had departed. Trepidation and excitement were replaced by a surge of strength now vying with nervous exhaustion. A strained drumming pounded at his temples; he felt as if he wanted to both run around and crash into a dreamless sleep. And yet, he'd never felt more revitalised. The naked audacity! The cheek, the sheer nerve, the gall! The gumption! He blew out a long breath as if blowing away all the tension that, up until now, had held his spine rigid and his mind so focussed.

Tommy Squire had played his part well — too well if Angel's smouldering possessive silence was any marker. Cobham and Sir Richard, too, though unwittingly, of course. Embroiling his upstanding cousin, Sir Richard, in his scheming gave Lando a pang of guilt, but already his nimble mind had an idea forming as to how he would make it up to him after this thing had been put to bed. Though of a reticent disposition, Richard's shrewdness was known and celebrated throughout the *ton*. Less well known was that an unpleasant young oik by the name of Ambrose Gartside had bullied him mercilessly at Eton, accounting for his crippling stutter and lifelong inability to communicate with the fairer sex. Returning to his comfortable bachelor lodgings at the Albany, Lando knew he'd mull the scheme well into the dawn. If he couldn't discern cracks in it, then there weren't any to be found.

In his turn, Gartside had watched Sir Richard like prey, his dull eyes flitting between Cobham and Lando's clever cousin. He'd hung on their every question, and there had been so many of them, one after another, like keen archers firing arrow after arrow at Lando's armour. Only his wealth, status, and unimpeachable pedigree blinded them to his scheming and the sham it was.

Dear Charles would have been so very proud of him.

Leaning against the drawing room escritoire, Lando rubbed at his weary eyes, still restless but fit for nothing more than his bed.

When he opened them again, Angel stood before him, an amused smile playing at his lips.

"I don't know whether to be awestruck or terrified, my lord," he murmured. "But I sincerely hope Lord Cobham didn't drink your port supplies totally dry. I'm in dire need of some to quell my nerves."

Lando huffed a laugh. "Help yourself."

Angel divested himself of his coat, and Lando watched while the other man unstopped the decanter and poured two generous inches. The satin of his tight-fitting waistcoat moved with him, closely enough to show the contours of his broad back. White linen billowed from his shoulders, and a few locks of his spirally dark curls had escaped the ribbon. His breeches fit snugly across his thighs.

Lando's thirsty eyes drank him in.

"This land," said Angel when he returned to where Lando hadn't budged from the desk. "It doesn't exist, does it?" He swirled the tawny liquid around his glass before taking a swallow. "I have to confess, my lord. I haven't quite grasped what you're up to."

"You hid it well." A smile pulled at Lando's lips. "And on the contrary, the land does exist. Though I have no intention of constructing mills on it. Rather, I'm of a mind to build myself a hunting lodge. It isn't quite as close to the mill as I led you all to believe. There is a thick copse protecting it from busybodies in every direction, and the views over the moors at sunrise are truly breathtaking."

Angel's hazel eyes crinkled at the corners. "Does His Majesty's most senior Custodian of the River, the North, and the Holy Grail approve of this wholesome plan?"

Lando chuckled softly and, unable to hold back any longer, stroked the tips of his fingers along Angel's pristine white sleeve. Plucking the fine linen between a finger and thumb, he tugged him a little closer.

"I might have to offer him a lure." Lando gave a peculiar smile. "One should never underestimate the power of simple enticements. Especially if they hint at the possibility of great fortune."

Angel studied him. "You're talking of something else, aren't you? The plan to hook Gartside."

Lando inclined his head a fraction. "Keep going." Again, he ran his fingers along the length of the white sleeve, grazing over the angle of Angel's elbow and up to the smooth swell of his bicep. "Engage that keen mind of yours."

"I'm trying to, but it's damned difficult when you're doing that." Angel's lips pressed into a thin line as he frowned. "You're promising them great riches in exchange for investing money up front. In land that exists but isn't for sale."

"I am," Lando breathed. His hand curled around Angel's bicep. He revelled in the firm heft of it.

"You're dangling untold wealth under the nose of Lord Cobham, a...an ageing baron with a hatred for Ambrose Gartside."

"Go on," Lando encouraged.

"And tempting Sir Richard, another wealthy baronet and of high social standing. Reeling in Gartside himself, a spendthrift and a rake, desperate to hold on to his fortunes."

Lando gave a low amused laugh. "Don't forget that dreadful American fellow."

"Most dreadful," agreed Angel. He chewed his lip thoughtfully.

"You want Gartside to bid for the project and outbid the others, don't you?"

Lando inclined his head graciously. "He needs to be ruined somehow," he agreed. "Which means he needs to be persuaded to part with what money he has left. And soon, before he spends it all."

"Yes," said Angel urgently. "That's it." Excitedly, he ran a hand through his thick dark locks. Lando could almost see the pieces of the puzzle falling into place. Lando's far-reaching proposal, the light in sensible Sir Richard's eyes. Cobham spotting it too. Tommy, playing that awful American perfectly, barely holding back his amusement. Purse-pinched Gartside's naked greed. And Angel in the middle, supposedly a government intermediary, an unknown, but trustworthy by virtue of his position. *I might have to offer him a lure.*

"So, Gartside will bid for a project that isn't for sale," Angel continued. "That's it, isn't it? To build mills that will never exist and expand a trade route not open for expansion."

Lando smoothed a path along Angel's collar bone with his fingers. "You're getting warmer."

"But he doesn't have the funds. Or he does, perhaps, but using them will take everything he has. And yet, by taking this chance, he can restore his fortunes. So he needs the deal desperately, far more than the others. At all costs, Gartside needs to win."

"Very warm," purred Lando.

Angel's chest was very warm, too, the heat of his skin a delicious distraction Lando planned to deal with very shortly if only Angel could join the dots… *I might have to offer him a lure…*

"You want him to bribe me, don't you?" Angel finished triumphantly. "You want Gartside to grease me in the fist. To break the law by offering money to an entrusted senior government official, a great deal of money in exchange for ensuring he wins the bid."

"Bravo." Lando smiled at the younger man's eager excitement. "And then?"

"And then, when he's won, he will need to sell his unentailed estate next to yours to fund the investment."

Angel suddenly frowned. Lando could almost hear his mind

whirring. "My lord, there's a flaw. A rather glaring one. *There is no investment.* The whole thing is a ruse. There are no mills. You are not building on your land."

"Correct."

Roughly, Angel ran his hand through his hair. "But don't you see? After he bribes me and he discovers that, he won't sell the estate. Which means he'll be in exactly the same position as he is now, except after our blood and demanding his bribe back."

Lando drifted his fingers lightly from Angel's chest, only to travel as far as one of the delicately embroidered buttons securing his single-breasted waistcoat. Not used to unfastening his own attire without assistance, Lando was pleasantly surprised how competently he succeeded in unfastening Angel's.

"Let me teach you something about a certain type of gentleman, Mr Angel," Lando began. "Knowledge gained from a lifetime observing them at close quarter."

A second button fell apart under his ministrations. There were only nine in total. In contrast, Lando's own waistcoat, lilac silk and double-breasted, boasted twenty-eight. A third button popped undone, revealing a mouth-watering crescent of snowy white linen. The fourth fell open easily too; he didn't understand why Pritchard made such a fuss.

"Some spoiled idlers," he continued, "are never satisfied with what they have or what they don't have. Whether they crave a finer stable of racehorses or a pair of double-barrelled Purdeys, a crested phaeton or a titled young bride, there is always someone with something better. Unless, perhaps, you are the king. But then, King Ferdinand of Spain may have even more. Who knows?"

Another button unfastened to the sound of Angel's breath catching in his throat.

"So, you must trust me when I assure you Ambrose Gartside will want to secure that business deal with every single fibre of his being. And nothing would give him more satisfaction than snatching it from the likes of Sir Richard so he, too, can be held in such high esteem."

Lando toyed with the next button. "You must appreciate that the good opinion of others is terribly important to a man as high in the instep as Gartside. Losing position in society, for a rake as odious as him, is akin to losing everything." Tipping his head back, he flicked his gaze up to meet Angel's.

"And that, my dear, will be the path leading to his ruination. With a gentle push in the right direction, Gartside will destroy himself. We're simply handing him the tools."

Two buttons and a stud remained at the top of his shirt. But to reach those, Lando had to untie the knot of Angel's cravat, a manoeuvre requiring him to sweep his fingertips along the length of the other man's angular jaw to reach it. In fact, he needed to perform the manoeuvre several times until the knot loosened. On the second occasion, the tips of his fingers had to linger awhile and fondle the marvellous golden hoop at Angel's ear.

"So, as I understand it," clarified Angel, still sounding uncertain and deliciously distracted, "Gartside is going to bribe me, and then you're going to expose him. What then?"

"Greasing the palms of government officials is a terribly serious crime." Lando tutted. "Even a baronet such as Gartside would be pressed to wriggle out of that. If you were a true official, who knows how the magistrates might disgrace him."

"But I'm not," pointed out Angel.

"No. But Ambrose Gartside doesn't know that. And he's never going to find out. Nor are the others. Because when he discovers that you have informed myself and Cobham and Sir Richard of his underhanded and unsporting behaviour, he'll face a far worse punishment than supping on gruel in Newgate."

"Will he?" Angel shivered as Lando slipped his hands inside his shirt, one of them exploring his bare chest.

"Yes, very much so. Because as well as forever checking over his shoulder and listening out for the heavy tread of the law, he'll be facing shame, ignominy, and loss of face. Cobham is an inveterate gossip, and neither Sir Richard nor myself are above whispering malice in a few well-placed ears. I assure you that, within a week, not a single drawing room in the *ton* will be open to him."

"That doesn't sound a terrible punishment at all."

"That's because you don't give two figs what the *ton* thinks of you," Lando answered. Lando didn't care much either. If he did, he wouldn't be rubbing the pad of his thumb across one of Angel's nipples.

"When the rumours begin to circulate," Lando continued, "his creditors will cease with their ever-so-polite reminders and bash down his door instead, demanding debts be settled. White's will quietly withdraw his membership. Invitations will dry up. His staff will leave when he can no longer pay them. The bank will foreclose on his London townhouse."

He stroked a finger into the notch between Angel's collarbones, following the path with his lips.

"Ye gods," muttered Angel.

"Precisely," Lando murmured against satiny skin. "And so

it will go on until he retires to his cold and draughty entailed estate in Scotland with his tail between his legs to beg pity from his sister and brother-in-law. Never to be seen again."

Lando tipped his head up at the same moment as Angel's cravat unravelled in a stream of snowy-white silk. "And at that point, my dearest Angel, I plan to step in and kindly ease some of his dreadful burden by offering to take a debt-ridden, unentailed estate off his hands."

He hovered with an eyebrow raised. "Which won't come for free, of course. And is in a dreadful mess. But he'll sell it for a song and, fortunately for me, I'll have recently acquired a ready source of blunt with which to put to good use in restoring it to its former state."

"Gartside's own money!" Angel ran his hands up Lando's arms, a wondrous grin of delight splitting his face. "My lord, you are…you are…" He shook his head. "Something else."

"I know. And, in case it has escaped your notice, desperate to be kissed."

Angel fell on him, crushing Lando's lips against his own. His hands tangled in Lando's hair as Lando wrapped his arms around his neck, pulling him down. As the heat of Angel's firm body pressed against him, Lando moaned with pleasure, pressing his own hardness back against Angel in return.

"Something is telling me the Chief Inspector of the River is not going to prove terribly difficult to corrupt," he gasped.

Angel's mouth widened with mirth around Lando's, and then he broke off. "Call me Kit, please," he panted. "Everyone else who knows me does, and our friendship has sailed well beyond pleasantries and polite terms of address; I hope you agree."

Mr Ange—*Kit's* determined fingers brushed against Lando's swollen prick as they picked at the buttons on the front fall of his breeches. Never mind pleasantries; Lando had sailed beyond rational thought.

"Tell me how I should address you, my lord," breathed Kit, licking and sucking on Lando's parted lips. "'Your lordship' is so terribly formal, is it not?" He paused in his lapping to shoot Lando a wicked grin. "Especially when my hand rests here."

A cool palm curled around Lando's member, startling a gasp from his throat.

"Lando," he sighed, pushing up into Kit's touch. "Address me as Lando. Almost *no one* else does."

At first, Kit did nothing but hold him, feeling the heft, while his scalding lips discovered new places to tease. Such as Lando's earlobe and the sensitive, shallow depression behind it. He paid a visit to the ribbon of flesh above Lando's high collar, too, before forging a new path along the blade of Lando's jaw. As if sampling every needy inch of him. "Lando." He breathed the wonderful sound of it against Lando's neck, drawing it out. "Much better. Henry Orlando Fitzwilliam Albert Duchamps-Avery is such a mouthful, is it not?" Sharp teeth nibbled tender skin as Lando let out a giggle. "When there are so many other things that I could be filling my mouth with?"

Gadzooks, the man was good. Lando let his head fall back, the line of his throat wide open to his new lover's touch. Kit's hand on his shaft closed more tightly, and he let out a whimper.

"Lando." Kit repeated it as he pressed kisses into Lando's quivering flesh before once more sealing his lips against Lando's mouth. How gloriously intimate. And how gloriously Lando felt his constrained, rigid composure melt under Kit's touch. As his breath quickened, Kit deepened the kiss. His member throbbed, hard as iron, against Lando's thigh as the slide of his palm up and down the length of Lando's satiny shaft intensified.

With an urgent whimper, Lando spread wider, arching into Kit's touch, swelling impossibly more in Kit's hand. Clutching at his behind, he drew Kit in further, hoisting his leg around his waist, as if by squeezing him close enough, he could climb inside.

Lando's chest rose and fell. His breath grew ragged, his kisses open and panting. His spine tingled with pleasure.

"I'm...yes...oh gosh, yes." With a cry smothered against Kit's mouth, his hot spend flooded Kit's hand.

"Kit. I'm..."

Whatever he was, Kit would never find out; the sentence remained unfinished. Limply, Lando dropped his head to his shoulder. Kit's arms came around his back, and he cradled Lando, pressing his lips to his hair.

When Lando finally stirred, Kit lifted his chin, smiling into his eyes still blurred with lust. Heat flushed his cheeks, and he let out a shy laugh. "I'm...thank you," he managed at last. "I ought to return the favour."

"No favour. The pleasure was all mine."

Kit planted a kiss at the end of Lando's nose, which he wrinkled. His hands dropped to Lando's behind and stayed there, stroking him. Kit kissed his nose again. "Lando," he said again. Lando didn't imagine he would ever tire of hearing it. "The name suits you."

"Your uncle Charles was one of the few people who have ever used it," Lando confessed. "Since our father passed, even my own sister addresses me as 'Rossingley.'"

"Then I shall use it freely," declared Kit, and he dropped a final kiss on Lando's nose. "And Uncle Charles had excellent taste in men. You, *Lando*, were extraordinary this evening."

"Only if Gartside plays along. Otherwise, all this will be to no end."

"I'll wager he will."

Lando gave a rueful smile. "I'm of the same accord. Which means I'm going to thoroughly ruin him, aren't I? Does that make me cruel?"

Kit shook his head. "He's going to thoroughly ruin himself one way or another. Like you said, you are merely nudging him along so fewer innocent souls suffer along the way. He's already devastated several other people's lives, perhaps it's time he tasted his own medicine. The only fly in the ointment is if your wealthy American friend persists in outbidding him or tries to bribe me too."

Lando fondled Kit's firm, high buttocks. "That…ah…won't happen. Our American will do as he's told."

Kit huffed. "I wouldn't be so sure. My, admittedly limited, impression of people from that nation is that they are a law unto themselves."

Lando arched an amused brow. "Not this one." He laughed softly. "I'll let you into another secret. When Mr Arthur Hamilton of South Carolina isn't imbibing my excellent port and winding Lord Cobham into a stew, he may be found treading the boards at Drury Lane and expanding his gambling hell empire. When he is not occupied with either of those, he is discreetly and expertly pleasuring rich widows in exchange for considerable sums of money, which he uses to fund the aforementioned expansion of his gambling empire."

Kit's jaw dropped. "Yet again, you have the capacity to astound me. Where on earth did you find him?"

Lando flushed. "Tommy Squire and I — for that is his true name — are old friends. I helped him out of a hole a long time ago, earning his undivided loyalty. And…and even in the depths of my mourning for your uncle Charles, I occasionally experienced some…base needs." He threw Kit a defiant look. "I'm not a monk. And Tommy is steadfast and…trustworthy."

"He's in love with you, that's what he is." Annoyance coloured Kit's tone. "Any fool can see that." He paused a beat. "Any fool of our persuasion, anyhow. I doubt your other dinner guests picked up on it. Your Tommy Squire would like nothing more than to be standing where I am now."

"He would," conceded Lando. "But he isn't. And although he has a deep affection for me, as I do for him, his heart most definitely lies elsewhere. Don't be cross that he deceived you. He makes a very convincing liar, as many have discovered to their cost. He will be well remunerated for his time and efforts."

"But not like this," insisted Kit.

Lando slipped a hand under the waistband of Kit's breeches. "No. I prefer my men one at a time."

Chapter Fourteen

ALONE IN THE early hours, after privately assuaging his own *base needs*, Kit spotted another flaw. Not in Lando, despite his disappointment that the man took himself off to his own bedchamber after their intimacy against the sturdy desk. In Kit's eyes, Lando was already approaching perfection from every angle, even flushed and unguarded at the peak of his crisis, and no man ever looked his best at *that* pivotal moment. But a flaw in their scheme to overthrow Gartside and, specifically, the parts affecting Kit himself. An uneasiness settled over him, a ragged thread of worry just out of reach. If his lust-soaked mind wasn't so intent on painting pictures of the earl in various stages of undress, he might be able to pinpoint it. Instead, he wrestled with the problem until dawn, which arrived misty and grey and devoid of a solution.

Breakfast distracted him further because Lando was already seated at the head of the table, sorting a mountain of correspondence into two piles whilst picking at a tiny bowl of figs. He was dressed immaculately in another beguiling robe, this one a delicate rose pink. Ye gods, the man was beautiful. Glacial until one laid one's hands on him, but beautiful, nonetheless. Any concerns Kit harboured that Lando might regret last night's brief interlude were banished when he greeted him with a warm smile.

"I was hoping you'd join me, Kit." Lando gestured to the sideboard. "Help yourself."

Holding up a gilt-edged card, he sighed. "I've been back amongst the *ton* for less than forty-eight hours and already the aspirational mamas are lining up their daughters. Unfortunately, being emotionally indisposed is not sufficient excuse to turn down a soiree at Lady Chalfont's."

He dropped the card onto the smaller of the two heaps. "This, here, is the *regretfully attend* pile." Picking up another, he examined the writing, then cast it aside without even opening it. He motioned to the larger heap. "This pile I have labelled *enthusiastically decline.*"

With a grin, Kit heaped sausage and eggs onto a plate and poured coffee. "Mamas the length and breadth of Mayfair will be distraught." After a sip of coffee, smoother than any he'd ever tasted, he set to tackling his breakfast. "You won't consider another marriage?"

"Gadzooks, no! I have my heir and my spare, thank you very much. And my younger sister seems set on breeding her own wolfpack should disaster befall them both." He dabbed his mouth with a lily-white square of linen. "Further efforts in that direction would be a huge waste of my energies." He popped a fig between his plush lips. "Especially when they can be spent on much more *fruitful* pursuits."

Dangling yet another item of correspondence between finger and thumb, Lando's pale eyes regarded Kit innocently. Why did every word spilling from this man's damned fine mouth provoke Kit's mind to flights of fancy? Was he flirting with Kit to distract from the morning's post, or had Kit simply lost control of his own concupiscence?

Either way, he delivered himself a sharp reminder not to make himself too comfortable. The rich coffee and the excellent breakfast were but temporary. As was their liaison. When, and if, Gartside was avenged, Kit would return to his humble lodgings and attempt to forge a more respectable lifestyle, and the earl would go back to…Kit was unsure, but harboured no illusions it would involve him.

"My sister has corresponded, by the way." The crisp sound of paper unfolding brought Kit back to earth. "She informs me that Anne is settling in nicely."

"Truly excellent news," answered Kit. "I must write to her, conveying my utmost gratitude and good wishes." Glancing at an older footman standing sentry by the breakfast room door, staring resolutely ahead, he dropped his voice. "My lor…Lando, I have a question for you. Regarding our plan."

"Only one?" Steepling his elbows on the table, Lando's eyes followed the direction of Kit's. "You may speak freely. Jones has been in my family's employ for thirty years. I have an extremely loyal household."

Yes, Kit was aware. His bruises were yet to fade. "No, not exactly. I have…um…several, in fact. But one is perhaps concerning me more than most."

"Ah." The earl's eyes glittered. "And I have a feeling I know what it might be. We should have discussed further last night. Except our evening quite ran away with itself, did it not?"

Kit cursed. There it was again. That damned fluttery, suggestive tone making coherent thought difficult. "Well, yes. The part I'm unsure about is—what happens afterwards? When I'm exposed for—" Despite Lando's reassurance, Kit lowered his voice, " —impersonating a senior government official?"

"Why do you think you'll be exposed?"

"Why do you think I won't? Sir Richard and Cobham will discover the truth sooner or later. And it strikes me as a crime associated with a lengthy prison sentence. Or even worse."

Images of sturdy iron shackles and his ankles attached to them flooded Kit's head. They portrayed a world far removed from rich coffee, crispy bacon, and a large comfortable bed. So, why did a nagging voice inside his head hint that one might be…payment for the other?

Shoving that train of thought aside, Kit pushed on. "Let's assume Gartside falls for it and attempts to bribe me. I agree with your assessment that he won't blab because doing so will expose his bribe and poor form. But there would be nothing stopping Sir Richard and Cobham when they discover I'm an imposter. Even though they won't have risked money, I'll still have made fools of them. To all intents and purposes, unless you intend to confess to your part in the scheme, it will appear that I'll have made fools of you and the *American* too." He chewed a mouthful of tender bacon, suddenly lacking in flavour. "Which may not concern you too much, but then it won't be your neck on the chopping block, will it?"

The chopping block? Where had that sprung from?

With sudden shocking clarity, Kit's niggling concerns of the night before fell into place, and he stared at his host in horror. Of course, that was it! What a fool he'd been! *Confess?* Why on earth would Lando do that? The earl would pretend, along with the rest of them, that he'd been deceived by Kit too. At worst, it would prove embarrassing for him, just as it would be for Cobham and Sir Richard. But not *life-threatening*.

Placidly, Lando contemplated his next fig. So calm, so elegant, so *controlling*. Of everything and everybody, including Kit, from the moment they kissed in the carriage. The assembled dinner guests had danced to his tune like marionettes on a string. And then, after the guests departed, the earl seduced him in their delicious episode in the drawing room, granting him permission to use his name. Kit remembered his hands working the earl's prick, gladly offering him pleasure and release.

And the act had not been reciprocated.

It was like a dreadful, third-rate operatic aria. Kit's own words played in his head: *It won't be your neck on the chopping block, will it?* But it would be somebody's. Somebody had to pay for setting up this elaborate scheme to bring down the baronet and to avenge his sister, the estate workers, and all Gartside's other victims. And that somebody was Kit. He was an utter fool not to have seen it before.

Nauseated, he pushed his plate away. It would serve him well to remember that his host, tranquilly sipping coffee and nibbling his damned figs, was the same ruthless person who had booted him out of his house. Twice. The same icy soul who had roughed him up against the wall of the stables.

"How terribly dramatic of you, Kit! Of course it won't come to that." The earl's amused cut-glass tones sliced through his thoughts. "The chances of anyone discovering you aren't who you purport to be are very slim."

"'Very slim' isn't very reassuring. You introduced me using my real name! I'm going to be running from the law for the remainder of my days."

Lando sighed. "Now, you're being ridiculous."

"Easy for you to say! I'm only relieved Anne used our uncle's name when she was in Gartside's mother's employ."

Stabbing at his breakfast, Kit wracked his brains for a way out. One that didn't involve Gartside escaping scot-free. He came up with nothing. Annoyingly, he liked the earl's daring plan right up to the part that he didn't, the last chapter. *Trust me*, Lando had said. And led by his bloody prick, Kit had.

Blind fury replaced his earlier panic, girding his loins. If he was going to the gallows, then it wouldn't be without a fight. And he'd damned well take Tommy Squire, the *American*, with him. He'd bet his bottom teeth that the slimy actor would waste no time implicating the earl if it gave him a chance of saving his own skin. Which would leave Kit where? A peer of the realm's word against that of a tawdry actor and a card-sharping pickpocket, already being hunted by the runners. Which meant, taking the whole thing to its logical conclusion: Lando would walk away free, and Kit and Tommy would be swinging from a rope. His stomach roiled.

"Kit," urged Lando. "I'm eavesdropping on your thoughts, and they're heading in an unnecessary direction."

"Unnecessary for you, perhaps." Kit cracked his knuckles,

quelling his overwhelming urge to throw something. "How wonderful it must be to have such station in life that one is above the law."

Lando narrowed his eyes. "Really, now you're being absurd. I'm telling you the law won't have anything to do with this because no one will ever find out!"

"Forgive me, *my lord*," Kit growled, "If I don't share your faith. Everybody in that room last night will be livid when they discover the whole thing is nothing but a ruse. Fleecing Gartside will be the least of my worries."

With a pained sigh, Lando shifted his letter piles to one side. "Right. Let's address your concerns one at a time, shall we? Beginning with Tommy Squire. Who obviously already knows it's a ruse."

"He'll talk. He'll gossip. People can't help themselves."

Lando shook his head. "No, he won't. I have no intention of divulging the exact story behind Tommy's association with me, but I can assure you that, at knifepoint, or even with the hangman's stool poised to be kicked out from under him, that man will never betray me." He turned over his palm as if tapping off his fingers. "Who's next?"

How coolly this harshly elegant man viewed him across the breakfast table. How chilly. He was once more behaving like the perfect stranger Kit first met in contrast to last night's lover, so soft and pliant, melting in his arms. If Kit didn't know better, he'd imagine the evening's finale had been nothing more than a combination of wishful thinking and an excess of rich brandy.

"Now, let's consider Gartside. We both agree he won't spill the tale, do we not? When his bribe comes to light, he will flee and likely never show his face again in society. Given that you have little intention after this is over of joining society yourself, the chances of either of you ever clapping eyes on each other again are as remote as me wooing and bedding a second bride."

Lando flashed a grim smile, exposing his small sharp teeth.

"What about the other two?" demanded Kit. "Their blunt may be safe, but they will lose a great deal of face. Lord Cobham is loud and brash. He has a short temper and won't take kindly to being hoodwinked, even if the principal victim is the scoundrel who cheapened his daughter."

Lando remained unperturbed. "Fear not, my friend. Within the last year, Lord Cobham has suffered two episodes of apoplexy, the second almost fatal. He has crippling gout, an excessive fondness for port, and a belly set to pop." Lando cupped a hand behind his ear. "Hark, the angels are already trimming their wicks. I wager he'll have hung up his dinner pail by the end of the year."

After witnessing the older man trying to catch his breath while waddling to the dining table, Kit was in private agreement with the earl's pithy assessment. Not that he would give him the satisfaction.

"When this is through," Lando continued, "you should lay low — I suggest Rossingley would be an ideal location." He smiled again, the seductive flirty one that had Kit so pathetically entranced despite his misgivings. "Until the poor man is sadly no more."

Kit huffed, still wanting to throw something. Not only was Lando devilishly attractive, it seemed he also had an answer for everything. "What about Sir Richard, then? He's in fine health, youngish too. And sharp as a rose thorn."

This time when Lando smiled, it seemed quite genuine. "Sir Richard will hear the truth. But not until it's all over."

"Why ever would you do that?"

"Firstly, he's my cousin. Blood is thicker than water and what reflects badly on me will undoubtedly reflect badly on him. Also, he detests Gartside as much as anyone—again, I am not at liberty to divulge why. Underneath that stuffy exterior, Sir Richard has a good sense of humour. In all honesty, he'll be delighted at our cunning." Another genuine smile. "And I am hoping to reward him in a manner that will please him, and possibly you, greatly."

Kit huffed again. "Let me guess; you won't divulge?"

"How well you have grown to know me," replied Lando sweetly, "in such a short space of time."

Damnation, the man was infuriating. And outrageously desirable, and with an answer to everything. He had a way of making Kit feel like he should trust him when it should have been obvious even to the blessed damask wallpaper, never mind the silent footman, that he shouldn't. And if anyone else were to dismiss his concerns for his own liberty with such unflappable high-handed self-belief, then Kit would probably succumb to his physical urges and plant his fist against the man's haughty, smug mouth. So why did he want to plant his own mouth against Lando's instead?

"Good. Now we have that little contretemps out of the way," said Lando, prising apart yet another wax seal with an exquisite bone-handled knife. "You still haven't asked me how it's really going to end."

"With me possibly swinging from a rope—I thought I'd

made that clear!"

The invitation card joined the *enthusiastically decline* pile, and the earl tutted. "Please don't be overly theatrical, Kit darling. It's far too early in the morning. What I mean is, you haven't asked how we get to that part. How Gartside's bribe becomes exposed without everyone discovering the entire land-selling scheme is a hoax."

"No, I haven't. It hadn't occurred, what with being more concerned with keeping my head attached to my body. I assume you're about to enlighten me?"

"Ah. Sadly not." A frown touched Lando's face. "You aren't the only one of us wrestling with this. I must confess, that part of the plan has so far eluded me." He examined another letter as if it mattered not a jot. "I daresay it will come, in time."

"Well, that's all right then," grumbled Kit. "I'll just sit around waiting until it does, shall I? Or do you have more shopping errands arranged for this morning? Or another pretty actor friend of yours, waiting to fool me and play the coquette with you and incite my…my ire? Unless you've tired already of jerking my puppet strings."

His little hissy fit was met with a look of mild amusement. "Jealous of Tommy? How delightful." Lando laid the back of a hand on his cheek. "Goodness, I'm blushing."

A desire to scream at the top of his lungs supplanted Kit's desire to throw something. God dammit, the man tested his patience.

"Alas, as much as I'd like to spend the day providing entertainment for you," Lando carried on, "I have a whole list of dreadful chores—a result of having neglected visiting London for far too long. So, your time is your own."

He waved one of the invitations at Kit. "Tonight, however, we are being seen. At Lady Chalfont's soiree, where I'll wager the whole *ton* will turn up to have a gander at me. Including Gartside, lending you an excellent opportunity to further your acquaintance. Along with my acceptance, I will send a note that I'm bringing an important houseguest."

As Lando rose from the table, he threw Kit a final smile. "Do you dance?"

To your tune? Yes, Kit was tempted to bite back. "Not if I can help it," he growled instead.

"Excellent. We'll dine here beforehand and arrive late. We'll do a couple of turns of the room then join in a card game or two, which is when you can chum up to Gartside and make him believe you are not only a customs official of the highest order but that you are also eminently corruptible."

"You are mistaking me for one of your friend Tommy's fellow thespian pals."

"Some of your time today will be well spent considering the topography and magnitude of our country's cotton industry," Lando carried on, overlooking Kit's gruff interjection as if he'd not spoken. "You will find my library has several excellent pamphlets and books on that exact subject. I expect my absence from your company will fly by."

Chapter Fifteen

"MY HOUSEGUEST AND I had...ah...a little falling out over breakfast."

Whilst Pritchard laid out his evening attire, Lando stretched the length of the tub, luxuriating in the exotic scents of citrus and bergamot.

"Bound to happen sooner or later," Pritchard commented. "Mr Angel's a poor young hothead, and you're a cold-hearted devil of an aristocrat. I'm not surprised."

Lando swivelled to stare at him, trying to keep a straight face. No man was a hero to his valet, thank heavens. A spoiled, wealthy one such as himself needed at least one person in his pay keeping him honest. "Just so you know, I don't care for that ex-planation, Pritchard."

Quick to temper, Kit had been mulish over breakfast, and nothing Lando had said managed to placate him. The meal had ended coolly; the young man had taken what he needed from the library up to his bedchamber and had not been sighted by Lando since.

"He's suspicious of my motives."

"Of course he is," answered Pritchard. "You've only given him half the plan."

"That's because I only have half the plan. I even admitted that to him." Raising it beyond the water level, Lando soaped his long, pale calf. "Which, in retrospect, did not provide the reassurance I hoped it might."

On the contrary, it served to make his young friend even angrier. He gave a frustrated hum.

"He's very different to...to Charles. He's fiery; he rails against the injustice of everything. And he's a thief, of course, which makes his belief that *I'm* the untrustworthy one even more laughable."

"But?" queried Pritchard.

"But..." Lando sighed. "I'm finding that I like him very much."

Wisely, the valet stayed silent as Lando voiced the words again in his head, testing the veracity of them. That he'd even compared his frivolous desire for young, pretty Kit to his deep, overarching love for Charles was astonishing.

"Unfortunately, Mr Angel is becoming less fond of me by the hour," he added, not allowing himself any more pause for thought. "He thinks I'm leading him to the slaughter to further my own gains, namely to obtain Gartside's estate for myself."

"How can you convince him otherwise?"

By getting him into my bed. Getting my need for him out of my system.

"By coming up with a suitable denouement to this wretched scheme. I have a couple of ideas, but I'm still not convinced they are the right ones. If I wasn't developing such a *tendre* for the fellow, I could have Kit arrested for accepting bribes. Publicly — or in front of Gartside, Cobham, and Sir Richard at least. As long as no one ever found out that he *wasn't* a true custom's official, then Gartside's humiliation would be complete."

"Tommy Squire should have plenty of friends who could dress up and play the part of a lawman," Pritchard observed.

"Mmm."

Paying one of Tommy's actor pals to take on the role of a Bow Street runner was the obvious solution. He could spring an arrest on Kit, arranged to occur in front of the others. Though the simplicity held appeal, it relied heavily on Kit's hitherto untested dramatic flair. More importantly, it relied on the individual to never tell. Which they would, naturally, because actors and scuttlebutt went hand in hand.

A much more definite conclusion, and one Lando dismissed on the spot, would be if someone let slip to the *real* customs officials that an imposter was trying to extort London gentlemen — Lando included. Then let Kit take the fall and subsequently persuade the magistrates to go gently on him. Gartside would still be humiliated, but it was a horrible plan with far too many ifs and buts for Lando's liking, and the chances of magistrates dismissing Kit, already wanted for a different set of crimes, was highly improbable.

He sighed, sinking lower in the tub. "Any news from Jasper?"

"Yes, my lord," Pritchard answered sourly. "Plenty. Starting with a declaration that the joys of valeting are not to his liking. And he's making certain that everybody below stairs is aware of it."

Lando laughed. "Surely dressing a man as comely as Mr Angel isn't that tiresome, is it?"

"Heavens, no. I'd give my eyeteeth to have at him."

As Lando twisted in his bath to stare him down, Pritchard added, "Obviously being *your* personal valet is a far superior and elevated position."

"Far superior."

"Though he is a fine figure of a man."

"He is that," agreed Lando. "In fact, I'm particularly taken by his broad shoulders. Though it sounds as if they are not sufficient to sway Jasper's low opinion."

Pritchard peered at Lando's midnight black evening dress, smoothing out an imaginary wrinkle. "No. Mr Angel's presence unfortunately serves to remind Jasper that the man has insulted you more than once. And Jasper's presence reminds Mr Angel of his lingering bruises. They are struggling to see eye to eye. Literally. Especially after today's run around."

Lando reached for a washcloth. "Do tell?"

Pritchard moistened his lips before launching into his tale. "Well, having spent much of the morning reading through that dull pile of books you left for him, Mr Angel tried to give Jasper the slip by sneaking out of a side entrance unobserved." Pritchard shook out a silk stocking. "He failed, naturally. Jasper followed him at a discreet distance, though God knows how that great one-eyed lump manages to blend into the background. Regardless, Mr Angel didn't spot him."

"Where did he go?"

"Vauxhall Gardens, my lord. Whereupon he strolled, aimlessly. Jasper had the impression he was spying out all the other young, well-dressed gentlemen with nothing better to do. And then deliberately contriving to walk alongside them and occasionally stopping to pass the time of day."

Annoyance bit at Lando's insides, and he scowled.

"But not walking *with* them," added Pritchard after a delicate pause. "If you catch my drift."

Lando breathed a sigh of relief. "I do, but the suspense you add to a tale is quite vexatious. And after Mr Angel's social meanderings?"

Pritchard's brow furrowed. "Jasper said it was most curious. After setting a painfully slow pace along the main avenue, as soon as he left the gardens, Mr Angel marched to Vauxhall Bridge like his arse was on fire, if you'll pardon the expression. Dived into one of the less salubrious goldsmiths, was back outside five minutes later, then headed here. Thankfully, Hargreaves made his usual song and dance over relieving him of his hat and coat at the front door, giving Jasper time to hotfoot it around the back and pretend he'd been loitering in the scullery polishing boots all along. Upon which Mr Angel inspected the boots and remarked that considering he'd been at it all afternoon, they weren't especially shined. Which put Jasper's nose out of joint something rotten."

"I imagine it did," replied Lando slowly, aware of a growing sense of unease. Perhaps his relief that Kit wasn't searching for male entertainment had been premature. Wandering around throngs of strangers then visiting a pawn shop? He knew precisely what Kit was up to, namely his light-fingered old tricks. For everyone's sake, Lando hoped the runner, Clark, was less observant than Jasper. Suddenly, his bathing was less sweet. "My towel please, Pritchard, and my robe."

*

WITH THEIR DISAGREEMENT and his worries still fresh in Kit's mind—judging from his expressive, downturned mouth—they dined in near silence. Lando's London dining table comprised fewer leaves than the expansive ocean at his country estate, necessitating Kit to be seated only a few feet away from him. Nonetheless, the distance may well have been the body of water separating England from France. How different this was to the atmosphere of their supper together at Rossingley, Lando reflected. And how well crisp evening attire suited his darkly handsome guest. Even if he was sulking. The man had quite a talent for it.

Whilst Kit chomped steadily through cook's excellent loin of pork with stewed apples, Lando only picked. For the first time since arriving in London and having Kit in his home, his thoughts turned towards Charles. At best, since losing his lover, his appetite had never been strong, but when faced with a stony companion, it was positively kittenish.

If such a wooden atmosphere hadn't prevailed, Lando might have been tempted to warn Kit that his modest home on Sindell Street was being watched, that perhaps even his pilfering at Vauxhall might be under scrutiny. Even Jasper wasn't infallible, for all that his one eye was surprisingly sharp. But if Lando did that, if he confessed to having Kit followed for no other reason than Lando's own naturally untrusting nature, then Kit would despise him even more.

"Tell me, Kit," he said, disturbing the empty stretch of time between clinks of silverware. "How did you come about your light-fingered skills?"

"Through necessity."

Lando waited for more. It was not forthcoming. He toyed with a morsel of pork.

"Whilst I appreciate your candidness, necessity does not enable a person to wake one morning with the required skills. Otherwise, every man down on his luck would be chancing his arm."

Kit speared a carrot, making Lando wait. "I'm not at liberty to divulge," he said after swallowing. "Isn't that your preferred expression? You're not the only one with secrets."

"I am, however, the only one of us behaving in an adult fashion." Lando's tone was sharp. "If you're having second thoughts regarding the whole scheme, now is the time to declare them. Before we wade out of our depth."

Kit laughed mirthlessly. "Wade out of our depth? It's a little too late for that, don't you think?" He waved his fork around as if searching for something to stab. "I want Gartside ruined. I may ruin my neck in the process. We've already established what's the worst that can happen." He thrust the fork into an unsuspecting roast potato. "So, for want of a better alternative, I'm going to have to go along with it, aren't I?"

*

"HENRY DUCHAMPS-AVERY, Eleventh Earl of Rossingley, and Mr Christopher Angel."

To describe a hush as settling across the room would not be an exaggeration. Followed by a noise akin to a swarm of a thousand bees as mouths whispered in ears and ladies murmured behind fans. At his shoulder, as erect and haughty as Kit had ever seen him, and utterly ravishing with it, Lando accepted the stares as his God-given due. Tonight, under his severe evening coat, the earl had selected a delicately embroidered sky-blue waistcoat. Though Kit had had opportunity at dinner to drink his fill, he still found himself sneaking admiring glances.

Once introduced to the matronly Lady Chalfont—from whom Kit only warranted the tiniest acknowledgment, given that his elusive aristocratic companion was far more interesting—a glass of punch found its way to his hand, and he was free to wander and act as if he belonged.

Even though he didn't, he found his evening entertainment fascinating and hideous in equal parts.

The ballroom and its occupants were a far cry from the country dances he'd endured growing up in the Kentish countryside. According to Lando, as they'd made their way across Mayfair in his crested landau, this wasn't a ball but a *soirée*, thus less grand and less formal. As Kit supped his weak fruit punch, lamenting a lack of fortification, his mind boggled as to how a ball could possibly be any grander. At least twenty servers waited on no fewer than sixty guests, entertained by a string quartet and a rather large gentleman belting out popular tunes on an overdecorated harpsichord. Assisted by garlands of flowers strewn across every surface and a cornucopia of lavish evening wear, the whole event was a dazzling riot of noise and colour, making Kit quite nauseous.

But no matter how many ladies in their flouncing finery wafted past on the arms of eligible young gentlemen, no matter how many mamas and timid second daughters engaged him in curious discourse, only the earl's slight figure ever caught his eye. *Doomed*, Kit thought miserably, sinking a second glass of over-sweet punch. Doomed to be infatuated by a man possibly plotting his downfall.

If Kit had hoped his lowly status as a provincial gentleman required to work for a living excused him from partnering ladies in dance, he was very much mistaken. No sooner had ten minutes elapsed before he was accosted by two young females of the plainer variety, both insisting he take to the floor. With Lando deep in conversation with a wizened patriarch, he had no alternative but to smile brightly and then stumble his way through a stately polonaise. Faring better in the quadrille, he manoeuvred the ladies back to their chaperone and then escaped the waltz by hiding behind an enormous potted plant bursting with flowers, which made him sneeze.

Lando, he observed, did not take to the dance floor once. In fact, as the dancing began in earnest, he hardly caught sight of his strikingly fair head at all. Sir Richard was not in attendance, nor Lord Cobham as far as Kit could tell, but he spotted Gartside during the second quadrille, surrounded by a rowdy group of young bucks already deep in their cups.

He heard him before he saw him, braying with a sneering kind of laughter, and for a second, Kit pictured the man leering over his poor sister, mocking as she cowered in fear. Flames of anger, still blazing away as though Gartside had assaulted Anne only yesterday, licked at his self-control. If it wasn't for a blushing young debutante and her sponsor attempting to ascertain his annual income through the medium of polite commentary, Kit would have marched over and socked Gartside on the jaw. Once he concurred with his female companions that the room was gay as a spring day and that Lady Chalfont did indeed gather the most delightful of crowds, Kit did the next best thing and took himself in search of a drink much stronger than bloody fruit punch.

*

HE MET UP with Lando in the card room, the earl's cool countenance and frosty hauteur as immaculate as on arrival. In contrast, Kit was sure he looked as hot and het up as he felt.

"People do this for fun?" he exclaimed as Lando cast an appraising eye over his appearance. "I've had three mothers ask me whether I'm a first or second son, and two daughters interrogate me on the number of bedchambers in my country home."

Lando's mouth quirked. "On a cooler evening such as this, I advise loitering on the upper balconies. It's an excellent deterrent. And if you select a windowed balcony with a long sash leading out to it, one can observe the vigorous goings-on inside without ever having to exert oneself."

"Did it not occur to you I might have appreciated those sage words in the carriage on the way here?"

Lando's pale blue eyes fluttered, full of mischief. "You were sulking. Magnificently."

He had a point.

"And," Lando continued, his delectable lips still twitching, "then I would have denied myself the pleasure of watching you dance."

Kit made a harrumphing sound. "Watch me long enough, and I'll be dancing on the end of a rope."

"Ah."

"*Ah* is not reassuring."

Kit's annoyance with Lando almost rivalled his desire. Which was a lot. Half of him wanted to strangle the man and the other half wanted to do something equally improper whilst a guest in another person's house. Instead, he had to satisfy himself with a further grunt and flopped into an empty chair.

"Do swallow your spleen, Kit, darling," Lando murmured. "There's a time and a place for anger, and it isn't now. All you're achieving with that thunderous face is a sore jaw from clenching your teeth."

"Gartside is despicable," Kit groused, ticking off the other reason for his poor temper. "I can barely manage to be in the same room as the man. Maybe I should lead him out onto one of those upper balconies, plant him a facer, then push him over it."

"Why don't you distract yourself with joining the next game of loo, instead." Lando's gaze flicked around the room. "You can take my position. It's Gartside's favourite, probably because it's one of the few games in which his small intellect grasps the rules. And at least then, you can mollify yourself with taking a few guineas from him while chumming up. Look, he's here to play now."

Having thrust him into the card game, Lando annoyingly vanished, leaving Kit once more having to control an urge to string Gartside up by his cravat. To make matters worse, he couldn't even temper his hunger for revenge by thrashing the man at loo. Which was damned infuriating as loo was one of the easiest games to manipulate ever invented. Tonight's game would have been child's play, seeing as every man around the table was already three sheets to the wind. All of them were determined to show off their purses too. Kit could have won every trick and every chip in his sleep.

Except he couldn't because a corruptible, gullible customs official—open to bribery—would be useless at cards. Why would he need to be corruptible if he won regularly at the gaming tables? So, if Kit wanted Gartside to think him a person keen to accept backhanders, he'd have to stew in his own miserable juices and lose his pennies hand over fist.

Which Kit did with remarkably good grace, putting up with the jeering, the sneering, the drunken braggadocio, and every other snide insult Gartside and his pals threw his way. When Kit could so easily have fleeced the lot of them.

As he congratulated Gartside on his meagre winnings, with a slightly too firm pat on the back, Kit retaliated in the only way he knew how—by dipping his nimble fingers inside Gartside's waistcoat pocket.

Chapter Sixteen

TOO RESTLESS AFTER the evening's excursion to retire to his bedchamber, Lando found himself wandering his own ballroom. In his mother's day, it had been a den of activity, one of the most utilised parts of the house. Now it sat bare, her beloved pianoforte and sticks of furniture hidden away under dust sheets. The view from the floor-length windows overlooking verdant Grosvenor Square, however, remained as good as it always was. Though he could barely see the outlines of the linden trees lining the leafy avenue through it, Lando took up a post at the window for a while.

Even in London, heavy silence ruled the dark hours of early dawn. In Lando's experience, it was a time best avoided. The melancholy that had settled around his shoulders during dinner still accompanied him, and his mind drifted to brood on those he'd lost — his parents, whom he'd loved, his wife of whom he'd been dearly fond, and Charles, whom he'd adored. At moments such as this, his loneliness knew no bounds, much like the rich velvet sky reflecting off the windowpane.

The nature of the silence changed when Kit joined him. He knew it was Kit; his presence thickened the air, enriching it in a way Lando had only ever known with one other person.

"You dance well," Lando remarked, not turning around. "Though you declined the waltz. At least three unmarried ladies swooned with disappointment."

"Alas, I do not know the steps well enough. Its fame hadn't reached Kent by the time I left."

"Oh, it's a dreadfully simple little thing." Lando contrived to sound bored. "But scandalous, according to the mamas, thus it has naturally become a firm favourite amongst their daughters."

Kit stepped farther into the room, his hard soles beating a steady rhythm against the polished wood. "Simple, yet you did not dare attempt it either. Or any of the others."

The heat of Kit's gaze caressed the nape of his neck.

"I avoid dancing through choice, not aptitude," Lando replied. "I have not danced since…" He swallowed away the words. "How long is of no consequence. I assure you my waltz is more than adequate."

Kit was so close, Lando heard his inhale, the soft rustle of his waistcoat, the creak of boot leather. "You don't dance, and yet you have this beautiful ballroom going to waste."

Lando continued to stare into the night. His other ballroom at Rossingley was more beautiful still. How was it possible he could have so much and yet so little? "Yes."

Quiet fell upon them once more, so much so that Lando

could hear the thrum of his own heartbeat. Minutes passed, maybe five or so, before Kit spoke again.

"I learned how to cheat at cards — piquet, loo, and brag mostly — from Sir Brandon Gower. Kentish winter evenings are long and dark; our neighbours were five miles away or more. We used to play for brass buttons. He himself learned during his time fighting in the hussars. He was a good, kind man."

"And picking pockets? Did Sir Brandon teach you how to do that?"

"No." Another few beats passed. "I learned that from my mother. She was half-Hungarian, descended from the Rom, though we learned never to speak of it. My father came upon her whilst fighting in Spain and brought her back to England. He married far beneath himself, but theirs was a love match and the reason we lived a quiet life in Kent. Picking one another's pockets became an amusing game. Anne is adept, too, though she has never used it to her advantage. Your own sister's belongings are quite safe."

"You have your mother's skin colour," Lando surmised. The man's honeyed tones and sulky hazel eyes had intruded on his thoughts on more than one occasion during the evening at Lady Chalfont's.

"Yes. Anne is fairer. She takes after our father."

More empty beats echoed through the ballroom as if even the silence listened and waited.

"Waltz with me, Lando." Kit's low murmur folded around Lando like a warm summer breeze. Or like the arms of his lost love tugging him close, whispering his name as if it were a secret shared between only the two of them. "Here. Now. Show me how."

Lando's eyes filled, and he made a sound, halfway between a laugh and a sob. "We don't have music."

"It matters not. Waltz with me." A command this time, not a question as Kit's breath gusted against Lando's skin, hot and damp.

If Lando turned, he'd find a willing mouth, willing arms, a willing body. And their dance would be so much more than a dreadfully simple little waltz because the body belonged to the only man who'd penetrated his frozen heart since Charles's death.

"Teach me," Kit repeated. "Dance with me. Like you used to with my uncle. In your even bigger ballroom at Rossingley."

Lando's cheeks were wet. "How do you know about that?"

"He spoke of it often, towards the end. Of how beautifully you dance. And of the pleasure you gained from it."

"It was foolish. *We* were foolish." Lando brushed a rough palm over his tears. "We thought what we had between us was…" He shook his head, defeated by the future he and Charles had once dreamed together. "Dalliances with men should only ever be a brief exchange of pleasure, nothing more. I know now."

"You do not truly believe that."

Kit's hand lightly touched Lando's shoulder, hovering as though he half expected it be shaken off. When Lando didn't move, it slid down his arm to settle at his trim waist. "One puts a hand here, does one not, for a waltz?"

"Yes." Lando huffed a weak laugh. "Lewd, isn't it?"

The space between them shrank until there was none, until Kit's torso pressed up against Lando's back, and the sturdy branches of his arms wrapped fully around him. "You and my uncle were blessed, Lando. Not foolish."

Kit's lips found the narrow column of his nape as Lando drifted against the rise and fall of Kit's solid chest, the cadence of his heartbeat, the shared warmth.

A minute passed, maybe longer, and then Lando turned elegantly as if already in tune with unheard music. He studied Kit's arms, still embracing his waist, unspent tears still filling his eyes.

"At Rossingley, our winters also stretched. Neither Charles nor I played cards. Though we were well occupied."

"I'm so, so sorry for your loss." Kit placed a light kiss on Lando's forehead, resting his mouth there. "I fear I possess two left feet, but may I offer myself as a poor substitute?" Stepping back, he smiled down at Lando before wiping at an escaping tear with the tip of his thumb. Such an intimate, tender gesture; no wonder another swiftly took its place.

Lightly, Lando brushed his hands along the length of Kit's arms. "You are far from that, Kit. I...I admit I do not know what this is between us. I cannot explain it. But whatever it is, it calms my soul. You are...you are not Charles. You are...you. And you have made me feel more alive than I ever believed I would again. I am...grateful."

He dipped his chin so Kit wouldn't see the flush of colour painting his cheeks. "Forgive me. I've said too much. Men do not speak to other men in such a way."

Kit barked a laugh. "They do not, I agree. But then you are not like any other man I have ever known." He lifted Lando's face up to his. "And I can't explain it either. Nor can I keep away or stay cross with you any longer. Not even when my trust in you hangs by a thread. You...you scare me, Lando." He shook his head, glancing up at the shadowy sky beyond the window. "And

I would not admit to that were it not dawn at the end of a very long and trying evening. You have me at a weak moment."

Lando's watery gaze locked onto Kit's. "Then we are both of us having weak moments. I would not shed tears or be so maudlin if I'd partaken of a hearty supper."

"I have yet to see you eat more than a few morsels."

"I…no." Lando sighed. "It is a family affliction, I think. In unhappy times. I cannot explain it. My mother also suffered."

Kit planted another kiss on his forehead and chuckled. "Then I shall endeavour to make you happy. And turn you into a plump cushion."

Lando smiled. "And you believe your waltz will achieve that?"

"I very much doubt it. But shall we find out?"

Relinquishing Kit's hold, Lando examined his dance partner's posture with pursed lips. "I'm a little out of touch, but both of your arms around my waist isn't the traditional stance. The *ton*'s decorum hasn't slipped that much in my absence."

"A great pity."

Trying not to laugh, Lando raised Kit's left arm, placing his own around Kit's broad back. "This hand belongs here, resting on my upper arm, almost on my shoulder. And your right hand rests as so, clasped in my left."

A puzzled frown pinched Kit's brow as he examined the position of his left hand. "You're leading."

"Yes. I am." Lando smiled again, an inviting, half-seductive and half-challenging sort of smile. "Although, when the mood takes me, I have been known to let other men take the lead," he added in a silky tone as he guided Kit across the dance floor.

"If not for the hard soles of our boots ringing out, I would hardly notice we're dancing," Kit murmured. "Charles was right. You are grace in physical form."

"And your feet are far nimbler than you led me to believe."

"If they are, then it is because you make them so."

When they reached a wall, Lando swept Kit in a turn, smoothly carrying the bigger man along. Kit had been correct about one thing, Lando mused. Music would have been superfluous as the fast beat of his own heart provided a rare old tune.

"You say you let other men take the lead," Kit began, his sinful gaze latched onto Lando's.

"Not all men," Lando corrected, then hesitated. "But I would allow you."

"You are both flower and gardener," Kit blurted, cheeks suffused with colour. And he promptly tripped over nothing.

"Nicely put." Lando laughed. "I am indeed. But your left foot should be mirroring my right. When mine moves forward a pace, yours steps back."

Staggering to straighten himself, Kit cursed. "I was right not to trust you. You lied! Your waltz is so much more than adequate."

With a brief pause before setting off again, Lando arranged him back in his hold. "Modesty becomes me. Now, pull your shoulders up and your chest out and stop looking down at those disobedient feet. Make them dance to your tune, not the other way around."

Kit found a rhythm and soon enough, they were tripping around the ballroom as if lighter than air. His confidence grew with it, enough to add light kisses on Lando's cheeks whenever they slowed for a turn. Then he abandoned the traditional hold altogether to shamelessly grasp Lando once more around his middle.

"I am picturing an imaginary audience of horrified snooty mamas," Lando said, amused. "This scandalous embrace would be the talk of the *ton*."

As if to prove a point, Kit squeezed him closer still. He whirled Lando around, moving on instinct. And if Lando's breath was taken away by the end of the dance, he'd know the damned reason hid behind the pair of sinful dark eyes laughing down at him.

"'*Trust me*,' you insisted," Kit said after one of his more exuberant moves. "Though it might be the most foolish decision of my short life, I have decided to obey." And with nothing but a determined look and a sudden swerve nearly toppling them both, Kit took the lead. Stronger and bigger, he swept Lando across the dancefloor in any direction he pleased. Kit went right, Lando went right. He sped up, Lando sped up. With all accuracy and timing abandoned, it was a ridiculous, made-up country jig of a dance, but it made Lando smile, it made him giggle.

"I'm unfamiliar with this one," Lando cried breathily after a most unaristocratic squeal.

"It's called 'The Angel.'" Kit pulled him into a twirl. "It will soon be the talk of the *ton*, you'll see. We'll be asked to demonstrate it in every drawing room from here to Piccadilly."

Another twirl followed the first. One hand slipped lower to rest on Lando's slim hip, the other grazed the dip of his spine, pulling him closer as Kit spun him around. A flood of heat ignited between them; Lando became aware of it at the same moment as

Kit's hooded gaze turned from amusement to something more restless. As if tethered, their steps slowed. They found themselves marooned in the middle of the empty dance floor.

When Lando tipped his head, only the smallest fraction, he found Kit's lips expectantly waiting for him, sweet and soft. Their tongues mingled in a tentative gasping exploration, filling Lando's soul with the purest, sturdiest, diamond-hard joy.

"We appear to have stopped dancing," Kit whispered when they broke apart. He stroked a finger down Lando's cheek, his gaze following the path as though memorising the contours. "If I kiss and dance at the same time, then an amateur such as I cannot give our kiss the attention it deserves."

"There is nothing amateur about your mouth." Lando tasted it again, just to be sure. "See? Your lips fit perfectly over mine. Your waltzing, however, is woeful. I am not convinced this new-fangled dance of yours will catch on."

"Then I shall save it only for you, for when we are alone," answered Kit and kissed him again, deeply.

Dawn light fell more and more brightly upon their heaving shoulders. Outside in the street, a cart rumbled by. Lando's servants would be about their business at any moment.

"We have danced the night away." Kit glanced towards the window.

"And banished my demons along with it," agreed Lando. "I am grateful. Sometimes they trail after me for days on end. Such a bore, especially as we have so much to do."

Kit cradled his face, his hand cupping Lando's cheek. He swayed slightly. "I'd like to take you to bed," Kit whispered.

"I'm..." Lando pressed his forehead into the warmth of Kit's chest. "I am not ready. I'm damaged, Kit. I should warn you. Difficult too. Spoiled even. I'm not always pleasant to those around me."

"If I were a true gentleman, I would disagree wholeheartedly and enlist all the ways you are not." Kit tangled his fingers in Lando's hair. "And God knows I'm flawed too. But the truth is that I find you to be all of those things and more. And yet…and yet, I still want you. As, I hope, you want me. I am prepared to wait."

"Be prepared to trust me, too," Lando pleaded. "However it might seem, however dark it might get, I promise I shall not let you hang."

Chapter Seventeen

KIT WOKE TO a man in his bedchamber. The wrong man, unfortunately. He'd bid farewell to the right one after taking him by the hand and escorting him to the bedchamber adjacent. An exquisite torture, but one which even now, as Jasper clattered the washbasin, hurled coals onto the fire, and yanked back the drapes, made his belly flip.

"I don't think you could make any more noise if you tried," Kit observed blandly.

"Probably not," agreed Jasper. "His lordship requests your presence in the breakfast room. *Sir*."

Kit almost replied that he requested the earl's presence in his bed, but somehow, he didn't feel his temporary valet would find that amusing. Jasper plonked a tray on the bedside table, sending coffee spilling down the side of the coffee pot.

"Would *sir* like me to shave him?"

"Ye gods, no. I prefer to keep my blood contained inside my body not spurting down my neck."

Sir wanted Jasper to bugger off so he might ablute in peace and mull over his wonderful encounter with Lando in the ballroom. Not carting him off to bed had felt right, as much as his aching cockstand had demanded otherwise. *Trust me.* Lando had a plan, that much was clear, from how he'd held him close. From how those pale eyes had beseeched him, had promised he'd come to no harm. From how he had clung to Kit as if losing him would destroy him.

Whatever had passed between them was more than a prelude to a simple tupping. And whatever Lando thought was wrong about men speaking words of love to one another was misinformed. He would show the man that Mr Christopher Angel was more than a damned passing pleasure vessel. And by the time he'd finished, the earl would never have eyes for anyone else.

*

ON KIT'S ARRIVAL in the breakfast room, Lando dismissed his footman. His fine features bore an expression Kit couldn't interpret. Was Lando now regretting his candour?

"Is something wrong?"

"Far from it." As the door closed quietly behind the servant, Lando rose from his seat and greeted Kit by reaching up and delivering a kiss.

"I've wanted to do that since I woke." His eyes roamed Kit's face. "But kissing you in front of Johnson, who has known me since I was a babe, would feel akin to kissing you with my father occupying the other end of this table, frowning behind his newspaper."

Lacing his fingers with Kit's, who still reeled with the idea of kissing Lando in front of anyone, let alone a parent, Lando led him to the laden sideboard. "So, we'll have to serve ourselves, I'm afraid."

Kit chuckled. "I expect I'll manage. But in exchange for only one kiss?" He plucked at the loose sleeve of Lando's silk banyan, the dove-grey one. "Wholly inadequate. Especially now I've finally got my hands on this."

A white linen nightgown peeked out from beneath the banyan; Lando's imaginary row of gossipy mamas must be clutching their pearls in horror. Unmarried gentleman did not parade in their nightgowns outside the bedchamber. Kit was learning by the hour that Lando's household was a little different.

Unhurriedly, he availed himself of Lando's upturned mouth, marvelling again at how the man yielded to him and how, in the space of seconds, breakfast had become his favourite meal of the day. His lover's shape under the banyan was everything the flimsy garment promised, his body hard and lean, wrought iron under soft, soft flesh. One part of Kit became very hard indeed, making his belly tighten with want. He deepened the kiss as his tongue sought out the corners of Lando's inviting open mouth. He bit at Lando's plump lower lip and then licked at the sweet taste of him. When they finally parted, they were both gasping.

"Will we be disturbed?" Kit asked. Kissing another (barely dressed) man in broad daylight with servants milling around was possibly the most daring thing he had ever done, far more daring than picking pockets or scheming to bring down a ghastly baronet.

"No." Lando shook his fair head, breathlessly amused. "They know not to enter."

Under Kit's fingers, the silk clasps of the gown fell away. "So I may do this, then." He drifted his hands lower towards the hem of the pristine linen.

"Yes. You will find that I am quite naked underneath."

A low grunt of pleasure escaped Kit's throat. What that fey, fluttery voice did to him. Bunching up the fine fabric, his fingertips encountered the backs of Lando's sleek thighs. His hands explored higher, roaming over Lando's firm buttocks and the twin dimples above them. Their kissing turned hungrier; arching into him, Lando circled Kit's neck with his arms, crushing their mouths as one. Kit glided his palm across a sharp hip bone, then travelled lower again between Lando's parted thighs this time, then up once more...to the treasure of Lando's long and slim prick, curving towards his navel from a nest of neat pale curls. Lando shuddered as Kit circled a thumb around the tip, dipping into the wetness.

"You are even more fine here than my hand remembered," he whispered, and Lando groaned into his mouth.

Kit began a slow steady glide, his own cockstand painfully throbbing against Lando's bare thigh. Lando desperately clung to him, panting wetly against the skin of Kit's neck, lost to Kit's hand on his shaft. Kit had bestowed this simple pleasure on plenty of men over the years and received the same in return, but with Lando, each breathy sigh and urgent moan felt like a treasure to be savoured.

Even as Lando spent in his hand, quietly and efficiently, his cool long fingers tugged at the fall of Kit's breeches while his mouth ran like silk over his jaw and neck.

"My turn," he whispered, his lips returning to Kit's for a long, liquid kiss. When Kit's prick sprang free, Lando allowed him one last delicious taste, then gracefully lowered himself to the floor.

Ye gods, was there a more glorious sight in all of His Majesty's great kingdom? Nay, the world? Swathed in dazzling white, Lando knelt at Kit's feet, his nose and mouth—God, his damned perfect mouth—not an inch from Kit's needy cock. Clasping his hands behind his back, he threw Kit a last lingering look up, then bowed his fair head.

Plush lips, as warm as sun-baked cherries, pressed tender kisses down his length. Teasing licks and nibbles peppered his lower belly. An undignified sound spilled from Kit's throat; roughly, he pushed his breeches lower in time for Lando's tongue to paint a stripe along the warm crease of his thigh. Ignoring Kit's heavy cock screaming for attention, Lando nuzzled into his balls.

Stringing together an entire stream of curses, Kit looked down again. Then wished he hadn't. Lando planted another teasing row of kisses along his shaft before lifting his gaze for an instant, eyes wide innocent pools of blue. Then, as if in prayer, his pale lashes lowered, and in one slick move, he swallowed Kit down.

"My God," Kit gasped, nearly spilling right then and there. "If you continue like that, I fear I shall not delay our breakfast much longer."

With a sound very much like a muffled snort, Lando withdrew to the tip, only to circle the slit with his tongue before sheathing him once more inside the velvet glove of his throat.

"My God," Kit repeated, grasping blindly for the sideboard. "Now you are simply showing off."

Lando's cheeks hollowed around him as he lathed Kit's cock with a punishing rhythm worthy of the devil himself. Kit's eyes shuttered tight. If he dared look again, he'd spend. But he needed to block off his ears, too, because Lando's tiny whimpers and moans as he sucked forth Kit's soul were more intoxicating than the finest French claret. Already, a tight tingling had started up in his spine, spreading to his groin. Stuffed in Lando's mouth, Kit swore his prick was thickening more than it had ever done before. As his breaths came in short, fractured bursts, Kit clutched at Lando's blond head, fighting his every desire to thrust deeper and harder.

"I'm…Lando…I'm…" This wasn't the first cock sucking of Kit's life, of course not, but never so expertly or so…ravenously. As his crisis swelled, he tried to push Lando's head away; one drank coffee at breakfast, not another man's cloying release. But it was too late. In a rush, his seed spilled from him to pour down Lando's throat.

"Lando, I'm sorry." Panting, Kit hauled Lando to his feet. "You are…"

His words fizzled out. On legs like jelly, Kit crushed the slighter man in his arms. Their hearts thudded against each other, and it was unclear who was supporting whom. All that mattered to Kit, as his blood returned to his brain and his mouth relearned how to form words, was that this precious, extraordinary, fragile soul knew how much he was loved.

"You…yes," Kit managed, his breath finally recovered, then stuttered to a halt again. *Loved*? Was that what this was? He pushed the thought aside. Only madness led that way. "You... your skills make a man feel quite lacking in control."

"One is only as accomplished as the tools one works with." Lando gave a lascivious glance down to where Kit's half-flaccid member was tucked away again within his breeches. "Though I accept the compliment, a measure of its veracity is whether breakfast is still warm." His reddened mouth broke into a smile, and he reached up to seal it with Kit's. Kit tasted himself on the other man's lips.

Arm in arm, Kit allowed Lando to lead him to the sideboard. He perused the lavish offerings and poked at a dish of crisp bacon rashers and plump sausages. "Toasty warm," Kit declared. "I am vindicated."

He piled his plate high with bacon and helped himself to sausages, suddenly starving. "There are so many jokes I could be tempted to make, but now that I'm an earl's lover and a man with his own valet, I shall refrain from doing so."

"Then allow me to do it for you." Lando smiled broadly as Kit took his seat. "Cook's sausages are a little on the small side this morning, don't you think?"

"And this chair at the foot of the table feels too large," responded Kit, patting his knee. "Care to share?"

He wondered what Johnson, the footman, would think if he could see his lordship now, daintily perched in Kit's lap and nibbling on delicate slivers of kipper, having already put away a coddled egg. If sucking Kit's prick was what it took to get the man to eat properly, then Kit would present himself as a willing volunteer every morning.

"Lord Cobham has sent a note," Lando announced.

"Johnson intercepted it. He requests a meeting with us both at White's later today. For dinner at four. Sir Richard and Gartside will be joining too. Cobham has asked that Mr Hamilton refrain from attending in order that he may talk more freely." He grinned wickedly. "Which is just as well as the matinee performance of Dick Turpin doesn't finish until five."

Kit smiled, too, but it was a timely reminder of the reason Kit was there in the first place. What with all the dancing and the kissing and other forms of amusement at the breakfast table, it had almost slipped his mind.

"So this isn't breakfast at all, but a last supper," he replied and rested his palm along the length of Lando's lean thigh, hoping it wouldn't be for the last time.

"Of course it isn't," insisted Lando. "You are very well pre-pared. You have read every government document front to back and back to front pertaining to that shipping canal, and if you for-get any detail regarding my land, then I'll cover for you. Having spent a month at the site after the purchase, I am well acquainted with it. And before you start, I'll do whatever it takes for you to walk away from this cleanly." He wrapped an arm around Kit's neck. "Now that I've found you, I have no intention of relinquish-ing you."

Kit wasn't ready to let go of their current playful mood. "Is that why you're sitting on my lap? Pinning me down?"

"No." With a naughty look, Lando wriggled his skinny backside up against Kit's tender parts. "I'm sitting here because it's by far the most comfortable seat around this table."

It was on the tip of Kit's tongue to confess that even if he did manage to walk away from the scheme unscathed, another obstacle blocked his path in the form of a tenacious Bow Street runner. But admitting to that would spoil this delightful breakfast and practically guarantee no more would be forthcoming. Kit despised his cowardice. He hated that he held his silence whilst Lando, proud and lonely Lando, had exposed his vulnerabilities to Kit so plainly and with such honesty. Harbouring this secret shamed him, yet he continued, nonetheless. Perhaps because the secret was shaming in itself.

"What if one of them has also visited the site?" he asked instead.

Lando seemed unperturbed. "Firstly, there has not been sufficient time. But even if they have sent an agent there, he will merely confirm that the Earl of Rossingley is indeed the owner of a busy mill next to a busy shipping route. If interviewed, my man in charge up there would truthfully report that I also own the vast swathe of land surrounding it. And, as I explained to our potential business partners, our venture is not widely known, so it would come as no surprise if my man claimed no knowledge of it."

"What about your relationship with Hamilton? And the plantation? What if they enquire about that at the mill, and your workers admit they don't know of him?"

"Documents pertaining to my relationship with the Hamilton's South Carolina cotton plantation are already in Cobham, Gartside, and Sir Richard's hands. They are an exact copy of the real ones I have with an entirely different cotton plantation in Savannah, owned by a man named Hamilton. Except, the fake ones are elaborated on to include the new proposals."

None of this was news to Kit, but hearing it again was reassuring. "What if someone at White's asks me if I'm acquainted with Mr so-and-so from the ministry? And plenty of the chaps there will know the Foreign Secretary. He may even be a member himself."

"They won't," said Lando swiftly. "Cobham has secured one of the private dining rooms. We shall not be disturbed." He gave a quick smile. "It will all seem terribly secretive and important to the regulars. Which will impress Gartside all the more. And with a bit of luck, after the favourable impression you made on him at Lady Chalfont's, he may not be far from making his move."

That favourable impression had almost blown Kit's cover. The man was a braggart and a drunk. As they'd played a few hands of loo, Gartside had tossed coins around like cheap enamel buttons, all the while boasting to Kit about someone else's daughter he'd taken a fancy to. Kit had had to smile and laugh in all the right places while digging his nails into his thighs and grinding his teeth. Cheating Gartside out of a handful of pennies and a gilt snuffbox had been small comfort.

"The sooner it comes, the better," he groused. "Every fresh occasion we meet brings me closer to wiping that smug expression from his hoggish, inbred, lubberly face."

With a snort, Lando wrapped his fingers around Kit's clenched fist. "I'm not sure His Majesty's Chief Customs Officer of the North would be quite so vulgar about a distinguished baronet."

"I bet he would if he had a sister or a daughter and spent five minutes with that bastard."

Bringing their joined hands to his mouth, Lando trailed his tongue across Kit's knuckles and gazed at him through his long, pale lashes. "You're awfully masterful when you're in a stew. I should endeavour to rile you up into one more often."

Kit's prick stirred, and he gave Lando a pinch. "Let a man have a good breakfast first."

It was hard to believe now that the playful man curled in his lap was the same grim nobleman who'd looked down his nose at him from astride that walloping great horse. Kit had heard of melancholia, of course, and was in no doubt Lando suffered from it. But whatever ailment afflicted him seemed like the blue devils and then something more added to it. It was almost as if he switched and became a different character altogether. Sometimes he was the distinguished earl and at other precious times, like now, simply Lando, a dear man in desperate need of affection and wanting nothing more than to bask in the warm touch of another.

Kit was willing to oblige with that too. In fact, he was beginning to wonder if there was anything he wouldn't do for this man.

He affected not to notice when Lando reached for a second bread roll.

As he slathered it in honey, Lando said, "You will be pleased to hear that when we meet later today, I intend to give the gentlemen a deadline of one week to place their bids."

"Good. My heart can't take the stress much longer."

And then what? Would Lando disappear back to Rossingley? And Kit back to his lodgings? Presuming, of course, he made it out of this hare-brained scheme without being arrested. And if Kit achieved that feat of survival, then he still had the problem of Clark chasing his tail.

But one thing was certain. If Kit did succeed in escaping with his head and shoulders intact, then he'd need to find new lodgings. Which meant one more trip back to Sindell Street to collect what few belongings remained and plan his future in pastures new. Perhaps Lando would help him find another secretarial post with a country gentleman as quietly amenable as Sir Brandon. One who wouldn't ask too many questions.

*

LANDO SUSPECTED THAT visiting the famously exclusive White's as a guest of the eleventh Earl of Rossingley would be daunting if Kit hadn't already experienced the opulence of Lando's Grosvenor Street residence and the unrivalled magnificence of the Rossingley estate. As it was, even alongside Lando, he seemed trepidatious. For the wealthy gentlemen of the *ton* such as himself, whose families had been members since it opened its doors over a century earlier, climbing the steps of the glamorous bow-fronted club on St James was much akin to paying a visit to a neighbouring nobleman and finding all one's old school chums already there.

As a member of staff fawned over Lando whilst divesting them of their coats and hats, he noticed Kit trying not to stare. The place was a maze of plush drawing rooms draped in fine upholstery, flocked wallpaper, and well-heeled gentlemen. The cheery clatter of dining came from one direction, the low hum of dice and card games from another. Two or three patrons stopped to exchange words with Lando, hopefully giving Kit the impression he'd been well-liked before his self-imposed exile. Aware of the scrutiny of curious stares, he was glad of Kit's excursion to his tailor, even if it did mean the poor man endured a daily tussle with Jasper to get the tight coat across his broad shoulders.

They were the last of the party to arrive, and Lando had a

suspicion the other gentlemen might have engineered it so, as already, they were seated with drinks. From Gartside's ruddy complexion, it was not his first.

After despatching greetings, Lord Cobham, accompanied by his solemn man of business, lost no time getting the meeting underway.

"We have questions, Rossingley," he barked rudely. At a snap of Cobham's fingers, his man handed over some papers. "Quite a few of them. Sir Richard and I have collated ours. Gartside here" — he cast him a disdainful look — "I daresay may have a few of his own too."

"I'm glad to hear it," answered Lando breezily, refraining from reminding the other of his more senior rank. "I'm nothing if not an open book."

And so it began: a thorough grilling, beginning with the arrival of the pease soup, continuing through the haricot of mutton, and even disturbing Lando's trifle, which was no trifling matter. Regardless, as the dinner dragged on, one aspect of the scheme became crystal clear. Lord Cobham and Sir Richard had both done their homework, whilst a half-sozzled Gartside clung to their coattails.

Having already reviewed the financial returns on Lando's existing mill and declared them favourable, Sir Richard homed in on his relationship with the Hamilton plantation and the various options of expanding his enterprise to other plantations should the American harvest fail. Cobham and his man had scrutinised the potential for expansion of the Bridgewater Shipping Canal with a fine toothcomb, demonstrating their depth of knowledge with alarming tenacity.

Gadzooks, Lando thought, wondering whether a second helping of peach trifle might settle his discomforting anxiety. His elongated and slightly unusual breakfast with Kit had imbued him with renewed vigour and appetite. And, despite the precarious nature of their current situation, he'd become terribly conscious of an extraordinary desire to *beam*. Never more so than when Kit brazened out an especially knobbly set of questions from Cobham's man by citing an ancient law, which Lando half suspected he might have conjured from thin air.

Regardless, Kit's time in the library had not been wasted, nor had Lando's. Where the younger man stuttered, Lando charmed, and when Lando's charm failed to pierce through Sir Richard's blinkered focus, Kit threw around a few complicated excise terms gleaned from God knows where, and all seemed well. And if Sir Richard's and Cobham's rows of facts and figures were designed to flummox and fluster and dampen Kit's forehead in a cold sweat, then Gartside's hulking presence served to remind them both of their true purpose. He'd been a gluttonish spectator for most of the meal, but as they passed around the brandy, he roused himself to participate.

"All well and good, Rossingley, but a man needs to know exactly how much blunt that peculiar American fellow is putting on the table."

"Irrelevant, my dear chap," soothed Lando. "He doesn't know it, but he could offer me the entire state of South Carolina, and I'd likely refuse. Simply put, on English soil, I want an English business partner. Someone whom one can trust." He smiled benignly. "Putting aside the slipperiness of foreigners, as Sir Richard's excellent précis has demonstrated, the American harvest failed in 1805 and only scraped through in 1811. So it would be damned awkward to have Hamilton as a fellow in business and then cease using his plantation, wouldn't it?"

"You're being obtuse, Rossingley! Of course you want a damned English partner — and a gentleman — anyone with half a brain would. That was never the question. But how much is he offering?"

"If I may be so bold, my lord," Kit intervened. "Sir Ambrose wishes to be sure that when he makes his offer, it is a winning one."

"If he'd bothered to put in a damned bit of effort, he'd have worked out a credible amount for himself," retorted Cobham.

"I h-have a calc-c-ulated f-f-figure in my h-head," offered Sir Richard and with uncharacteristic boldness added, "but I'm n-not g-going to share it."

"Couldn't bloody tell it to me anyhow with that godawful stutter," grumbled Gartside, giving Kit one more reason to despise the man.

With a little thrill of excitement, Lando pressed his foot very carefully down on Kit's under the table. Surely, he must be feeling it too. Gartside's question revealed everyone's hand, namely, that Cobham and Sir Richard wanted in. Trusting their judgement, lazy Gartside was also throwing his hat into the ring, though he had no idea how to secure it. Which meant he would have to find an alternative, underhand way of making the deal his. Crossing all his fingers and toes and avoiding Kit's gaze as Kit returned the steady press of Lando's foot with one of his own, Lando upped the ante.

"Mr Angel, here, is keen to get this thing wrapped up and

return to Manchester. As am I. No doubt, I'm not the only investor with cotton assets ripe for expansion. And, as Mr Angel has outlined to us all, the Bridgewater Canal is ripe for improvement."

His penetrating gaze travelled around his companions, skewering each of them. Did it linger slightly longer on Gartside?

"I'd like that project to have my name at the top of it," Lando continued, "next to one of yours. But time is not on our side, gentlemen. Thus, I am requesting all bids in by midday a week today. Then I suggest we meet here again at six to commiserate with the losers and toast my new business partner."

Chapter Eighteen

"GADZOOKS." LANDO FLOPPED into the carriage seat. "I feel like a hollowed-out rag doll."

Kit couldn't have put it better himself. As he collapsed into the seat opposite, they eyed each other for a few moments.

Sighing heavily, Lando shook his head. "Possibly worth it though. Did you see the look Cobham gave to Sir Richard at the end? I do believe we've fooled them."

"I bloody hope so. I don't think I have the stomach to go through that again. If his man had asked me one more question about the tidal patterns across the Atlantic and how they affected the currents at the estuary, I might have had to slip outside and bash my head against the nearest brick wall."

Lando chuckled. "You coped admirably."

"Only because you had my back."

Lando had been magnificent, in Kit's opinion. A heady mix

of cleverness, confidence, and cunning. If Kit had the strength, he'd haul the earl across the carriage onto his lap and ravish him, gawkers lining the streets of London be damned. Watching him now, as immaculate as ever and with only a flush to his cheeks hinting at the gruelling last few hours, that word *love* raised its meddlesome head again, whispering its madness in his ear.

"Seeing as we are now playing a waiting game, I'm taking the liberty of going away for two nights," announced Lando, making Kit's tortured heart sink. "I'm afraid I'm leaving at first light. I must journey down to Eton to visit my boys."

"I shall miss you," Kit answered. And blushed. The man was travelling forty miles south, not flying to the moon.

Lando tilted his head to one side. An amused quirk played at his lips. "I shall miss you too, Mr Angel. It seems we have only now become properly acquainted. But Eton is a simple journey from London—it can be done in half a day. I would be foolish not to take advantage whilst I am here."

"Of course," agreed Kit, pulling himself together. "And if we're not mistaken, then Gartside will make his move any day now, especially since you've stipulated a deadline. Perhaps he will be more likely to do so without you around."

"Quite. And if he doesn't, then I shall regrettably inform the other parties of my acceptance of the American's astonishingly high offer, and no one shall hear any more about it."

Kit nodded. The gentlemen would curse at the earl's volte-face and at the time wasted but then go on their way, none the wiser the whole thing had been a ruse. Alas, Gartside would not be venged, and Kit's acquaintance with the earl would cease. Both of those outcomes had become equally undesirable over the last few days.

Kit's disappointment must have still played across his face because Lando leaned forward to clasp his hand.

"But on my return, I would very much like us to…carry things forward. If you want that too, Kit. My…my bed has been far too large for far too long."

As a flame of hope kindled, Kit caressed Lando's dry, smooth palm before bringing it to his lips. "Then I am already counting down the hours."

For the remainder of the short journey, Lando's hand rested in his, and Kit comforted himself with the thought that the earl's absence would at least render him opportunity to return to his lodgings. Whereupon he would be able to collect his residual belongings without any questions being asked as to his whereabouts. He squeezed Lando's hand, picturing their reunion on Lando's return.

"How should a senior customs officer alone in a strange city amuse himself whilst his host is away?" he teased.

"I'm very glad you asked." Lando gave him a lopsided smile. "Pritchard informs me that Gartside can be found most afternoons riding his ugly mount through Regent's Park. The north side is his usual hunting ground, where he can be sure to be seen. I'd like you to take the grey mare from my stables and contrive to bump into him. Drop hints that he's my preferred choice—that I'm worried Cobham's health is too poor to last the duration, and that I believe Sir Richard too cautious. Perhaps arrange another hand of cards for a few days' time, just the two of you."

If he never cast eyes on Gartside again, it would be a day too soon. Nonetheless, Lando's idea held merit. If stroking the man's ego and enduring another round of drinks and cards was what it took, then Kit would comply. Somewhat revived, Kit sat forward and ran his hands along the inner edge of Lando's thighs, wishing the interior of the carriage wasn't quite so visible from the busy street outside and that the journey was longer. "Bedding you would be much more preferable."

"So, I imagine, would the pox," answered Lando, drily. "But needs must."

*

KIT WONDERED IF Gartside filled his stables according to size. His mount, a bulky, unappealing beast, was by far the biggest trotting along Regent's north avenue. In that regard, it was not dissimilar to its owner. Whereas the elegant eleventh earl rode as if his horse was an extension of his streamlined self, Gartside rode as if he he'd quarrelled with his an hour earlier. Never had Kit seen a mount less enthused at being ridden by his master. Admittedly, his own equine skills were modest, but the grey mare was placid and, like everything Rossingley, effortlessly stylish.

Gartside rode alone, so it proved no difficulty for Kit to arrange to be in his eyeline at a fork in the track.

"Ah, Angel," he barked. "How the devil. I was just thinking about you." Gartside cast a sharp glance over Kit's shoulder. "Rossingley not choosing to partake of the air?"

"His lordship is travelling to Eton," explained Kit, hoping he sounded as if earls travelling to Eton was part of his normal daily parlance. "To visit his sons. He's away for two nights."

Gartside nodded, his fleshy chin wobbling. "Always surprised me a tulip like that ever begat sons. Ride with me."

Several replies to Gartside's snide insinuation and imperious order were ready on Kit's tongue, but he obediently swallowed them all and fell in alongside.

"How are you finding London?" Gartside queried. "A little more cut and thrust than the provinces, I daresay? A few more pleasurable diversions?"

An image of Lando, head bowed around his cock, flashed through Kit's head. "Very much so. Though I am enjoying myself, I confess to looking forward to wrapping this business up and returning to Manchester. I have several commitments there and had to leave at a very inconvenient time."

"Yes?" Gartside inclined his head, and Kit pushed on.

"No rest for the wicked, I'm afraid," he replied with a hollow laugh. Ye gods, how easily he found stepping into the role since he'd decided to trust in Lando. "I have several other parties clamouring for my attention—land is being bought up left, right, and centre. One can scarcely keep pace with it all."

"Is that so," Gartside said carefully.

"I've had to take on another secretary to help manage the rush." Kit made a show of glancing around as if ensuring they were alone, then dropped his voice. "Between you and me, if one has the readies, I wouldn't be investing it anywhere else this year. What with all the newfangled machinery coming in, men such as the earl are set to make a very pretty penny."

"Hmm."

They trotted in silence for a few moments, Gartside deep in thought and Kit endeavouring to appear suitably grave.

"And you're the gatekeeper to all these business deals, yes?" Gartside asked.

"Well." Kit feigned modesty. "I don't work entirely alone, of course. I answer to the Foreign Secretary first and foremost, but with Manchester being so far from London, it wouldn't be wrong of me to admit to having some degree of autonomy. Parliament is so dreadfully busy, you understand, and one does have a significant amount of first-hand knowledge of the workings of the goods importing business. Like my father before me, I have lived and breathed imports and exports my whole life." He gave a tinkly laugh, making himself cringe. "One might say it runs in my blood."

"How the dickens do you whittle down which chap to sell to?"

Kit pretended to contemplate. "As long as the gentlemen interested in investing are of sound finances and background, Sir Ambrose—and a man such as yourself would be an excellent case in point—then I'm very much left to my own devices. Someone such as yourself—" He gave a simpering smile, detesting himself for trying to be so ingratiating with such an odious man. "—would have no trouble persuading me you were the right person for the job."

"Naturally," said Gartside briskly. "I am a baronet. Of impeccable standing."

A true gentleman would never need to remind another of that fact, Kit thought.

"Of the highest," he agreed, feeling nauseous. "As are Sir Richard and Lord Cobham. Although..." He broke off, pressing his lips together as if he'd said too much.

"Although what?" Gartside's tone was sharp.

"Although..." Kit attempted to appear discomfited. "I take

my position of being in the earl's confidence very seriously, Sir Ambrose. Thus, one does not wish to speak out of turn or on behalf of another."

"There's no one to overhear. Say it, man. I insist."

Wincing, Kit directed the grey mare closer to Gartside's and dropped his voice. "I only wish to say, in order to further your own interest in the matter that..." He hesitated again.

"Yes?" Gartside huffed with impatience.

"I have made the reasonable observation that Lord Cobham is in poor health. And whilst he has shown excellent financial prudence in the past, I fear his health matters may, shall we say, override his ability to manage his affairs if they were to deteriorate further. And I am of the opinion the earl shares similar reservations."

"Does he now?" Gartside nodded once more. "Rum fellow, Rossingley. Sharp as a tack but rather too fond of peach flowery waistcoats for my liking, if you get my drift."

It was all Kit could do to prevent himself from bursting into laughter.

"Nonetheless, one would do well not to underestimate him," Gartside added with relish. "Man owns half of bloody Mayfair as far as one can tell. And much of Wessex. Wasted on a dandy like that. Bloody good at holding onto his money."

"He is," agreed Kit, like the diplomat he was pretending to be. "One would do well to side with him."

"Sir Richard is of the same opinion," grumbled Gartside. "Though God knows why Rossingley is considering him. Man's a coward and a dimwit. Can't even bloody speak properly."

"Mmm," Kit concurred, hating himself. Of all the people

they were hoodwinking, that Sir Richard was one of them bothered him the most. Quiet and affable, Kit rather enjoyed his company.

Pressing further, he added, "Of course, my role is only to advise. Ultimately, the decision will rest with the earl. But, if I could be so forthright, having been in his acquaintance for quite some months now, I do believe I have his ear. It wouldn't be beyond the realm of possibility for me to find myself, if sufficiently incentivised, in the position of being able to…sway him."

He finished with a long, hard look at Gartside, praying he hadn't gone too far yet also hoping he'd gone far enough, given the man's below-average intelligence. As it was, he could almost hear the cog wheels chugging.

They reached another fork in the road. Two dashing young fellows in a yellow phaeton were signalling for Gartside's attention.

"Ah, there they are," he said. "Beefy Allington and Poodle."

Poodle. Daft buggers, these aristocrats never grew up. As Kit drew up his horse, Gartside threw him a distracted wave, already dismissing him for acquaintances with more merit. "My route takes me this way, Sir Ambrose," Kit declared to his companion's half-turned back. "So I'll bid you farewell. I have a stack of papers to read through on my return to the earl's residence."

"You are still his guest?"

"I am, indeed. Until our meeting at the end of the week. Most afternoons, I am alone in the library while the earl conducts his business elsewhere." Kit tipped his hat. "Good day to you."

Chapter Nineteen

KIT GLADLY ESCAPED Grosvenor Street the next morning, even if it was only a trip to his old lodgings. In the eleventh earl's absence, with much to say and no one with whom to share it, he wandered aimlessly, his feet echoing along the hallways and stairways of the enormous residence.

Like motes of dust trapped in candlelight, everyone shone a little brighter in Lando's presence, Kit decided. The lavish breakfast had tasted less pleasing without the beguiling earl curled up in his lap, and even the rose bushes in the stone urns either side of the imposing front door appeared to bloom less enthusiastically. As he made his way down the wide stone steps, the majestic linden trees across the square seemed to no longer care whether they gathered their leaves about them or let them sail away on the breeze.

He headed towards Bond Street to hail a hansom. His restlessness had a name. *Love*, and it disrupted his thoughts like a troublesome toothache. Kit held it responsible for every single one of the poetic flights of fancy cramming his head when he should be concentrating on his future. It was the reason for his stumble over a loose cobblestone, for failing to hail a hansom and having to hunt for another. *Get a grip*, he admonished himself. The roses around the bloody doorstep were fine; they were thriving, as were the lindens. Kit had no idea why he'd bloody noticed them anyhow.

He'd walked halfway to Sindell Street by the time he managed to secure a driver. Which gave him plenty of time to resolve to come clean to Lando regarding the runner, Clark. Shame had prevented him from confessing earlier when Lando first mooted the Gartside plan, shame that Lando would think less of him. Admitting one's flaws to oneself was painful enough, never mind to a ravishing and wealthy earl with whom one had fallen headlong in love, and who had readily admitted all his weaknesses to Kit. Whether his love for the earl was reciprocated or not, frankly, he was undeserving of it anyhow. If, after the whole farrago was over, he and Lando parted ways, then it would be nothing less than Kit warranted. He'd crawl into the darkest of dark corners, lick his wounds, and if God and the honest employment market were willing, slide back into his appropriate level of society a better, more trustworthy man.

Sindell Street was its usual grimy, bustling, smelly self. Kit used to barely notice, but now he had an urge to cover his nose and block his ears. He'd discarded Lando's fine clothes for the expedition, not wanting to draw attention to himself, and a jolly good thing too. His new supple leather boots were far too nice to gather muck.

Love and *ton* living had made him soft; he hardly bothered to glance up and down the street before crossing over to his lodgings. Having ransacked the place weeks earlier and deduced Kit was not to be found, Clark had hopefully moved on to hound some other poor bugger scratching out a nefarious living. Rather wishing to avoid an unpleasant encounter with his landlady, Kit threw thruppence to a bundle of rags clutching a mangy dog, then slipped down the dank side alley, fumbling in his pocket for the heavy key.

His abode was as depressing as on his last visit. His few clothes and books were still carelessly tossed around the place; Kit didn't think anyone had been back. And why would they? There was nothing worth stealing. If he was honest, there was nothing worth him coming back for either. Except that his other woollen coat had been passed down from his father, and he had a pointless, sentimental attachment to a dogeared set of playing cards from his youth.

And they belonged to him, dammit. Which was as good a reason as any.

Add in a couple of his favourite books gifted from Sir Brandon's library, a worn greying towel, a shirt requiring repairs, and two cotton handkerchiefs, it was a pathetic haul to show for three and twenty years. Hefting his small bag across his shoulder, he took a last look around the room. Whilst a week from now he'd face an uncertain future, hopefully not involving Newgate, he knew he wouldn't be coming back.

The first blow landed from nowhere, as he was closing the alley door silently behind him so as not to draw the attention of his landlady. More of a stumble really, a sharp strike against his leg. For a fleeting instant, Kit cursed himself for tripping over someone else's rubbish in the gloom, unbalanced by his heavy bag. But stumbles didn't push back or thump a second fist low in his belly, accompanied by a grunt. A hot flare of pain shot through his hip as he smacked against the damp wall. "What the…?" A third breathtaking whop to the small of his back had him lurching forwards.

"Oy! Get off!" Abandoning his bag, Kit thrashed indiscriminately at his unknown attacker, barrelling into him and knocking the other man off balance. For a moment, they scrapped, cheek to jowl, Kit's head still reeling as he determinedly dodged the blows. Blood from a thick gash across his forehead spurted into his eye, and he lashed out half-blinded. One of his blows hit home as his assailant made a sound like a yelp, then hollered, bringing a new set of footsteps pounding down the alley.

Kit's chest burned. The stink of the other man's rank sweat mingled with the taste of his own blood. His attacker's accomplice drew closer just as someone else shouted from the other end of the alley. Kit's heart skipped with fear. One ruffian, he had a sparring chance against, two or three, and he was only staving off the inevitable.

The second man was bigger; Kit barely had time to brace before one swift boot to his flank had him breathing hard and choking on his own iron-tinged gobs of spit. A follow-up with an open fist, and Kit lost his footing completely, tumbling towards an ungainly sprawl across the cobbles.

The final lightning punch, a practised roundhouse swipe squarely on his temple as he was on the way down, he never even saw coming.

Chapter Twenty

"AN EXPRESS RIDER waits in the parlour, my lord, with an urgent message for you. He's ridden hell for leather from London."

Exchanging a puzzled look with Lando, Pritchard took the proffered letter, roughly folded, from the trembling housemaid. Reassured that his beloved, rambunctious sons were in their usual high spirits, Lando would be taking to the road himself after a light breakfast. They were anticipating a leisurely ride, pausing for lunch during the change of horses and arriving back in Grosvenor Street with plenty of time to spare before nightfall. Lando was quite anticipating nightfall; he planned on spending it renewing and extending his acquaintance with Kit most thoroughly.

"Oh, God." Pritchard clapped a hand over his mouth, his face ashen. "My lord, it's from Jasper. We're to come at once. Mr Angel has been attacked. He's suffered a severe blow to the head.

Your physician is tending to him now."

For a second, Lando stared wide-eyed in disbelief before snatching at the note. *A severe blow to the head*? How could he have? Kit was staying at his house, sleeping in the rose bedchamber, and riding the grey mare in Regent's Park. How on earth could he have been attacked?

But there it was in Jasper's poor hand clear as day.

A severe blow to the head.

The paper fell from Lando's fingers as a sudden tautness assailed his chest. Dark spots danced in front of his eyes, and he grabbed for the chair behind him, collapsing into it. *His Kit, his darling Kit.* For a sickening moment, as his thoughts tumbled into the abyss, Lando felt he might pass out.

Pritchard was first to gather his wits, turning to the housemaid. "You, girl. Send for a porter at once to help with the bags. Have the horses saddled and the earl's carriage brought to the front. There'll be a sovereign in it if we're ready to leave within a quarter hour."

Pritchard didn't waste a second as the girl scurried away to begin tossing the remainder of their belongings into bags. Lando buried his face in his hands and squeezed his eyes shut.

"Now, now, my lord. We'll have none of that." Pritchard efficiently folded away Lando's shaving things. "Your Mr Angel is made of strong stuff. He's had Jasper's boot on his backside twice and still come back for more. There weren't many Frenchies who could boast that."

"A severe blow to the head." Lando could summon little more than a whisper. "That could mean…"

"It could mean nothing more than a cheerful clip round the

ear," Pritchard interrupted. "You know how Jasper overeggs the pudding. Mr Angel will be sitting up in bed drinking ale and demanding to know what all the fuss is about by the time we get there." He held out Lando's travelling coat. "If his lordship would please stand up, we can get this on and be on our way."

Lando hoped to God Pritchard was right. Kit Angel brought lightness to his soul. He was like the sun, warming his bones from the inside out. With his charm, his touch, his kiss, his damned earring and ribbons, he'd driven darkness from Lando's heart, taking his melancholia of the past three years with it. In a single, throbbing moment of sheer terror as Pritchard eased the coat around his trembling body, Lando knew love.

And was petrified of losing it.

"He will be fine, my lord. I promise."

As Pritchard climbed into the carriage, he paused to address the inn's groom. "The express rider. Tell him to take some food, exchange horses, then ride directly to Rossingley and ask for Mr Robert Langford. Mr Langford will see he's well compensated for his efforts." His eyes darted across to his employer, mutely folded in on himself in a corner of the landau, and Lando gave a tiny nod. "And ask him to tell Mr Langford to ride to his lordship's London house with all haste."

As roomy and comfortable as his crested carriage was, for once, Lando regretted they hadn't travelled in the phaeton or on horseback. As he was needful of Pritchard's comforting presence, his valet sat alongside him as the horses flew over ruts and swerved around bends back towards London. More than once, Lando's tense gaze met the calm grey eyes of his loyal valet, drawing strength from them. It was all he could do not to clutch the other's hand. Nonetheless, by the time they reached Grosvenor Street, he was more composed though no less concerned.

His butler, Hargreaves, greeted him at the door.

"Where is he?" Lando was already marching towards the sweeping staircase, barely breaking stride to remove his hat and gloves.

"In the rose bedchamber, my lord. The physician departed not an hour ago. He has left instructions for his care and will return tomorrow. Mr Angel's condition remains unchanged."

Thank goodness. So he was alive.

Lando, his heart thudding, was met with near darkness as he pushed open the door. Faded sunlight filtered through the draped windows, dappling the heavy oak bed moored in the middle of the room and casting long shadows over the man lain very still upon it. He froze in the doorway, not daring to take another step, trembling with fear at what he might find — a fear of the kind he'd hoped never to experience again.

"He's going to live," pronounced a gruff voice. "Daft pillock."

Lando's gaze swung to an armchair stationed near the head of the bed, finding Jasper in attendance.

"Him, my lord. Not you."

On shaky legs, Lando ventured closer as Jasper vacated the chair, gesturing for the earl to sit whilst he stood almost to attention beside him. Together, they gazed down at Kit's waxy face.

"Is he…what did…"

Nausea swirled in his belly as Lando scrabbled to formulate the words. Kit's lips were parted and his eyes closed, the thin lids covering them so fragile-looking they were almost blue. Tufts of thick hair poked out from a clean bandage circling his head. An angry bruise blossoming on his right cheek provided a grim splash of colour.

"He's woken a couple of times," Jasper added. "Once, when the physician stuck a great pin in his foot. And once, when he wafted a candle over his face and peeled his eyes open. Unconscious again now though. But his pulse is good and strong."

Not caring that Jasper was there, Lando took one of Kit's cool hands in his.

"He's got cuts and bruises in tender places, and he's done a few ribs, I reckon. Nothing time won't fix. He'll have a sore head when he wakes though. That took the brunt of it."

Lando swallowed, his mouth dry. "What…what happened?"

"Silly sod went back to Sindell Street, didn't he? Nearly lost him 'cos he ducked down the back way so as not to be seen. Trouble is, that Bow Street runner who's after him had that beggar I told you about keeping a weather eye. By the time your man here came out, a 'scallion and his two chums were waiting to bash him. Poor bugger didn't stand a chance. Two of 'em roughed him up while another went to fetch the boss. He'd have been right pissed off when he got there and found out I swiped him. Mind you, one of 'em got me right square in the ballocks. If you'll pardon my French, my lord."

Lando wasn't entirely certain which part of his language Jasper was apologising for. None of it was fit for his employer's ears, but he really didn't care. Not only had the former soldier saved Kit's life, but he was also completely overlooking the fact that Lando was clutching Kit's hand as if he'd never dare let go.

"I'm forever indebted to you, Jasper," he said. "You may go and rest. Tend to your own injuries. And I would be grateful if you would instruct Hargreaves to prepare for the arrival of my brother. I expect he will be with us tomorrow."

"Yes, my lord." Jasper pointed to a glass bottle and wrinkled his nose. "There's laudanum there for if he wakes and is restless, on the instruction of the physician. Don't truck with it myself. I've seen too many men lose themselves to it. Brandy's better. But I daresay a few drops won't hurt."

For a long while after Jasper left, Lando sat unmoving, never taking his eyes from the heavily sleeping man. Only time would tell if there was lasting damage, for all of Jasper's bravado.

Twice, Pritchard came in with attempts to coax him away, offering one of the footmen to take his place so he could eat and rest, and twice, Lando refused. On the third occasion, Pritchard brought Jasper back with him in the company of two housemaids.

"My lord," Pritchard said. "Your vigil is a credit to your fortitude, no doubt honed from hours of the vicar of Rossingley's dreary sermonizing with your derriere perched on six inches of hard wood. And not of the pleasurable variety. But you are no nursemaid, and I would not be your loyal valet if I didn't point out that the time has come to extract you from your crumpled travelling attire."

Pritchard extended a finger towards his companions. "Gertie and Emily will wash Mr Angel and change his bedding with Jasper's assistance, and you, my lord, will accompany me to your own chamber and will eat, rest, and bathe."

"I am not hungry. Nor am I weary." Neither did Lando feel in need of bathing, but there were serving girls present.

"But you are stubborn, my lord," Pritchard countered. "And your stubbornness is overriding your intelligence. When Mr Angel awakes, he will not want the first thing he claps eyes on to be a rumpled, starving heap of creased wool and silk. And you are not yourself when you are hungry." He treated Lando to a stern look. "As we have all found to our cost."

Chapter Twenty-One

A MOST DISAGREEABLE churning in his belly jolted Kit awake along with a dizzy hammering at his temples, compounded by his feeble attempt to move his head. Prising open one eye, he sensed he was not alone. A warm body lay curled next him, and for a moment, he had absolutely no idea where he was.

And then, as bitter bile rose to his throat and the warm body shoved a basin under his chin, it all came flooding back, and he closed his eyes once more.

The next time he awoke, the nausea and pounding were no better, but the dizziness had receded, and his mind felt more alert. When he dared open an eye, a blurry image of the window and hazy bronze sky beyond danced into two and then back to one again, indicating it was most likely early morning. And still, a warm body nestled against him.

On his third waking, the warm body had gone, though a

person with a hand in perfect ratio to his own had their fingers entwined in his. The same person, he thought, was murmuring softly, promising him everything would be all right. *Lando.* He'd know that sweet voice anywhere, no matter how hard he'd been smacked around the head.

How Kit wished that were true. He wanted to reply, to tell Lando everything wasn't all right, but a different person was rolling him from side to side, turning his peaceful bed into a choppy ocean and making him seasick. A soapy cloth was swished around private parts of his body reserved for no one but an intimate, and he didn't care for it, certainly not while lying in bed and certainly not in front of Lando. The indignity!

If he'd been feeling more himself, he'd have protested. But he wasn't, and so he didn't. Instead, he accepted the sips of something wet and warm pushed through his dry lips and fell asleep again.

Two days after his beating, Kit roused a fourth time, and this time, he stayed awake for longer. The warm body was back in his bed, filling his battered senses with the delicious biscuity smell of sleep and freshly laundered linen. For a few minutes, he inhaled it while simultaneously trying to ascertain if he would cast up his accounts. Then, gingerly, so as not to cry out in pain, he lifted himself onto an elbow. His stomach complained — as did his head, his ribs, and his right hip — but ye gods, the effort was worth it.

Henry Orlando Fitzwilliam Albert Duchamps-Avery, Eleventh Earl of Rossingley, dressed in nothing but a stark white nightgown, was tucked up alongside him, his blond waves fanned across the pillow like a spilled sheaf of golden corn.

A sight almost worth taking a shoeing for.

After drinking his fill, Kit flopped down again. Though his head was spinning, and his eyes weren't working entirely as they should, he knew the vision was real. He was in his bed in the comfort of the rose bedchamber at Grosvenor Street but with very little recollection of how he'd arrived there. He remembered the beating, being set upon by two ruffians as he exited his lodgings, and he had a fair mind as to who had set them upon him. He also recalled his efforts to fight back before being overpowered. But how he'd then escaped remained a mystery his poor ill-treated brain hurt too much to comprehend. Abandoning all efforts, Kit drifted in and out of sleep until his companion stirred a little while later.

The earl even woke elegantly, with a languid stretch of his long limbs and a soft sigh. When his leg brushed against Kit's bare one, causing Kit to move, he started, and his silvery-blue eyes sprang open. For a second, they were unfocused, and then a slow smile spread across his features.

"Kit," he breathed, and his eyes filled with tears. "My dear Kit." He brought a hand up to Kit's face and traced a finger along the line of his lips. "Thank God. I was so scared I'd lost you."

Kit's voice was husky with sleep, his mouth dry. Even talking pained his ribs. "Not that easily."

"Are you...do you...do you feel quite awful?" Lando's beautiful eyes worriedly searched Kit's face.

Despite feeling as if he'd been run over by the mail coach, Kit managed a small smile in return. "Not at all. How could I possibly, waking up next to you?"

A wince spoiled his gallantry as he tried to shift onto his side to face Lando.

"Shh, lie quietly." With a gentle but insistent palm, Lando pushed him down again. "The doctor said you must rest. There is laudanum should you require it."

Kit's head spun enough already. "Perhaps. But not yet." He twisted his stiff neck to the side, taking in the empty room. They were alone. Of course, because, scandalously, the eleventh Earl of Rossingley was in his bed. "You must leave through the adjoining door before the servants awake," he whispered in as urgent a manner as his pains allowed.

"There is no need." Lando sounded amused. "I think my fondness for you is now quite apparent to all members of my household."

After drawing himself up, Lando reached across to the chevet where a glass of water waited. "Drink, but only a few sips until you can be sure your stomach is settled."

With Lando's aid, Kit found a comfortable position on his pillows, half reclining. The cool water tasted divine; if his nursemaid allowed it, he'd gulp it all down. Deeming him to have had his fill, Lando replaced the glass and took Kit's hand in his.

"But…but…you're in my bed," Kit croaked. Fondness between gentlemen was all well and good, but clearly, Lando had not yet grasped the nub of the problem. "They will know what… what you are."

Lando's lips twitched. "Yes, I do believe that has become quite apparent, too, over the last few days. Reinforcing what they have already known for many years."

He turned Kit's hand over and kissed the rough palm, laughing softly. "Rest assured, Kit. I am not the first or only… ah…sodomite at Rossingley. And I daresay I won't be the last."

Kit's black and blue brain felt quite muddled. "You…what? The other…earls?"

Lando laughed again as he trailed off. "Yes. One could describe my household staff as *specially curated* over several generations. We Duchamps-Averys have always prided ourselves on looking after our people, and in return, they serve us well, with utmost loyalty and discretion."

That blow to Kit's head must have been even worse than he'd believed. "So they know your…your…um…preferences?" He'd had a suspicion Pritchard might be aware of his lordship's proclivities, but Kit was hard-pressed to imagine others were also privy.

"Gadzooks, yes." Lando chuckled again. "The Duchamps-Averys are a rare breed; we manage to procreate and keep the line strong despite our naturally inverted tendencies. Not every generation, but more of my ancestors than one would expect are afflicted. My grandfather, for instance, had many a tale, by all accounts, though he did his duty and sired five children."

Kit was puzzled. "You call it an affliction." In brutal honesty, his head swirled so strangely, he would not be surprised to learn this whole conversation in his bed was nothing but a disconcerting and wonderful dream. Life could be damned confusing sometimes.

"Is it not?" Lando raised his eyebrows in surprise.

Blearily, Kit regarded his loveliness. "From where I'm lying? No." He felt himself blush. Damned head injury had made him soft. "If I had the strength, I'd gather you up in my arms and cover you in kisses."

"Then I look forward to your strength returning," replied

Lando, his smile widening.

"It's… How the blazes did I get here, Lando?"

"You took a heavy blow to the head."

"That part I'm very aware of." Kit dabbed around the edge of his dressing. "Several, I'd wager."

"You were mugged. Jasper fought off your attackers, then brought you back here."

If his brain hadn't felt ready to fall out of his skull, Kit might have queried why the dickens Jasper was there in the first place. And then confess to Lando that his beating wasn't a mugging. That a chap named Clark was on his tail. That Clark might prove a fly in the ointment of *the plan*. But, overcome with weariness, those ideas did nothing but tickle the edges of his bruised consciousness, and he yawned widely.

Lando drew himself up. "And to that end, I should leave you in peace. You need rest. Jasper will be here soon with your breakfast and to help you eat and wash."

"I am thoroughly spoiled," Kit replied, and then, a little needily, "Are you going?"

"I must." Lando placed a firm kiss on his bare shoulder. "You need some breakfast and then more rest. Though I will return to see how you are faring later. My brother awaits."

"Brother?" Kit's fuzzy mind wasn't sure if it recalled a brother.

"Yes." Lando kissed him again because he could. "His name is Robert. A soldier, a spy, a countryman, and my father's favoured by-blow."

*

"I CANNOT RECALL a time when you looked happier," pronounced Robert without preamble. "Not in recent years, at any rate." Placing the book he'd been idly flicking through down on the breakfast table, he threw Lando a crooked smile.

"Kit is finally awake and much recovered." Lando took a seat opposite him and selected a breakfast roll. "Though he is drowsy still. He has not yet pieced things together." He buttered the roll, then reached for the honey pot. "Tell me, have you tracked down Clark yet?"

Robert rolled his eyes as he sugared his coffee. "Did you really need to ask?"

"I daresay not, but don't leave me in suspense. I have enough of that from Pritchard. Who is pining after Inglis terribly, by the way, and it's making him quite the pepper pot."

Robert chuckled. "I'll convey that message so Inglis can brace himself for the onslaught when you finally make it back to Rossingley."

"Soon, hopefully. I have my fingers crossed that Gartside will be tempted to place his bribe any day now." Lando caught a drip of honey on his tongue, savouring it. "So if you have any useful thoughts regarding how we can disentangle Kit from this whole thing, then now would be a good time to share them."

Leaning forward, Robert laid both arms on the table. "I have a friend at Bow Street. A discreet and helpful one."

"I expected nothing less. Only the one?"

"Who had a great deal to say about Clark," Robert continued blithely. "Not all of it good. The man is hard-working and diligent but not...well-liked. Or trusted. My chum described him as slippery as seaweed."

Music to Lando's ears. "Go on."

"Our Mr Clark has a predilection for the finer things in life and is rather familiar with a small wharf just outside Wapping. Derelict, at first glance — nothing but a tumble-down granary. On closer inspection, however, it is a well-oiled drop-off point for free-traders, and one of those free-traders happens to be Clark's older brother. Tea, principally. Some tobacco. Our friend Clark has been known to grease the palm of the local preventer on his busy brother's behalf. Acting as a sort of go-between, as it were."

"Hmm." Lando frowned as he pondered Robert's thinly veiled suggestion. "So you think the threat of him interfering further in Mr Angel's doings can be dispensed with, given sufficient inducement."

"I do," agreed Robert. "It is my belief that, with the right combination of words whispered in his ear, he could be persuaded to forget he ever stumbled across a serial pickpocket named Angel at all." He regarded Lando over the top of his coffee cup. "Assuming, that is, Mr Angel ceases his nefarious activities."

"If our Gartside scheme is successful, then Kit will have no need."

A small weight eased from Lando's refined shoulders. Enticing a God-fearing man to wipe Kit's name from his memory by dangling bags of coin in front of him had not been entirely to his liking. The problem being that bribed men became terribly good at spending their ill-gotten gains and soon developed a taste for more. Gleaning unsavoury facts about a person such as this troublesome Mr Clark and then levering them to your advantage was much more palatable.

"You will encourage Angel to keep the bribe?"

"Some of it," Lando agreed. *If he gets out of this in one piece as a free man.* "If I'm able to persuade him. The money Gartside offers should primarily be put to good use righting a few of the wrongs on his estate. But a portion of it should go to Kit—which he will undoubtedly pass on to his sister—to recompense him for his troubles."

Lando frowned again, the strands of an idea tugging at his thoughts. "Perhaps this Clark can be persuaded to…" He stopped again, trying to picture the steps. "Hear me out, Robert. When, and if, Gartside attempts to bribe Kit—any day now with luck—we need his impropriety to be exposed in front of myself, Cobham, and the others. Ideally, by a highly respected person of law."

As his brain hummed with possibilities, Lando took a larger bite of his breakfast, suddenly ravenous. "Who better than a Bow Street runner with a secret to hide?"

Tilting his head to one side, Robert acknowledged the idea. "Who, indeed? I'm struggling to think of anyone."

"Mmm." Lando leaned back in his seat. "So am I. Except, somehow, our corrupt runner must be blinded to the master plan." Pursing his lips, he nodded thoughtfully. "By a distraction of sorts. Yes… I do believe… I may have a solution. Do you have to rush back to Rossingley?"

"I fear so. My fallow acres on the eastern border are brimming with turnips to harvest, preferably before this fine dry spell turns. And the crops in Fernley Field won't rotate themselves, you know."

"Will they not?" Lando sighed prettily. "A pity."

Robert pushed his chair back, stood, and brushed himself down. "By leaving now, I may, however, have time for a short detour to Bow Street. Only if his lordship wishes it, of course." He endeavoured an obsequious pose and failed. The man had not a deferential bone in his body. "Perhaps Jasper should accompany me. I always find a display of muscles comes in useful upon these occasions, do you not?"

Lando grinned. "I've always been a fan of a muscular display; you know that, darling. On any occasion." He took a dainty last bite of honeyed bread. "Which reminds me. I must retire back to bed."

Chapter Twenty-Two

WHEN HIS FIRST conscious thoughts on waking no longer circled around casting up his accounts but on his hungry, rumbling belly, Kit deduced he was on the mend. In fact, he was well enough to note that, from the play of bright colour on the ornate ceiling above the bed, the hour must be late.

But as he immediately discovered, brilliant morning light wasn't merely streaming through the chink in the drapes. It was under the bedclothes with him, exhaling soft puffs of air, its pale, elegant form folded around his own like a second skin.

Kit's hunger stretched in a new direction.

That damned white nightgown, now rumpled and formless, had no right to be so beguiling. So as not to disturb the sleeper, Kit laid his palm gently upon the thin layer of linen covering a lean arm draped across his chest. Lando hummed, wriggled, then settled once more, and Kit's morning cockstand responded happily.

His hand didn't stay still for long; his fingers itched to explore, to travel where his mouth couldn't, not while Lando slumbered. As he skimmed them lower, skirting under the bunched hem of the garment, he imagined he was kissing Lando through the tips of them, nuzzling at his warm creases and intimate folds, pressing his lips up against miles of flawless skin.

His wandering hand's first discovery was a weakness for a taut slim thigh hitched across his, for warm supple flesh curving into a soft swell of buttock. He swept slow circles up and around the firm meat of it, each stroke laying down a new layer of intimacy as his fingertips grazed ever closer towards the shallow divide dipping between one perfectly rounded buttock and the other. Lando hummed again, a contented rasp low in his throat as he burrowed deeper into Kit's side. If Kit's cockstand were the yardstick—and it was starting to feel as if it approached that length—then he was definitely on the mend.

When the pad of his finger skimmed across Lando's entrance, Lando's breath hitched, and he raised his leg higher. When his prick dug into Kit's thigh, and Kit answered with another drift of his fingers down Lando's divide, Lando snuffled a laugh.

"Pritchard would vouch I am loathsome when awoken before I have requested it. But you are forgiven. Your touch is better than any of my dreams."

In one glorious manoeuvre, Lando divested himself of the nightgown, then shifted over, aligning his body above Kit's. Resting on his elbows, he looked down between them, Kit's chest and belly dark and hairy, his own milky and smooth. Their cocks greeted each other for the very first time, and Lando almost purred with pleasure. "We are like night and day, you and I."

"More like alabaster and rough-hewn granite." Kit scratched a nail across one of Lando's pale nipples before sliding his fingers higher up Lando's chest to cup his chin. The man had barely sprouted a whisker overnight, whereas Kit already sported what some boasted as a full beard.

He groaned as Lando rolled his hips above him. "You are unreasonably handsome, Lando," he teased. "And you wield your beauty like a sword with which to slay me."

Lando's laugh was throaty and full of want. "I had no idea rough-hewn granite could be so poetic."

He rolled his hips again, his long pale prick gliding alongside Kit's thickly veined one. "You are no stranger to a sword yourself," he pointed out, then dropped his lips to Kit's to deliver a soft kiss. "And I want your sword," he whispered in a breathy gust. "So, so much. I want your sword to lead this dance."

Kit's wide eyes said all where his voice failed. His lover's meaning was unmistakeable.

"We have the necessary in the chevet," murmured Lando, kissing a trail along Kit's jaw, his throat, his shoulder, his... Ye gods, yes. *Take the lead.* Be buried deep inside Lando.

Assailed by his urgent need, Kit heaved himself up to reach for the oil. Then barked a yelp as the ribs on his left side screamed a protest, his hip bone rattled in its socket, and his right temple throbbed a chorus of disapproval. Ye gods, no. He flopped back down against the pillows.

"There is nothing I would like more," he confessed with a frustrated growl. "But I fear...I have a grave concern that the level of vigour required for proper swordplay may cause my head to topple clean off my neck."

Lando giggled against his shoulder, and Kit joined in before groaning as his hard length brushed once more against Lando's.

"Damn you, if you do that one more time then," Kit said, arching up into him, "I wonder whether I might live quite well without it."

In one swift motion, Lando was up and straddling his hips. He leaned forward to plant his mouth on Kit's. "I have become exceedingly fond of your head. I do believe we should preserve it a little longer. Allow me to assist."

Giddily, Kit gazed at his lover as he reached across him to the chevet. His mouth watered as his greedy eyes feasted on Lando's lithe form. A form Kit had fallen stupidly in love with; whatever the outcome of the next few days, his heart would never return to its former dimensions.

"I'm right, you know," he breathed, "You are unfairly handsome."

Once more, Lando straddled him. The sweet musk of jasmine filled the air as he massaged oil into that hidden part of himself, moaning softly. His other hand was at his ballocks, fondling them. His lips parted as his breath quickened; his cheeks flushed with warmth. Sore limbs and throbbing head forgotten, Kit's own cock leaped, and he pinched himself, wishing he could feast on the spectacle for hours but fearing he would burst with desire if he did.

"More of that, Lando, and I may spill before I am even inside you."

Biting his lip and flicking Kit a naughty glance, Lando's palm curled around his length, and he self-pleasured. As if Kit wasn't there.

"Now you are making sport of me." Kit arched his back towards nothing, seeking out relief, and cursed.

A single pearl beaded at Lando's tip. He swiped it with his thumb, bringing it to his mouth. He licked his tongue across it. "And you are making a king of me."

It was time; Kit could wait no longer. Sensing it, Lando's hand left his own shaft to hold Kit's in place. Then, very deliberately, he lowered both his gaze and his body.

Kit watched himself—nay, tortured himself—disappear inside his lover. Only the tip, at first, but so hot and tight, melting Kit from the inside out. His lungs filled with the heady, musky scent of jasmine, and already, he spiralled to high oblivion.

"Yes," he breathed.

After a beat, during which Kit thought his expanding heart might cease to function entirely, Lando pressed deeper. Then barely eased back before sinking down again. A long shuddering sigh escaped him as his channel accepted the blunt intrusion, sending a rush of heat all the way to Kit's toes.

"You are magnificent," he whispered.

Lando's dark pupils, ringed in silver, met Kit's as he sank to capture his lips. "And you are…ah…substantial."

Lando rode him with the same elegance and expertise as he drove forward his sleek black stallion. Under Kit's hands, his thigh's ropey muscles flexed and softened, flexed and softened as he rocked back and forth. Kit's bones dissolved to nothing as Lando let out a blissful low hum, his silvery-blue eyes fluttering closed, his pale hands gripping the thick fur on Kit's chest. Injuries be damned, Kit raised himself up and tugged Lando down, clasping his flushed face between his strong hands, plunging his tongue into the sultry treasure of his lover's mouth.

"This…" he panted, his soul full of Lando, "…is too much."

Kit's need for release was building fast. Lando's, too, Kit knew from the tautening of his belly, the tension in his thighs, the choppiness of the rhythm. One of his hands found Lando's weeping cock, clumsily he fisted it, loving the sounds pouring from his beautiful lover, loving how Lando's head fell back, loving their shared sweet surrender.

"Yes." Lando cried. "Yes, Kit."

Stuttering and shuddering, Lando rode him through his crisis and beyond until Kit's member could take no more. Where he began and Lando ended, Kit knew not, and as Lando spilled across his chest, his neck, his face, he'd have been hard-pressed to remember his own name. All he knew was to drag his lover against him, to crush him against his chest, and hold him close as if he'd never be parted from him.

*

FOR HOURS AFTERWARD they lay entwined. Though the sheets were sticky from lovemaking, neither were desirous to move. They talked of nothing and everything, of how Lando's release matted Kit's furry trail, of how he insisted nothing compared to that first sinking down onto another man's cock, not even a willing open mouth. How they were well-matched for height. How Lando had lain every night in this bed since Kit was brought home and much of each day too. How he had cleaned and dressed Kit's head wound under Jasper's instruction while Kit slept. How he'd ordered new velvet ribbons for Kit's hair in every conceivable shade of midnight blue and a few in a bright magenta, too, simply because he could. How he'd like to bind Kit's wrists up in his pearls and ride him as he'd just ridden him. How Kit would never again breathe in the scent of jasmine without recalling this precious moment and the precious man with whom he shared it.

Their fingers were interlaced. Lando's head made a pillow of Kit's chest, while once again his thigh found a home across Kit's hips. One of Lando's slim calves even snaked around a sturdier one of Kit's. If his time was suddenly called, Kit would shuffle off his mortal coil a happy man.

So, it was with a heavy weight resting upon his heart, he felt obliged to spoil things.

"I must make a confession, Lando." Staring up at the plain white plaster ceiling, his head felt clearer than it had in days. "A grave one."

"Out with it, my darling," Lando answered sleepily. "Confession is to be encouraged. It empties the soul, making room for more sin." His fingertips trailed down Kit's bare flank to rest at his hip. "And sinning with you has become my very favourite way to pass the time."

Kit's own hand closed over Lando's, stilling it. Was it too late to change his mind? He could confess to weariness, dizziness, hunger, or a sore head. He could feign ignorance of the whole beating, and Lando would be none the wiser. A head wound was an excellent excuse for convenient amnesia.

Except, past deeds had an annoying way of catching up with one, whether one sought them out or not. His temple throbbed, serving to remind him that Clark had not forgotten him, and that wily Jasper, coming to his aid, might know there was more to the episode than opportunistic thievery. And his dear, honest Lando, with whom he could not deny he had fallen deeply in love, deserved to hear the truth.

So if not now, when?

"The ruffians who set upon me," he started. And exhaled deeply. "They were lying in wait when I returned to my former lodgings. A dogged Bow Street runner, determined to bring me to account, paid them for their services. I...I am a wanted man, Lando, no better than my assailants."

Already, he felt washed clean. Even if he now faced a mountain to climb to regain Lando's trust. And a silence to fill; once he had begun, he couldn't stop.

"I have rather made a mull of things. I do not deserve your forgiveness but seek it anyhow. Your belief in me and your fondness has been misplaced. I fear my previous actions may put our scheme in peril. This runner will not stop until he has a noose around my neck."

Lando said nothing, but neither did he move away. If Kit hadn't just admitted his duplicity and shallow nature, he would imagine the other man slept.

When Lando eventually made a sound, it was very much like a low chuckle. "Poor Pritchard. I shall be quite swimming in lard this evening."

What the blazes?

"He wagered me a florin that you'd not spill unless I held a knife to your throat." Lando twisted to press his lips against Kit's chest. "I disagreed. A most scrupulous heart beats underneath this irascible shell. This very fine and um...*quite hirsute* irascible shell."

Kit cursed. Every time Kit thought he had the measure of

him, Lando surprised him anew. "My lord," he spluttered. "I am at a loss to understand your mirth. My head must ail me more than I first believed."

The cool hand on Kit's hip strayed lower, commencing a lazy and thoroughly undeserved stroking of his ballocks.

"Your head is fine." Lando rubbed his nose along Kit's pelt, breathing him in. "And I am not your lord, even when you are demonstrating your irascibility perfectly. I have been abreast of our perseverant *Mr Clark* since you first disclosed your habit of picking pockets. Which, of course, was a truth you were courageous to share, given that you sought my assistance at the time."

"How the devil do you know his name?" Kit cried. The ballock stroking continued unabated. "And stop distracting me!"

His lover seemed even more amused. "Were you not paying attention when I described my brother Robert's varied attributes? There is very little he can't unearth if he puts his mind to it."

"But…what was…did he?" Ugh. That hand. This man. Never mind being unable to think straight, Kit's mind zigzag-hopped all over the place.

Taking pity on him, Lando withdrew his ministrations from Kit's tenderest parts to raise himself onto his elbows. His damned silvery eyes glittered like precious diamonds. How had Kit ever believed them cold and icy?

"I have a confession of my own, Kit, darling. Do you recall your feeble attempt to blackmail me?"

"I've tried to block it from my memory," Kit bit out. "I was an ass of the highest order."

Lando inclined his head. "Be that as it may, I am a cautious man, as one who is breaking the laws of the land by lying here

with you has to be. I don't share my bed with anyone, you understand."

"Glad to hear it." He'd be sharing it with no one except Kit
from now on if he had any say in the matter. Even if his smart
lover was damned annoying.

"My loyal Jasper has been trailing after you since we arrived
in London. On my instruction. For both your protection and
mine."

So that's why the great one-eyed lug had insisted he person-
ally deliver Kit to Sindell Street that first time. And to the tailors.

"I suppose I should be grateful," he grunted in a most ungrateful fashion. "Your suspicious nature has saved my life."

"It has." Lando nodded. "Thus, I'm grateful to myself."

He sounded a tiny bit smug. As well he might. Shaking his
head, Kit smiled to himself. Annoyance was futile as, indeed, was
any sort of defence against this man.

"And I don't have an irascible shell!"

"You are blessed with *a lot* of hair though."

Chapter Twenty-Three

TWO DAYS LATER, when a footman arrived at Grosvenor Street with a note forewarning them of Sir Ambrose's imminent visit, the sated lovers were knee-deep in playing cards. Or rather, Kit was cheating at three-card brag, and Lando was attempting to spot his deception. He'd declared—rightly– that Kit's loose left sleeve was somehow involved, but, to Kit's delight, Lando was failing to fathom it. Notwithstanding, sprawled in the armchair next to Kit's bed, with a wooden tray balanced on Kit's lap serving as a makeshift card table, his lover appeared to be thoroughly enjoying his failed attempts to get to the bottom of it.

"He's arriving at four." Lando perused the missive as if it might contain clues to the sender's intent. "To pay you a visit. Not me."

A fluttery sensation pooled low in Kit's belly. They exchanged a look, the cards forgotten. Lando's hand slipped into

Kit's. "Do you feel well enough?"

On the physician's orders, Kit had remained confined to bed for several more days. Lando, his faithful nursemaid, had ensured he followed the order to the letter, forbidding Kit all activities unless they involved him and were strictly horizontal.

"I shall have to be, shan't I?" He fingered the purplish bruise above his right eye. The bandage had been removed the day before, but the wound was far from healed. "I can hardly receive him here in my nightgown."

Truth be told, Kit was feeling much improved. His headaches had receded, his vision returned to normal, and his appetite stronger. His libido was ravenous. Indeed, he could have ventured from his sick chamber earlier, but if Lando wanted to coddle him a little while longer, then who was Kit to complain?

"Meet him in the library," Lando instructed. "The light is dimmer there. You shall appear less pale."

Jasper appeared to help him bathe and dress. In his previously weakened state, the practicalities of those activities had taken up all of Kit's strength, leaving him far too exhausted for awkward exchanges. And though his heart held but a very small amount of affection for the surly ex-soldier — a sentiment reciprocated, he was sure — it sat there alongside a deep well of gratitude, which he could no longer ignore. Even though spitting out the words pained him. Especially when Kit was marooned in the middle of the bedchamber wearing nothing but his underclothes, with the ex-soldier holding his breeches to ransom in his great paw.

Clearing his throat, Kit addressed the man's solid back as he bent over the washstand, preparing for Kit's shave. "I would like to take this opportunity to express my gratitude to you, Jasper, for rescuing me from a rather threatening situation."

"Beg your pardon, sir." Noisily, Jasper tipped water, no doubt only tepid, into the ceramic wash basin. "Missed that." He tapped his ear, turning to face Kit. "Deaf in this one. Musket blast six inches from it back in 1814."

Kit gave him a long hard stare. Whenever Lando reminded Jasper that it was time for Kit to drink some vile medicinal concoction on his physician's advice, the man's hearing was perfectly intact. Jasper's single eye roamed over Kit's exposed legs.

"I said," he repeated through gritted teeth. "You have my sincere gratitude for rescuing me from an…an awkward encounter."

Jasper made a sound suspiciously like a snort. "I've heard a good thrashing called a few things in my soldiering days, but never an…"

"All right, all right. Good grief, man. Just…thank you. You saved my life, and I'm eternally grateful and forever in your debt, et cetera, et cetera."

Jasper returned his attention to the washstand. "Didn't do it for you. Did it for him."

"Yes, well. I rather presumed that to be the case." Kit exhaled through his nose, and his fingers twitched, almost as if he wanted to wrestle something. He would very much like to be wearing his breeches. "His lordship is terribly grateful too."

"He's a good man. One of the best. Like his father before him."

"So I understand." Still on the weak side, Kit sank into the chair by the washstand. "You are…um…obviously content to be in his employ at Rossingley." He leaned forward as Jasper roughly folded a towel around his neck. "It's a fine part of the world. There are certainly much worse places to live."

"There be that," agreed Jasper. He proffered two soap bars. "Would sir like the jasmine or orange?"

Ye gods, they were having a normal conversation. "Orange. Thank you." Now was not the time for jasmine; his meeting with Gartside required his full concentration. "Do you miss Rossingley?"

With a fingertip, Jasper tested the sharpness of the blade and gave a satisfied nod. On a silent prayer, Kit shut his eyes tight. "Can't wait to get back. London folk aren't to my liking."

"You include me in their number, I'll wager." Kit grinned. "I daresay you're looking forward to leaving me and this valeting behind, too, getting back to your old job."

As Jasper scraped the blade with more care than he ever had before across Kit's sensitive, bruised flesh, he let out a mirthless laugh. "Leaving you behind? Fat chance of that. Not if his lordship's got anything to do with it."

"My home is here in London," answered Kit, puzzled. "You've seen it. You've seen how straitened my circumstances are. Thus, you understand as well as I that I do not have the luxury of swanning about the countryside as the guest of an earl. No." He shook his head, earning a glare from Jasper. "I shall find another set of suitable lodgings when all this Gartside business is over and seek gainful employ."

Jasper scoffed, dipping the blade into soapy water. "Lodgings? You won't be going back to living in them again. In your shoes, I'd get out of London."

He had a point. "Maybe I'll go to Kent," Kit argued sulkily.

"l know the area well. I'll be sure to find suitable employ after this has died down. His lordship will surely give me references of good standing."

Patting his chin with a soft towel, Jasper shook his head. "There's a fair few miles between Kent and Rossingley. My lord won't allow it."

"He is not *my* lord." Indeed, Lando had said so himself. Kit jerked his head to glare at Jasper. "I am at liberty to go where I like."

Jasper jerked him back towards the light again, his strong fingers clamped around Kit's chin. "You'll be coming with us," he growled in a tone brooking no disagreement. "For good. He'll kidnap you if he has to. Mark my words."

*

"WHAT THE BLAZES has happened to you?"

Gartside strode into the library as if he owned it. Kit grimaced. So much for poor lighting. They exchanged polite nods, Kit's cracked ribs protesting at a hearty clap on the shoulder. With his legs still a little shaky, he gratefully fell back into a chair.

"Took a tumble from that grey mare," he explained, his eyes darting to Jasper in attendance by the door. Staring straight ahead, the footman was a model of subservience. "Damned creature was spooked by a passing stage."

Gartside harrumphed, taking up a stance by the window. Though his seated position put Kit at a disadvantage, it was preferable to swooning at the odious man's feet. A sheen coated Gartside's brow, and he dabbed at it with a white handkerchief. Kit smiled to himself; he wasn't the only one beset by nerves.

"I'd wager a man in your position doesn't have the leisure or blunt to properly understand quality horseflesh. Wouldn't mind riding that prime bit of blood myself." With his hands clasped behind his back, Gartside examined Kit down his nose before turning back to the window.

"No, sir," Kit agreed. The man really was utterly loathsome. "A deep regret, but a consequence of one's station in life, which one must bear with stoicism."

"Quite."

There was a pregnant pause, during which Kit had the distinct impression Gartside, staring out into the park, was building himself up. Unless he had a particular fascination for linden trees.

"Rossingley has returned from his trip, I assume?"

"He has," Kit confirmed. "In good spirits. If you wish for further information from him regarding his proposition, perhaps I could send Jasper here to enquire as to his whereabouts?"

Indisposed to visitors, Lando was taking a leisurely scented bath, which Kit planned on interrupting as soon as Gartside left. "He is keen to have this business wrapped up so he may return to the country."

"His presence won't be necessary," said Gartside in a clipped tone. "I'm sure you are perfectly capable of furnishing me with what I need."

Another delicate pause followed, during which Gartside's fists flexed. Kit exchanged another glance with Jasper. Since his beating, he found the man's presence reassuring.

"And may I enquire as to what might that be, Sir Ambrose?"

Apparently satisfied with the foliage outside the window, Kit's visitor turned his attention towards Kit. "Yes, you may." He wiped a fat finger across his damp upper lip. "I understand you have the ear of Castlereagh, the Foreign Secretary."

"Yes," confirmed Kit, schooling his features into the solemn countenance of a man who did indeed spend his days advising Parliament how best to conduct a portion of its import and export affairs. "When he travels north."

"And of Rossingley too."

Kit nodded gravely. "I do not wish to appear immodest, but yes, these past few weeks his lordship has leaned quite heavily on my thoughts and experience."

And on other parts of him too.

"Is that so." Gartside's lips pursed as he peered at Kit, much like one might a bug under a microscope. Kit resisted the twin urges to both avert his eyes from Gartside's piggy scrutiny and to gabble. If his card-sharping days had taught him nothing else, it was that fast-flowing words were a ready sign of duplicity. Instead, he met the odious man's regard with a level one of his own and tried not to fidget.

"You are fond of the finer things in life, I believe." Gartside's eyes flicked up and around the well-appointed library. "Good tailoring and horseflesh and so forth."

Blushing on cue was beyond Kit's acting repertoire, so he settled for lowering his gaze to the carpet. "I admit to those weaknesses, yes."

Gartside inhaled in a noisy sniff. "Good. In which case, sir, I have a proposal for you."

He spun around to face Jasper, who eyed him impassively. "You, man. Leave us."

As if of his own choosing, Jasper strolled out, taking his time.

With another harrumph, Gartside returned his attention to Kit. "You have one minute to accept or decline. If you decline and word gets out of my offer, then I shall be left with no alternative than to suggest that it was *you* who made the offer to *me*. And I shall report you to your superiors. Do I make myself clear?"

Kit dug his nails into his palm as he fought a desire to punch the air. "Crystal, Sir Ambrose," he answered in a steadier voice than he imagined possible.

"Humph." Gartside gave a brisk nod. "Very well. Two hundred pounds will be delivered direct to your pocket by my manservant tomorrow evening if you can provide me with your word that I am to be selected as Rossingley's business partner. Another fifty when the deed is done."

Kit's dull nagging headache vanished. *Two hundred pounds?* A gentleman could run a small household on that for a year and not feel the pinch. That was a larger sum than he'd seen in his life. A thrilling fire coursed through his veins as he pictured what all of those pound notes would look like, heaped in a pile. Or thrown up in the air with abandon. Even his broken ribs were quiescent.

"What say you, sir?" added Gartside with a jerk of his wobbly chin.

Kit made himself count to ten, determined not to let his excitement, almost too big to be contained, overpower his intelligence. *Two hundred pounds.* This was it! Bar a small portion for his sister, the remainder he'd hand over to Lando so that Gartside's ill-treated tenants might survive the winter. Vindication for his sister and every other poor chit the man had abused was so close he could almost taste it.

The sum Gartside offered was even bigger than they'd imagined. So pompous, so arrogant, yet the man was a fool of the highest order. Kit felt like punching him for being so stupid. To be on the safe side, he extended his count to thirty.

"I say...I say that you will make an excellent business associate for the eleventh Earl of Rossingley's cotton ventures. Sir." A smile of immense relief, itching to break out, spread across his face. Fortunately, misinterpreted by Gartside.

"Then we have a deal." Darting forward, the baronet vigorously pumped Kit's hand, forcing him to stand. Kit's hiss of pain as an equally hearty backslap threatened to topple him went unnoticed by Gartside, too busy congratulating himself on his excellent deal. "I knew you'd see reason, Angel. Spotted you as a man of sound mind the minute I clapped eyes on you."

"I'm...thank you. Flattered to be sure." And then, as Kit felt obliged, he added, "Can I offer you some refreshment, a toast perhaps?" His eyes watered. *Please decline.* Every single one of his ribs had felt that backslap and his legs had suddenly liquefied, although that might have been secondary to the two hundred pounds bribe.

Lando had been right, this odious baronet's character was the instrument of his own downfall. Gartside's ruination was so close, Kit almost smelled it in the air.

"No, Angel. I shall be on my way," Gartside answered curtly, his tone making no bones about the fact that socialising with Kit was far beneath a fellow of the upper orders such as himself. Thank God. "We shall reconvene on Rossingley's appointed schedule. Whereupon I anticipate some excellent news."

Chapter Twenty-Four

KIT HAD NEVER entered Lando's bedchamber, though the hidden door in the panelling had tempted him more than once. Being invited into this private space was being granted permission to unveil another even more intimate layer of the man.

Muted, classical simplicity was very much à la mode in and around the *ton*. The clean, sleek lines of Grosvenor Street's reception rooms were replicated at White's, at Rossingley, and had even reached the home of Kit's former employer, Sir Brandon Gower, out in the provinces.

The fashion had bypassed Lando's sumptuous bedchamber. As Kit stepped farther into the room, his dazzled gaze flitted like a butterfly from flower to flower. Far above his head, gilded hunting scenes ran amok across the plaster ceiling in lavish detail fit for a king's drawing room. Below, his boots sank into the richly patterned fitted carpet as though standing on a mattress made of goose feathers. The white marble chimneypiece was wide enough to home a small family, the inferno merrily blazing away within sufficient to warm an entire village. Red silk walls and opulent upholstery complemented cream-and-burgundy silk bed hangings, themselves enriched with panels of delicate ivory-coloured embroidered flowers. The bed was a warm hug, an inviting haven of indulgence, steeped with pillows, throws, rugs; every item beckoning him closer.

Naturally, all of this passed him by in the blink of an eye because of…Lando, naked, in a huge claw-footed tub facing out towards the park. Shrouded in fragrant steam, he idly sponged a long pale arm while enjoying the view. Unable to tear his eyes from an entirely different view, Kit reached out a hand to steady himself, sucking in a deep inhale. What a glorious scent. What a glorious sight!

"I sense you bring excellent news, darling." A ripple accompanied Lando's greeting as the arm sank underwater. In proportion with the vast bedchamber, the bath easily hid his body, leaving only his head and shoulders visible, his blond locks damp and curling at his nape, resting on a cushioned pad. Around his neck looped a heavy rope of pearls.

"W…what?"

The thick pearls circled his long neck twice, glistening. Two droplets of water trickled down his cheek.

"I said, you must have excellent news. Your fists are hanging by your sides and unclasped."

"Yes." Kit's limbs took on a loose, fluid quality. "Forgive me, I was…"

With a tilt of his chin, Lando indicated to the fireplace.

"Pritchard has towels warming. Would you be kind enough to pass them? The water is cooling."

"Of course."

Kit thought back to his own ungainly clambering out of his bathtub earlier that day, accompanied by much cursing and sloshing of water, despite Jasper's assistance. Lando's graceful transition from lying to standing, shamelessly bare, was seamless. Generous streams of water cascaded down his chest, sheening his flat belly, slicking the treasure lying long and pale between his thighs. The man was as flawless and polished as the white marble of the chimney breast behind him.

"You are wearing pearls," Kit stated needlessly. "While bathing."

"For your rendezvous with Gartside." Lando flashed his small, neat teeth. "For luck."

Lando made no effort to cover himself. Or, in fact, dry himself. Kit drank in the perfect arrangement of shoulders, limbs, chest, and belly.

"The...ah...towels?" Lando murmured after a minute or so. Raising a slim hand to his neck, he fingered the pearls. His lip curled in that suggestive, crooked way he had.

"Yes." Kit swallowed, his gums and tongue thick and sluggish as if unsure of their purpose. "You are wet," he added uselessly.

Lando brought the pearls to his mouth. He ran the tip of his tongue around one. "One normally is after bathing. You could dry me off."

The towels were thick and soft. Warm, too, from the fire. Kit began with Lando's face, tenderly dabbing at the dampness.

Lando stayed perfectly still.

"Gartside. His visit," he prompted as Kit rubbed the towel in slow circles across Lando's chest. Lando's member was half hard now; Kit's own arousal throbbed painfully against the placket of his breeches. As he swept the towel lower to catch a few drips making their way down Lando's belly, he ghosted over Lando's arousal and a possessive, needy sound escaped his throat.

"You are so…ugh…" Kit breathed.

A pearl clacked against Lando's teeth.

"You are…" Kit tried again, a coherent response failing him. "That man's name has no place in this bedchamber," he managed instead. "Not now. Not here with…" His eyes were drawn to where Lando mouthed the pearls. "You need drying very carefully."

Lando chuffed, and with a circling of his hips, brushed his shaft against Kit's thigh. "Look. I'm still very wet down here."

If Kit looked, he might explode. "So is your back," he answered. "Turn around."

As Kit swept the towel down the valley of Lando's shoulder blades, he traced its path with his tongue, his open-mouthed kisses claiming every inch of hot damp skin. He rested his hand at Lando's hip, holding him lightly in place as he trailed the cloth along the curve of his spine, lingering on the swell of his pale, smooth buttocks. When he dragged an edge down Lando's divide, Lando arched back into him with a moan.

"I need drying there *very* carefully."

"You are soaking," Kit agreed hoarsely.

His desire was too loud for words. Too intrusive. Unstoppable. Palming himself through his breeches, he dragged the towel up again, a little deeper this time. Lando widened his stance, gripping the side of the tub for balance. As Kit dried that hidden part of him most thoroughly, with his other hand, he squeezed Lando's bare buttock, rubbing himself against it.

It was not enough.

Abandoning the towel, he sank to his knees. Like succulent ripe fruit, Lando's two pert mounds hovered inches away from his mouth, arching back into him. Tempting him. Kit had never performed such an intimate act—had never desired to—but then, he'd never been presented with such a delicious spectacle. Spreading Lando with his thumbs, he licked an obscene line down Lando's crease and was rewarded by a sharp gasp.

He pulled back. "Too much?"

Lando pushed into him with a sigh. "Not enough."

Kit licked again, this time keeping his mouth there. Lando writhed in pleasure, spurring him on. Kit lapped at the delicate pink star quivering under his tongue, tasting it, mouthing it. The taut flesh softened, he watched it unfurl and open, aware of his own shaft leaking like a lead pipe and just as hard. Lando's sounds of pleasure echoed around the room in counterpoint to Kit's obscene slurps.

"I am spoiled..." Lando gasped, writhing away from him. "No bath shall be complete until you undo me like this afterwards. I shall demand it after every single one."

"You shall have it, my lord." Ye gods, how wonderfully indecent Kit felt, himself fully clothed and his lover splayed open for him. "Whenever, whatever you wish, it is yours."

"I wish to kiss you."

Kit stood, spun Lando around, and pulled him into his arms.

Frantically, he claimed his mouth, bruising Lando's ripe lips with the intensity of it. Dragging him closer still, Kit closed his fingers around a clutch of pearls. As his own need threatened to drown him, he pushed Lando backwards. "And I wish you to be on the bed. Now."

Kit loosened his cravat, urgently extricating himself from his finery. Spread out waiting for him, Lando toyed with his damned pearls. With his other hand, he fondled himself, teasing the hood of his prick up and down.

"Damn your tailor," Kit cursed, wriggling like a worm on a hook. There was a slight tearing sound. "This coat is too blasted tight across my shoulders."

The buttons were cursed, too, all ten pretty enamel ones adorning his waistcoat. A series of soft chuckles erupted from his lover as he wrestled with them, gaining in delight as Kit shook off his undershirt like it housed an angry wasp. He sat for his boots, in the nick of time remembering he hadn't been put on this fine earth purely for Lando's entertainment. Considering his lover was the one stark ballock naked and dripping soap suds, he shouldn't be the one now chortling like a burst drain.

"It's those blasted pearls." Kit flung his stockings across the room, then groaned, clutching his sore ribs like a loon. Hip, head, and ribs be damned too. "They have addled my brain. You will be the death of me, Lord Henry Orlando Fitzwilliam Albert Duchamps-Avery." With a sudden move, Kit pounced on his squealing lover. "But, by heavens, it will be a most marvellous way to go."

Wrestling Lando higher onto the pillows, Kit took charge. Both of his man and the damned jasmine oil. As Kit's slippery finger sought entry between his parted thighs, Lando's eyes widened. Already slack, he arched up into Kit's touch. As he whimpered, Kit smiled.

"You like that, don't you? Pleasure yourself on me."

Lando shuddered, and one finger became two. His head fell back, and Kit sucked and nipped at his neck. He buried his tongue in the hollow behind his ear, shared his hotly gasped air. Kit was thoroughly spoiled, too, for any other man.

"Now," Lando panted, "Now, Kit. Please?"

How Kit loved that little desperate please. Kneeling up, he helped himself to some more oil and took himself in hand, coating himself from root to tip in a showy, generous manner.

Then he lined himself up.

Nothing compared to that first thrust. Unhesitating and unapologetic. In that moment, he swore Lando's soul was tangled with his. Buried to the hilt, he held still, mesmerised by his lover's parted lips, his silent cry of pleasure. Pulling almost all the way out, Kit poured himself into him again, his hips slapping against the back of Lando's thighs. Lando slid down the pillows, and he grabbed onto Kit's shoulders, his nails digging into the firm flesh.

"Hold on tight," Kit gasped. He had one hand around his lover's neck, the blessed pearls caught up in his palm, the other wrapped around the bedframe. As his lover opened up, he pounded into him, harder, faster, deeper until Lando was laudanum running through Kit's veins, and Kit, a hungry, greedy addict. Between them, Lando's shaft lay hot and heavy; with every stroke, Kit rubbed against it between them. Lando trembled, his channel tightening around Kit's prick.

"I am close to spending," he breathed, his mouth merging with Kit's.

Kit squeezed a hand between them, closing it around Lando's leaking member.

"Then spend for me, my love. And I shall do the same."

*

"I MUST ADD bedsport to your list of talents, Kit," observed Lando lightly. Still damp from his bath and now from his exertions, his blond locks curled sweetly across his forehead. "My mattress may never recover. And your...your tongue —" His cheeks flushed a delicate hue. " — is singularly gifted."

"I have never done that...there until now," Kit confessed. "In fact, I have never lain in a bed with another man until you, though I have partaken of my share of men. But not lain with them. Not like this."

Those faceless mollies and Lando didn't warrant the same sentence. Pillowing his head in his arms, Kit sleepily gazed up to the complexly patterned ceiling and the swashbuckling adventures played out upon it. He frowned. On closer inspection, some of those innocent hunting scenes weren't what they had first seemed. That swarthy knight, for instance. Kit blinked, then blinked again to be quite sure. The one without the helmet and the exaggerated codpiece. He wasn't...with that...that other knight. Was he? And was...was that his memb...? Ye gods.

"Quite." Lando gave a little cough. "You were saying, darling."

Flushing, Kit turned his regard to the safer, plainer silk hangings draping the bed, adorned with lilies, though rapidly averted it to the carved wooden scrolls at the foot because those water nymphs were…good Lord. Closing his eyes was simpler.

"I was saying I've never tupped in a bed."

"And is it to your liking?" Lando's nimble fingers curled around the trail of thick dark hair tracking down the centre of Kit's belly.

"I'd say so. Mostly, I've done it stood up against alley walls or bent a man over in a dark corner. An occasional swift tumble on a well-used sheet in the back room of the coffee house down on Field Lane when funds have allowed. But never like this, never on a soft mattress made up with linen sheets." *And never with one as fine as you.*

He turned to where Lando lay on his side, drowsily watching him from under the lids of those silvery eyes. Like a lazy lion waiting to pounce. "And…and I've never taken the role you…you have just taken," he admitted. "But I wonder, with you, whether it would give me pleasure."

"Then I should find it most pleasurable too."

Closing the gap between them, Lando rested his head on Kit's chest. His ribs didn't mind one bit.

"This is new to me also," Kit remarked. "Lying here afterward and speaking my heart." He huffed a laugh. "Tupping you makes me garrulous."

"In some ways, this can be the best part." As Lando's cool fingers trailed up and down Kit's side, Kit didn't think he was wrong.

The fingers tapped on his chest. "Though no conversation or music is so pleasant to my ear as your strong heartbeat." Lando turned to press his lips against the skin overlying it. "Every second and every minute you lay unconscious spoke only of my empty future."

With a shake of his head, Lando tutted, his breath fluttering against Kit's thick pelt. "How selfish I sound. You, so unwell, and me, only thinking of myself."

Kit squeezed Lando's fingers, bringing their hands, now knitted together, to his mouth to kiss them. "If I had been capable of conscious thought, then I daresay I would have been thinking of you too." He grinned down at the blond head. "You consume far too many of my thoughts these days, my lord."

"Then may these days stretch forever."

Kit kissed his fingers again. "Amen to that."

Sighing contentedly, he nuzzled against the top of Lando's head. He'd never felt a need to kiss a man as much as his lips sought any part of Lando and marvelled that his need for him was not sated despite their recent exertions.

"Gartside offered two hundred pounds." Kit allowed himself a quick flare of satisfaction. "If I secure the deal as his, and another fifty pounds when it's done. I accepted, naturally; the money will be delivered here by this evening."

"Then we should celebrate. We have him in our grasp."

"We do," agreed Kit hesitantly.

Lando tilted his chin up to look at him. "I sense it does not give you pleasure."

"Oh, it does." Kit half-smiled. "That vile man is trapped; this will not end well for him. Though…" He shifted. "I still have a suspicion it will end awkwardly for me too."

"Shhh." Lando pressed a finger to Kit's mouth. "Don't say that."

"I must. I cannot deny the uneasiness in my bones. It heralds a natural end to our association too. As cocooned as I am now in this…this—" He swept an arm encompassing the opulence surrounding him. "—splendour, nonetheless, I am masquerading as someone I am not and fear being apprehended by the hour."

"You know I will do everything in my power to prevent it," replied Lando swiftly. "Robert and I have an idea and though I confess to not having the finer details thought out, if it fails then I am a peer of the realm. Even in these enlightened times, my word carries weight. It pains me, too, that you are at risk."

"I chose of my own free will to go along with your plan," countered Kit. "I knew the consequences. And Gartside's downfall is worth it." He sighed heavily. "But even if I wriggle through this, there still remains the thorny problem of Mr Clark. Granted, he is trouble of my own making and should be of no concern of yours, and yet, he is on my trail. I have broken the law on many occasions, and I do not wish for you to become tainted by an association with a common thief such as I. When this Gartside business is put to bed, if I walk away a free man, then I must escape his clutches by returning to Kent. I will use Sir Brandon's and my uncle's connections to seek honest employ." He pecked the tip of Lando's finger then let it go. "And Rossingley is quite a few miles from Kent."

Lando drew himself up onto his elbows, his worried eyes roaming Kit's face. "Do not speak of that now. Not when we have this…us. We are a beginning, not an end. It does not have to be that way. My brother, Robert, thinks we may come through this unscathed. He has made enquiries regarding Clark. You must put your trust in him. And in me."

Trust. It walked hand in hand with love, even if occasionally it lagged behind. As Lando offered it so sincerely, so bravely, how Kit wished he could grab it with both hands.

"I am saddened that I struggle to see the future as clearly as you, Lando. But I must carve my own path. Regrettably, that cannot be at Rossingley, where I have neither home, family, or connections, nor here in London. Most definitely not here in London, not if I wish that path to be a lengthy one. Though, it pains me to say it, as I wish for nothing more than to spend my days in close acquaintance with you."

Lando's glittery eyes beseeched him; he looked anxious. And beautiful. "Then let us not try to see the whole future" — his voice trembled with hope — "Let us live by the day. Let us see to the end of this Gartside business and then speak again as we do now. Frankly and openly as lovers and friends. Can you do that for me, Kit?"

His lips met Kit's urgently as if showing the future to Kit if only he had the courage to believe in it.

As they broke apart, Kit answered, "I have said it before." He smiled and shook his head. "There is nothing I will not do for you. Especially when your body lies naked on mine and your lips" — he chased them again — "taste so sweet."

Lando's fingers stroked across Kit's mouth as if learning the shape of it. His gaze dropped. "I know it is not polite to speak of one lover whilst in bed with another. But if I may, there is something I must share with you." He toyed with Kit's earring, rolling it between his finger and thumb. "I hope it is not too much too soon. But I can think of no other way to reassure you that I shan't allow anything dreadful to befall you. Robert and I will never let that happen."

"I shall try my utmost to believe that to be true."

"I grieved Charles's passing terribly, Kit. For three long years. And yet, at the same time, even in the depths of my melancholia, I understood all things must pass and even grew to accept that he had been my allotted portion of joy." He gave a rueful smile. "That the precious short time we had together was my due. And I did not complain. Mourned, yes. God, how I mourned. But not complain."

He swallowed as if it pained him. "And…and then you came along. And it seems our Lord has seen fit to afford me a second allocation of joy. One I shall not squander. So, though your path today may be covered in rocks and stones, it will not be that way forever. When all is said and done, we shall be together. I promise."

Chapter Twenty-Five

AS A RULE, anxiety's nimble tread tiptoed through Lando's mind and out the other side with nary a pause. Melancholia generally stayed a while, and when absent, Lando was not averse to vanity's dancing feet. Though he'd deny it all day long. But anxiety and a weakness of the nerves never tarried, which was why today's vacillation was all the more surprising.

"If I forewarn Kit of our plans regarding Clark, then I'm convinced he will give himself away to Gartside," Lando fretted for at least the fourth time. "We must use the element of surprise to our advantage, and I fear if Kit is in on it, then he might not behave in front of the others in the manner in which I intend."

Pritchard's expression told him he'd begun to find Lando's fussing quite wearing. Along with London life in general. The sooner Pritchard was back at Rossingley and enjoying the comforts found within Inglis's capable hands, the better his valet's humour would be.

"He is not half the actor Tommy is," Lando continued. "He wears his heart too close to his sleeve; he'll give us all away. But if I don't forewarn him, he will suffer such a dreadful shock he might loathe me forever after, even when all is revealed."

Pritchard tutted. Again. His well of subtlety had run dry, evidently. "My lord. If you believe that bag of moonshine, then I'll be wondering if you also took a cudgel to the head. Loathe you? Fat chance of that. The man is besotted."

They were returning in the phaeton from Coutt's on the Strand, having deposited Gartside's two hundred pounds for safekeeping. Wracked with nerves on the drive out, on account of being laden with so much money, Pritchard's usual gripes regarding his employer's penchant for speed had been forgotten. Now, with an empty purse and a nagging headache borne of his lordship's wittering, they returned in full flow.

"And if you don't slow down, there will be nothing left of you to loathe, my lord. Really, that last bend was not designed to be taken with two wheels in the air."

"But afterward, Pritchard, when all is revealed, do you truly believe he'll forgive me and accept my invitation to return as my guest to Rossingley?"

"No, my lord. I think he'll slice off his apples with a rusty blade and join a Cistercian monastery. And I also truly believe that lovesickness is a disease mostly suffered by those in the company of the infected person. Lovesick earls don't have to endure listening to themselves."

He threw Lando his sternest look. "And if you don't stop this thing bouncing over every blasted pothole in the road, I might choose to go and join him in the monastery. Keep both hands on the reins! Begging your pardon, my lord."

"Pardon absolutely refused." Snorting with laughter, Lando gave him a poke in the ribs. "And if you continue in this vein, I'll tip you over the side. I've told you before, it is not the done thing for an earl to be seen about the *ton* giggling with one's valet."

Reining the horses in a fraction because he was nothing if not considerate, Lando indulged himself in daydreams of the future: Waking with Kit alongside him, planning their day together in Rossingley's cosy breakfast room while admiring the flowers in the walled garden; serving him food from the sideboard while he poured Lando's coffee; watching him eat, watching him chew, watching him swallow; becoming insatiably aroused; dismissing the footmen so he could initiate amorous congress amongst the kippers. He mused over innocent, harmless reveries, so it was such a pity Pritchard's next words carved through them.

"Though Mr Angel may feel inclined to join you as a temporary houseguest, I feel duty-bound to remind you that it is also not done to have a permanent male house guest. Rossingley might be eighty miles hence, but one can never be too careful. Whilst your staff are loyal and discreet, visitors from the village and beyond may gossip. And—" He raised a finger to silence Lando's protests. "I grant that Mr Angel is as nauseatingly taken with you as you are with him, but have you considered whether he actually wants to live the life of a...a concubine? He's young, strong, and virile. He'll soon tire of loafing around your great pile while you're out doing your...whatever it is you do to keep your swathes of acreage shipshape."

"Oh." Lando pouted. "I...had not considered that."

"Hence, I'm alerting you to it. I'm not merely here to pick out waistcoats, you know."

To the delight of the matched pair and the dismay of Pritchard, the reins slipped loosely through Lando's fingers again as he sank into deep thought. Beyond their declarations of love, he hadn't fully pondered what Kit would *do* at Rossingley, only that he would be there. He had dismissed Kit's foolish insistence he should return to Kent to earn blunt, but now he reconsidered. As his valet had so forthrightly put, a prideful young man such as Lando's beloved would not be content in the role of unpaying house guest and lover. Pritchard was right. Kit wasn't of Lando's class — he would be no more comfortable living as an idle gentleman of leisure as Lando would clambering up sooty chimneys. He would have to *do* something.

"Given that you are in such an insightful mood, Pritchard, what do you suggest? You have presented me with a problem but offer no solution."

White-knuckled, Pritchard clutched the rail. "What I was going to add, my lord, if you would just slow this godforsaken contraption down for half a second, is that removing Sir Ambrose Gartside from your neighbouring property constitutes only half a plan. You will be improving the lives of many, but not of your own." He let out a yelp of terror as Lando's arms crossed over the reins as they went screaming around a stationary stage.

"You were saying?" Lando queried, unruffled.

"I was saying that this plan of yours is looking after everyone except for yourself!"

Muttering under his breath, Pritchard made the sign of the cross. "Removing Gartside would be excellent for all concerned, except yourself, who will not only inherit a multitude of tribulations to overcome in addition to managing your own affairs, but you would still be alone."

"Mmm," replied Lando with a brisk jerk of the reins. A rather brilliant idea had just occurred. "Unless, of course, I remove Gartside and place someone capable in his stead. Someone in desperate need of a home near to Rossingley. Someone...young and strong and virile, for instance." Taking his eyes off the road, he glanced at an ashen Pritchard. "Do you imagine that might be a feasible solution to our Mr Angel problem? Might it assuage his pride?"

"I have no idea. But if you don't rein in these satanic horses right now, then I swear to our Lord God Almighty, neither of us will live to find out."

Such a spoilsport. With a click of his tongue and a twitch of the reins, Lando brought the phaeton's speed down to a gentle trot. A huge smile spread across his face. Under duress, his valet could always be relied upon to unearth pockets of absolute genius.

"Thank you," Pritchard whimpered. "I shall live to see my Inglis again, after all."

Still grinning, Lando gave him another nudge. "It is I who should be thanking you, Pritchard. And before it escapes me, may I take this opportunity to praise your choice of the word *concubine*. It really is one of my very favourites. Terribly *exotic*, don't you think? Invariably puts me in mind of leather and thick strapping."

"Always here to please," Pritchard answered primly. "Although, if you ever drive this thing at those speeds again, I shall take a leather strap to you. And unless I'm mistaken, Grosvenor

Street is that way. Where the devil are you taking me now?"

"Oh, didn't I tell you?" Lando grinned evilly. "The bids are in. From Cobham and Sir Richard. Delivered by hand this morning. So, we're off to share the good news with Tommy."

"Drury Lane?" cried Pritchard, aghast.

"Well, he's hardly going to be found propping up the mantel at White's, is he? If we get a shuffle on, we can make the interval of the matinée performance. I hear Tommy's portrayal of Dick Turpin is terribly vulgar. It incited a riot two days ago. A brawl in the street! But I'm sure you'll be fine if I pop in for a few minutes."

*

THE DAY OF the rendezvous at White's drew bright and cheerful. As if eager for the afternoon ahead, the wind blew in teasing gusts, sending leaves flying from the trees and swirling around the landau in a mosaic of colour. Autumn, dazzling at its very best.

Kit, floundering in a soup of trepidation and foreboding, felt he was anything but. His form-fitting coat was trying its hardest to suffocate him. He was hot, and his head throbbed with all that hung heavy on his mind. Half an hour hence, he would be congratulating Gartside as the victor in a business proposition that didn't exist, disappointing two honest and innocent gentlemen of the *ton*. And then, somehow, Gartside's deceit would be exposed, while his own would remain magically secreted away, intact. Gartside would slink off into the night a broken man, and everyone else would happily go their separate ways. Believing all that was a rather tall order, despite the reassuring presence of Lando's cool hand gripping his. *Trust me*. By this point, Kit didn't have much choice, even though Lando was keeping him in the dark.

Dressed in a severely cut charcoal coat and unadorned navy cravat, his lover looked splendid and maddeningly unruffled, as if they were off to the theatre or a pleasant stroll around Vauxhall. Which only served to add to Kit's growing irritation.

"You're glowering, darling," Lando murmured, rubbing his thumb over Kit's tensed knuckles. "You know the effect that sulky mouth has on me. If you don't stop, I shall arrive in a state of heated arousal, which will quite ruin the line of my breeches."

Despite himself, Kit smiled. They had made love that morning, indolent and unhurried — a measured grinding of hips, Lando on top and Kit below, slippery with sweat. Whispered endearments had flowed between them, promises and reassurances, and in the moment, Kit had believed anything was possible, including a bright future in his lover's arms. Afterward, with the earl curled up alongside him, sweetly drowsy and pliant, Kit had shut his eyes tight so he might hold on to the sensation as long as possible.

"You would still be the most handsome, well-dressed gentleman in London," Kit replied gallantly, though his belly curdled. *And I would still be a common thief.*

*

TOMMY SQUIRE, PLAYING the role of Mr Arthur Hamilton, was undeniably handsome too. Artfully so. Like Kit, he wore his hair longer than the current fashion, but where Kit was also unfashionably broad and solid, Squire was slight and agile. And where Kit lacked guile, Squire was fox-minded; his calculating gaze travelled around each member of their small party, only softening when it fell on Lando. Kit fervently wished this would be his last ever encounter with the man.

"Lord Rossingley," Mr Hamilton drawled in that accent, which Kit now knew to be fake but, for the life of him, couldn't fault. Impeccably attired, the man occupied an armchair near the fire, looking for all the world like a seasoned member of the club. As his shrewd eyes raked over Lando, obviously approving of the view, Kit clenched his jaw. "My offer for your tailor to accompany me back to South Carolina still stands." He sighed — that was fake too. "Though, I suspect his skilfulness is greatly flattered by your fine figure."

"I think that's quite enough of the pleasantries." Lord Cobham's bark precisely mirrored Kit's thoughts. With a bandy strut, he took up a wide-legged stance in front of the great hearth, mopping his brow. "Let's get this thing done, shall we?" He glared at Mr Hamilton. "With less of the theatrics."

Theatrics? The man had no idea how closely he skirted the truth.

Other than greeting his cousin warmly, Sir Richard had said nothing, too busy quietly observing the others. An impatient Gartside paced the room. He'd barely acknowledged Kit, though he'd shot him one or two furtive glances, which Kit had returned as calmly as a fellow could whilst simultaneously trying to stop his heart from beating out of his chest. He noted Gartside perspired, too, even though the room was cool.

Only Lando, effortlessly drawing everyone's attention, seemed totally at ease. Quite still, he had arranged himself in a highbacked chair of claret-coloured silk. One slim leg was drawn back and the other stretched out; his hands rested easily in his lap. His refined features were inscrutable, reminding Kit of the dispassionate, frigid nobleman he'd first encountered that wet and windy evening at Rossingley. It seemed an awfully long time ago now. Since, Kit had learned to recognise the pose and the hauteur for the facade they were. He blew out a breath. Ye gods, Kit hoped his lover knew what the blazes he was doing. If this was to be one of his last few nights as a free man, he had no desire to spend it in this company.

With a light clearing of his throat, Lando spoke, reaching directly to the heart of the matter. "All of you have made your interest known regarding my proposal to construct four new mills on my land, in addition to expansion of the shipping routes. I thank you."

His silvery gaze turned to Kit. "And I also extend my gratitude to Mr Angel for most thoroughly fulfilling all I have asked of him." His lips twitched faintly; if Kit hadn't been sensitive to his lover's every move, he might have missed it. "Without his company, these last few weeks would have been much less...satisfactory."

Kit gave a modest nod in Lando's general direction, praying his cheeks didn't appear as heated as they felt.

"I'll begin with you, Mr Hamilton," Lando continued smoothly. His expression softened to one of sympathy. "As fervently as I wish our arrangement regarding the export of your raw cotton to continue unabated for as long as the hot South Carolina sun continues to shine on your crops, alas, you have been comfortably outbid in your efforts to establish your enterprise on English soil. As we both suspected would happen."

Not only was Mr Hamilton's accent authentic, at least to Kit's untutored ear, his disappointed pout was a highly credible performance too. Slapping his thigh *and* clicking his fingers might have been a step too far, but for all Kit (and the other assembled gentlemen knew), perhaps Americans employed a host of bizarre rituals to cope with disappointment. As if reading his mind, Hamilton slapped his other thigh.

"Well darn," he replied, elongating the vowels. "But I thank you for your consideration, Lord Rossingley. And never you mind. I'll sail on home, count my blessings, and still be a winner. As we like to say back in America, you're only a loser if you don't enter the race."

Kit suppressed a wince. If Americans truly spewed uplifting homilies like that in response to defeat, he sincerely hoped he never had cause to visit the place.

"That's very…gracious of you," said Lando thinly. The lack of empathy from the other three gentlemen in the room was deafening. "Regardless, your family will continue to profit from my business association with one of these gentlemen gathered here with us. So may I trespass further on your valuable time by inviting you to stay a while?"

Hamilton rubbed his hands together. "Why, thank you kindly, Lord Rossingley. Wouldn't miss it for the world."

Lando's attention switched back to the others. Steepling his fingers under his chin, he regarded them contemplatively. Like the charged seconds before a thunderstorm, anticipation hung in the air. Twice, Gartside tugged at his cravat, his eyes darting towards Kit, and twice, Kit managed a polite smile in return. He felt a tad hot under the collar himself, though he'd die before showing it. Refreshments were unforthcoming; he'd have killed for a jug of ale.

"You all delivered your bids into the hand of my butler earlier this week." Lando adjusted his cuffs, the only outward sign of the strain he must surely be feeling. "I am most grateful for your promptness. Mr Angel and I have had time to discuss them at length. You have all been most generous." He gave a cryptic smile. "Clearly, I approached the right fellows to assist me in my venture."

Gartside rocked on his heels, unable to keep still. If Lando didn't declare him the winner soon, Kit wagered the baronet would combust.

"Lord Cobham, Sir Richard." Lando's voice was solemn. "You delivered almost identical bids. I salute your diligence and sharp minds. The opportunity to work with either of you would be most humbling. And profitable. Alas, you were both handsomely outbid by Sir Ambrose here, who not only surpassed my expectations by offering a substantial source of funds for expansion but also brought to the table his own brand of wisdom and perspective."

How Lando managed to say the last few lines with a perfectly straight face was anyone's guess. At that moment, no one paused to ponder it because two of the gentlemen regarded each other with identical expressions of disbelief. One fake American gentleman endeavoured to hide his enjoyment of the whole charade behind his hand while Lando's glittery gaze had trapped Kit's, the two of them silently sharing all the words they couldn't speak in the company of the others. Gartside, of course, being the poor winner Kit anticipated, clapped his hands with delight, revelling in the sweet taste of victory. He might as well have shaken a triumphant fist under the noses of the other two, such was his elation, an ugly mix of glee and condescension. Enjoy this moment, Kit thought, for it shall not last long.

A disgruntled Lord Cobham had seen enough. "I shall be getting along, Rossingley," he announced briskly, throwing Gartside a curt glance. "Let this *gentleman* have his day."

Gracefully rising from his seat, Lando proffered a hand. "Then I'll wish you a pleasant evening Cobham. Let's ring for someone to show you out. And once again" — he treated the portly baron to his most ingratiating of smiles — "I am eternally grateful for your time and your patience. No doubt, there will be other ventures we can explore together."

He wheeled the lord in the direction of the doorway, to where a waiting footman proffered his hat and coat, and in a whirlwind of activity, Cobham was gone.

"The old man's a buffoon," chortled Gartside, all traces of his prior anxiety vanished. "Good riddance, I say. The man lost his wits years ago. Even had the nerve to accuse me of compromising his damned youngest daughter at Vauxhall. Bloody cheek. If it wasn't for his father and mine being old chums, I'd have called him out years ago."

"As to the unsavoury matter of his daughter, I cannot comment," answered Lando coolly. "Though I have heard conflicting accounts. Regardless, I happen to hold his intellect in high regard."

"Hear, hear," said Sir Richard, earning himself a spiteful glare from Gartside. With a nod to Kit, he made a move to leave. Lando stayed him with a hand on his sleeve.

"I wonder, Sir Richard, if I could trouble you to remain behind a little longer. A family matter."

"Of course."

Strolling to a long window providing excellent views of the lush parkland opposite, Lando looked for all the world like a man with his affairs about to be wrapped up.

"Age and infirmity will come to us all one day," he observed. "God willing."

"We should call for drinks," Gartside declared, jubilantly ringing the bell. "The cellar's finest claret. I have much to celebrate."

"Why not," agreed Lando, turning. "Do you care to join us, Mr Hamilton and Mr Angel, in a toast to our new business partner?"

A knock at the door heralded a wave of relief all around. A footman entered, bearing glasses and a silver decanter. Awkward small talk had filled the interim, mostly provided by Mr Hamilton, whose voice had an uncanny knack of grating on the stretched few nerves Kit had remaining. Lando, no doubt filled with a similar growing sense of unease as Kit, indulged his chatter, while Sir Richard stayed silent, his plain features set in a slight frown. Gartside, oblivious to the tension, helped himself to a very generous slug of claret and would have downed it in one if it wasn't for a commotion at the door chopping short his celebration as suddenly as it had begun.

"What the dickens?" Gartside exclaimed.

A thick-set man, younger than Cobham but older than the rest, marched into the room.

A beleaguered footman dashed in after him. "Sir, you are not invited. Sir, I do insist you return to the…"

"I'm here on business," snapped the intruder, holding up a

hand. "Official magistrate business."

The man removed his hat, revealing a pallid, fleshy face below a balding pate. A harsh face, one Kit had only glimpsed once, as he'd raced down an alley and vaulted a low wall. One he'd prayed to never see again. *Magistrate* business. Bow Street magistrate business. The floor beneath him suddenly dropped away.

"Yes, but I insist…" tried the troubled footman again but to no avail. This interloper didn't care for the rules of White's, he had no patience for fancy gentlemen and *ton* etiquette. Clark—for it was he—took up a position in the centre of the floor, brandishing his scroll of paper like a dagger.

"I'd say I'm sorry for the interruption, gents." He smiled without mirth. "But then I'd be lying."

Kit's heart raced as Clark swept his keen gaze across his audience. It settled on him, of course, and the man sneered. "There you are, my friend."

Once more, the footman tried to intervene, once more, he was brushed aside.

"Mr Christopher Angel, last known abode Sindell Street, London," Clark began in a condescending nasal tone. "I'm arresting you for heinous wrongdoings against multiple honest gentlemen of the town. For false representation of yourself. For misleading others. For gross larceny amounting to more than one shilling against Sir Ambrose Gartside, amongst others. Crimes punishable by certain death."

Outside the window, a carriage drew up. Maybe two from the loud clattering that reached into the room. Gentlemen arriving for an evening hand of cards perhaps. Maybe even some of Lando's acquaintances, not that Lando would be of a mind to see them tonight. Kit didn't want to look at his ashen lover, didn't want to see the pain of failure written in his sculpted features. Didn't want to read goodbye on his lips. He might cry if he did, and God knew a man like him should never show fear in front of a man like Clark.

"Let me see that," ordered Lando, his chilly voice stretched taut.

Holding it at arm's length, as though poisonous, he scanned Clark's sheet of paper, an imperious scowl marring his fine features. He regarded Clark dismissively before turning to address his fellow noblemen.

"This arrest warrant is signed by a magistrate, giving this man, John Clark, the powers of a Bow Street runner. Everything seems to be correct. It would appear, gentleman, that we have a suspected criminal in our midst."

With barely an icy glance at Kit, Lando examined Clark with open disdain. "Your interruption to our evening is most reprehensible, sir. Cuff him and be gone."

Chapter Twenty-Six

AS CLARK PRODUCED a set of cuffs from the depths of his coat, Lando looked away, shielding himself from his lover's wounded gaze and horrified disbelief. A coward's response, and he hated himself for it, hated himself for deceiving Kit so publicly, so humiliatingly. Sick to his stomach, every fibre of his being screamed at him to run to his mate. But he couldn't; they'd come too far to ruin it now. Gartside's disgrace was within their grasp. If Lando lost himself for only a second in the dark pools of those hurting hazel eyes, he feared he'd blurt the truth.

"I'll be damned," swore Tommy from his front row seat.

"What the devil?" Gartside blustered. "Who...what..."

"W-w-what is this n-nonsense? Rossingley?" For once, Sir Richard and Gartside were in accord, both speechless.

Only his lover's voice failed to break the stunned silence. Framed against the late autumn sky, docile as a lamb, Kit held out his wrists. His penetrating gaze never wavered; Lando's skin prickled with the heat of it. Sucking in a shaky breath, he steeled himself to play his part as well as Tommy was playing his. Kit, too, if only he knew it. With a thumping heart, Lando dragged his regard back to where Kit stood, as lifeless as a statue, and affected a mask of noble distaste.

"I am at a loss to explain," he declared.

A metallic snap sliced through the air, signifying the cold, unyielding embrace of iron meeting flesh as the handcuffs snugly encircled Kit's wrists. After a mechanical click, Clark pocketed the keys. The room seemed to hold its breath.

"Right, *sir*," he pronounced, wrapping his meaty fist around Kit's arm. "You're coming with me. And don't try any funny stuff unless you want me knuckles in yer face."

Surprisingly, Sir Richard was the first to find his voice. "S-S-stop a moment." He held up his hand. "Of S-S-Sindell Street? Here in L-London? I unders-s-stood Mr Angel to h-hail from M-M-Manchester."

"On the corner of Canon Row and Sindell, to be precise, my lord," confirmed Clark. "Though I don't expect you 'ave much cause to travel that way. Big boarding house. Can't miss it. Took me a while to track 'im there, mind." He gave Kit's arm an unnecessary tug, and Lando's bile rose.

"S-s-so..." Sir Richard's clever mind flew ahead of his mouth, his brow wrinkling in puzzlement. "So h-he's n-not..."

"Goodness, are you quite all right, Gartside?" Lando interrupted. If Sir Richard gleaned much more information from Clark, it might ruin everything. "You look quite green, as if you've seen a ghost."

All eyes turned to where Gartside had staggered to the fireplace, gripping the marble mantel as if his life depended on it. His usually ruddy features had taken on a corpselike hue. Even his lips were barely there as if all the blood in his head had sunk to his boots.

"This man…" Weakly, he pointed at Kit. "He's…he's…"

"'E's a common thief, my lord, that's what 'e is." Clark's strong fingers twisted into Kit's arm. "Pinched your pocket well and good, ain't he?" With a curt nod, the runner addressed Lando. "Now if you'll excuse me, my lord, I'll be on my way. There's a pretty reception awaiting this one."

With a click of his heels and a vague, mocking bow in Lando's direction, Clark was gone, dragging Kit with him. The four men left behind stared at one another in bewilderment. Well, two of them, anyhow; the other two deliberately avoided each other's eye.

"I-I-I don't…I'm d-damned confused," admitted Sir Richard, sinking back in his chair.

"I'm afraid that makes two of us," said Lando. "I'm…at a loss to explain what on earth is happening. Mr Angel is…"

"What else is in that note?" interjected Tommy. "The note the runner handed you. It must have more on it than the magistrate's stamp. More details, surely. Read it out."

"I…I…yes. Certainly." Lando looked down at the now crumpled paper. Tommy had hit his cue perfectly. "I…gosh, this is all dreadfully absurd."

With the eyes of the others on him, Lando unfolded the sheet once more, his trembling hands nothing to do with his acting skills. On a deep inhale, he pretended to read it again, then clapped a hand across his mouth.

"Oh my."

"What?" Gartside, sweating profusely, wiped an arm across his sodden brow. "What is it, Rossingley. Dammit, man!"

"It's…" He dropped the letter face down in his lap then picked it up again. Really, Pritchard would have been most proud of him; they'd practised this dramatic gesture several times. "It says that an arrest warrant has been issued for a Mr Christopher Angel of Sindell Street, London." At this, he glanced at Sir Richard. "For gross larceny and for —" He swallowed and blew out a breath. " — for masquerading as a senior member of His Majesty's Customs and using this exalted position to extort and bribe moneys from unsuspecting gentlemen by means of promising them…by promising them favourable business deals."

He flopped back in his chair, laying a palm across his forehead. "Bribes? Extortion? Gentlemen, I do believe we have…I do believe we have been taken in by a scoundrel."

"Good lord," exclaimed Sir Richard. "Good l-l-lord. The man's an imp-p-oster!"

"Well, knock me down with a feather." Tommy slapped his thigh. "Masquerading as a government official? I'll be damned."

Out of the corner of his eye, Lando peeked across at Gartside, instantly regretting that Kit wasn't alongside him to bear witness. The man was a picture of anguish. Distraught, he stared into the fire, seeing nothing except perhaps his own crumbling future. Sweat poured from him. Unashamedly he wrenched apart the knot of his cravat.

"I…I'm at a loss for words," said Lando. A blatant lie; he knew exactly what he would say next. He and Tommy had the script memorised to perfection. "Why, I was actually growing fond of the fellow! And to think this imposter has been living as an esteemed guest under my roof."

"D-d-done a lot of p-p-preparation too." Sir Richard sounded almost impressed. "He kn-knew his s-s-stuff. Man's w-w-wasted as a c-c-con man."

"As far as I see it, we've all had a damned lucky escape," agreed Lando. "Gosh. It doesn't bear thinking about."

"If the bloodhounds of the law hadn't been on his tracks," pointed out Tommy, "the devil might have scarpered with a king's fortune! Who knows? You might have handed hundreds, nay, thousands over. Maybe some fellows already have." He raised an eyebrow in the direction of Gartside, who appeared on the brink of casting up his accounts.

"Absolutely." Lando wrung his hands together. "Not to mention the dreadful shame of it." His wretched anxiety for poor Kit aside, he was quite enjoying himself. "If Angel had succeeded in his dastardly plan, one would never be brave enough to show one's face in society again for fear of being made a laughingstock. One's reputation as a man of intellectual soundness would be ruined."

A pained whimper interrupted his flow.

"Are you sure you're quite all right, Gartside?" he queried. "You're still dreadfully pale. Is it something I said?"

"I..." Gartside shook his head. "The..."

Sir Richard's brow pinched, his mind clearly whirring. Lando couldn't have chosen a better unwitting accomplice. "W-why d-d-does the arrest m-m-mention you?" His lips thinned. "Sp-sp-specifically. The runner s-singled you out. Y-you..."

Breaking off, his cousin pinched the bridge of his nose between finger and thumb as if trying to drag the information from inside his skull. The man was so close, practically doing Lando's delicate task for him. He held his breath.

"May I offer up a suggestion, my lord?" A glint of mischief danced in Tommy's eyes. "I'm but a simple gentleman from across the pond, so I don't have much care for the rules of your damned society. But it looks to me, and correct me if I'm wrong, but Sir Ambrose is doing a damned fine impression of a man with something to hide."

"Goodness, Mr Hamilton," began Lando in mock outrage. "Whether you are familiar with society or not, that is an awfully bold accusation. As my privileged guest here at White's, I must warn you that gentlemen of the *ton* don't take lightly to—"

"You…you've already g-g-given him some money, haven't you?" cried Sir Richard. "You…you b-bribed him, didn't you? To s-s-secure the deal." He laughed, scarcely believing what he'd just dared say, but knowing it to be true. "You…you swine!"

Even if Lando and Tommy hadn't been abreast of the truth, there would have been no escaping it, writ large across Gartside's waxy face. On the cusp of finishing his accusation, Tommy clamped his mouth shut. Clever Sir Richard had done it for him.

"Good heavens, no." Lando endeavoured to appear aghast. He turned to his cousin. "That is an…no, Sir Richard. I beg you to retract. That is simply…well, it's—"

"It's the truth. Isn't it, Gartside? As t-t-true as I-I'm sitting here!"

Gartside's voice was barely a whisper. "Yes. I gave the swine two hundred pounds."

A dense hush followed as the enormity of what he'd done sank a little deeper. Lando counted a minute under his breath, and then another, trying to prevent a faint smile touching the corners of his lips. After a suitable interval, he sat up a little straighter, patiently waiting for all eyes once again to return to him. As he once again took command of the room, a frosty hauteur swept across his still features. It never hurt to remind everyone of his senior rank as the eleventh Earl of Rossingley. When his silvery gaze pierced Gartside, even Sir Richard seemed cowed.

"How jolly...unsporting of you." Like icicles, his words crystallised in the air, each one clear and precise. "How...ungentlemanly. Your dear father, rest his soul, would be appalled."

Tilting his head to one side, Lando studied the stunned, broken creature in front of him. Waiting for him to respond, he counted to ten once more. Would he sob like a baby or lash out like a cornered animal? Under Lando's instruction, there were footmen positioned outside the door.

Eagerly, Tommy leaned forward in his seat. "Hey, do you fellas still duel?"

Lando's gaze never left Gartside's. "No longer to the death. More's the pity."

Reeling wildly, Gartside took in all three seated men. "Angel's made fools of you too." Spittle flew from his lips as his arms flailed. "Have you thought of that? We'll all of us be destroyed if word of this gets out."

Tommy laughed. "Not me." He rubbed his hands in glee. "All I've got is a fine old tale to tell back home, even if I can't add a duel to it."

"N-n-not me either. I d-d-didn't give the m-m-man money, d-did I?"

"And nor did I," added Lando, twisting the knife. "Therefore, just one of us will be ruined, it seems. I believe Lady Butterworth is hosting the first ball of the season tomorrow evening. Were you hoping to attend, Gartside?"

"I…yes, damn you!" Gartside clutched at his hair. "All this is your fault, Rossingley! You and your blasted mills. Should never have listened to you. Any of you."

"Or you could have simply bid for the venture in the conventional way," suggested Lando. "Like a gentleman. And then, imposter or not, all of us would have walked away with our finances and our honour intact."

As pleasant as observing Gartside's world crashing around his ears was, Lando was very keen to move things along. Somewhere out there, his poor Kit must be at his wits' end. And more than anything, if he could help it, Lando didn't want to spend another hour apart from him.

"I suggest you avoid Lady Butterworth's." He flicked his eyes up to Sir Richard, struggling to hide his glee. "In fact, I suggest you avoid the *ton* altogether for the time being. Your continued presence will…well, it will not end happily for you."

"Are you threatening me?" Gartside's eyes had a menacing unruliness to them.

"No. I'm merely pointing out the truth. In a word, your character is besmirched. Beyond repair. And that's before Cobham discovers tonight's goings on. You know how he likes to tattle. And he's not terribly fond of you to begin with, is he?" Lando straightened his cuffs and stood. "I think it's time I rang for a footman to show you out, don't you?"

Lando's hand hovered over the bell. Gartside shook his head, knowing he was beaten. "I will see myself out. Good day."

Everyone watched him walk to the door with much less alacrity than he'd entered. Lando almost felt sorry for the man until he remembered Kit's poor sister and the tales of his hungry by-blows sleeping in draughty barns.

"One s-s-second." Sir Richard leaped from his chair, halting Gartside in his tracks. "You forgot something, Ambrose." He marched up to where Gartside stood, eyeing him coldly.

"Did I? What?"

"This."

Before Gartside saw it coming or had time to duck, Sir Richard swung his arm back, clenched his fist, and socked him on the jaw. It was a blow so masterful they could probably feel its after-effects all the way to Piccadilly. Looking for all the world as though he might do it again, Sir Richard rubbed his knuckles with satisfaction.

"That's f-f-for Eton. You bastard."

Not much shocked Tommy Squire. Sir Richard, however, had succeeded, Lando observed. As Gartside staggered from the room, Tommy rose to his feet.

"I do believe I've had enough excitement for one evening, gentlemen. It's been...well..." He extended a bracing handshake to Sir Richard. "Here's to hoping I never find myself on your bad side, my good sir."

Turning to Lando, Tommy threw him a private wink, then swept a low bow. "I'm heading back across the pond first thing in the morning. So, I'll wish you both a very good evening, gentlemen. Lord Rossingley? It will be a pleasure to continue doing business with you."

After he'd gone, Lando poured himself and Sir Richard a thimble of port, then collapsed back in his chair, no longer trusting his legs. "All those afternoons at Jackson's have paid off, Richard." With a quick grin, he downed his drink in one gulp then blew out a sigh of relief. "My, oh, my. It's been quite the afternoon."

"Y-y-you're up t-t-to something, aren't y-you?" Sir Richard said.

Cocking his head, Lando regarded him, abstractedly running a finger around the rim of his glass. "How terribly perceptive of you." He'd leave, too, in a moment, once his legs stopped shaking. "And quite correct. I apologise for embroiling you in the whole affair, but I needed another potential business partner, one I could safely spill the beans to if things became desperate."

"A-and d-did they? Become d-d-desperate?"

Lando made a sound somewhere between a laugh and a groan. Strangely, he felt rather choked. "Yes, they did, as a matter of fact. But not now. Now, I hope things will turn out rather wonderfully."

"G-G-Gartside is r-r-ruined." Sir Richard held out his glass for a victorious clink against Lando's. "That's w-w-wonderful enough for me. So whatever else y-y-you are up to, I d-d-don't care. But I'm s-s-sorry about M-Mr Angel. I l-l-liked him and d-didn't s-s-suspect a thing."

A warm feeling settled in Lando's chest. He scrunched up the note, still in his lap, and tossed it onto the fire. "I liked him too. Very much."

As the strong liquor permeated his veins, Lando finally loosened his own cravat. A wave of weariness swept through him and a desire to crawl into his bed and sleep for days. And he would, as soon as he was able. God willing, he wouldn't be alone.

"My dear fellow," Lando said, examining his cousin fondly. "We really should see more of each other. The fault is all mine. I have been rather a glum hermit of late."

"I d-d-don't get out m-much either."

"I'd like to invite you to Rossingley very soon," Lando pressed on. "And once there, I will regale you with this whole tale from start to finish. I am confident it will be to your liking. And then, when we are suitably reacquainted, I propose you go on to pay a visit to my sister at Horton. She has a young governess staying with her at present. A scholarly, quiet young lady — the niece of my very good friend Captain Charles Prosser. Do you remember him? Excellent fellow. I think you and she will find each other's company most satisfactory."

*

IN THE GLOOM of an overcast evening, Sir Ambrose Gartside's Belgravia residence stood dismal and unlit, evidence suggesting the master was not home. Lando, however, knew differently. Pritchard had (with poor grace, naturally) shadowed the baronet there after his rapid departure from White's. Now, the valet was seated alongside Lando in the phaeton, eyeing the building with distaste.

"I suspect it may be many years before this property opens its doors again to the *ton*," Pritchard commented as Lando alighted. He followed this pronouncement with an exaggerated shiver. "If you are too long inside, I'll be frigid as an icicle on your return."

Lando shot him a long-suffering look. "Darling, it's the middle of a mild October. And this shouldn't take more than a few minutes."

"My lord, will you — at risk of sounding as if I truly cared — will you be quite all right in there?" Pritchard jerked his chin in the direction of the house. "He'll be as cross as two sticks and desperate to pin the blame on someone. And you are not a large man."

Lando gave his valet's arm an affectionate pat. Gartside lacked intelligence, to be sure, but he wasn't an utter fool. "Whilst I applaud your cheap attempt to invite yourself into the warmth, I'll be fine. Ambrose Gartside is an odious bully, nothing more, nothing less." He smiled thinly. "And I am no victim. It is my experience that if you grip a bully by his cravat, you will invariably find it comes off in your hand."

He peered up at the forbidding grey stone house. "I'm not convinced there's much warmth inside, anyhow."

*

GARTSIDE'S BUTLER LED Lando into a dim parlour with the air of a man counting down the hours until he secured a position elsewhere. Slumped in front of a parsimonious fire, his employer made no effort to rise and greet his guest.

"You're an odd fish, Rossingley." Gartside threw him an ugly look, not aided by the purple bruise blossoming on the left side of his jaw. "And you have some gall showing your face here. Your blasted mills are the reason I'm in this hellish mess."

"In addition to your own underhand behaviour," Lando felt obliged to point out.

"That damned weaselly bastard made a fool of me."

"He made fools of us all, Gartside."

"And you seem uncommonly cheerful about it."

"Do I?" Lando smiled amiably. "Perhaps that's what comes of a clear conscience."

He gazed around the room. It had been a few years since he'd visited—a raucous card evening if he remembered, many years ago, ending with him much richer and Gartside and his cronies poorer. And, goodness knew, Lando was no card player; he'd simply been able to resist the lure of showing off. More paintings had hung from the walls then. He recalled a small Canaletto catching his eye. And, if he wasn't mistaken, a very fine inlaid Hepplewhite table had sat near the mantel. "So, you've taken my suggestion not to stay in town?"

Gartside harrumphed. "What do you think? I don't have a lot of choice, do I? Sir Richard will be first through the door at White's come tomorrow, hunting down Cobham. Unless you beat him to it."

"I have no interest in malicious talk," Lando replied. "Though I cannot vouch for the others. And I can't deny Cobham may relish a sense of *joie maligne.*"

Abruptly, Gartside stood. Coatless and cravatless, he was a dishevelled mess. "Then my reputation is ruined." He rubbed a hand across his bruised jaw. "I'm leaving for Scotland at first light. There's nothing else for it."

Lando could practically taste the panic.

"Short on blunt too." Gartside's eyes slid away from Lando

on the admission. "Borrowed the two hundred pounds from my brother-in-law. I'll have to bloody sell something to cleave that back."

"How…" Lando hesitated as if uncertain how to phrase his delicate question. "If that is the case, then how were you planning on funding our joint business venture?"

Gartside huffed. "The estate bordering yours is unentailed. One of my old school chums was interested in buying it. Snuffy Pallister, now Duke of Beaminster. Rich as Croesus. His father died six months ago—Snuffy's taken the title, but his land is all the way up in bloody Northumberland. He wanted something closer to town." He barked a laugh. "Won't want it now. If this gets out, I'll wager he won't even recollect my name by the end of the week."

"Mmm." Buying himself some time, Lando pretended to examine the heavy oil painting to the left of the fireplace. A fearsome, ugly woman stared back at him, her flabby breasts spilling from a too-tight corset, her mouth painted in a perpetual snarl. That she was one of Gartside's ancestors left no room for doubt.

"Rossingley has had two poor harvests from the last five," Lando began casually as if still admiring the portrait. "My man of business informs me barley yields have been particularly low across the whole of the south. Especially Spratt, if I'm not mistaken. All the signs are that next year will be equally dismal."

He regretted not paying more attention to Robert's ramblings; if Gartside asked him what those *signs* were, he'd come terribly unstuck.

"Never known such temperamental weather," grumbled Gartside. "Or farmers. Blasted fellows more trouble than they're worth. That land's made a loss hand over fist ever since I took over the place. Not that I shared *that* with Pallister," he added gloomily. "Too bloody late now, at any rate."

Lando let his eyes flutter closed. Drawing stale air into his lungs, he let his shoulders drop, clearing his mind of everything except what he was about to do.

"I suppose I could always take that damned estate off your hands," he offered in a languid drawl. "After all, we do abut. And I suppose if I hadn't thought of you as an excellent potential business partner in the first place, this dreadful affair wouldn't have happened, would it?"

He sauntered back to Gartside and arranged himself in a chair. "Mind, it would be a bit of a bore. I'm certainly not looking to expand Rossingley; there is quite enough to keep my heirs busy for many a good year. And, as you know only too well, I'm quite preoccupied with my ventures in the north."

He let his offer dangle for a few seconds, then added, "But, to help out an old friend, perhaps I could be persuaded. And, seeing as we are such old chums—" The earl flicked at an invisible mote of dust on his lapel. " —I might be able to encourage Sir Richard to keep the scuttlebutt to himself. At least until you are safely ensconced in Scotland and a new scandal emerges."

Selling the estate would wipe out all Gartside's debts, as well as the one he owed his brother-in-law. Fascinated, Lando observed Gartside's mental and facial contortions as he attempted not to leap at the idea too eagerly. Hungry babes in arms were more inscrutable. No wonder the man lost every time he took a seat at the card table.

Taking pity on him and because he was keen to be on his

way, Lando added, "Shall I put you in touch with my man of business? You may take your time coming to a decision. I'm in no hurry, no hurry at all."

"We can shake on it now," blurted Gartside, holding out a hand. "The details can be thrashed out later. That way, I'll be able to promise my brother-in-law his blunt."

They shook, Gartside's grasp clammy, the earl's crisp and smooth.

"Do you want to discuss some loose terms?" Lando pulled a pained face. "Wearisome, I know. Or shall we leave it to our men?"

"Snuffy offered 18 000 pounds. You can relieve me of the damned place with half of that if we shake on it now."

He really was horribly desperate. If Lando had offered to take the land off his hands in exchange for his oldest boots he had a feeling Gartside would have obliged.

"Excellent. Most satisfactory. Consider it done." Lando pulled out his silver fob. "Dear me, it's late. I must press on. I'm travelling to Rossingley at first light. I've been away far too long."

He gave Gartside a clipped nod. "Look after yourself, Gartside. I expect it will be some time before our paths cross again. If indeed, ever. It's been a pleasure doing business with you."

Chapter Twenty-Seven

AS KIT WAS dragged, handcuffed, though the narrow, unlit corridors of White's staff quarters, the lump of humiliation lodged in his throat threatened to choke him. Being arrested in front of the likes of Gartside and Sir Richard was bad enough, but being paraded in fetters in front of gawping staff — some of whom a few days earlier had waited on him at dinner as if he *belonged* at the club — was somehow even worse.

And then there was his dear Lando. He couldn't even begin to think about him. Not yet. *Trust me*, he'd said, and those silvery, glittery eyes had searched Kit's face as if it held all the answers to the universe and beyond. And Kit *had* trusted him. He still did, even now, though Lando had as good as denounced him in front of Clark. Who could blame him? Their Gartside scheme would have toppled if he hadn't, and all their efforts would have been reduced to nought. Whatever he and his brother had concocted, had been too little, too late to change the course of the tides. Clark had caught up with him, as he always would, and that was that. Even his precious, clever Lando wasn't infallible. Or above the law.

But how the devil had Clark tracked him down to White's? Perhaps he'd staked out Grosvenor Street or sent a lackey in his place after someone had caught sight of the Rossingley crest when the carriage had pulled up outside the boarding house. Not that it mattered now.

Mr Christopher Angel of Sindell Street, London, I'm arresting you for heinous wrongdoings against multiple honest gentlemen of the town. For false representation of yourself. For misleading others. For gross larceny amounting to more than one shilling against Sir Ambrose Gartside, amongst others. Crimes punishable by certain death.

Such an exhausting, convoluted way to pronounce a man a common thief! Despite the invidiousness of his position, Kit almost smiled. Any sum amounting to more than one shilling was, indeed, punishable by death according to the letter of the law. But it was a damned fancy way of calling out a purse-snatcher and a card sharp. He wondered why Gartside had been singled out — the snuff box during their game of loo, probably. That alone was enough to get a man hanged. It was the last item he'd pilfered and one of the nicest he'd pinched in a while, that shiny bauble would have fetched a tidy penny. But it was nothing compared to a two-hundred-pound bribe. Imagine if Clark got a whiff of that? Kit would be hung several times over.

The bawdy chatter and cheery clatter of the front rooms receded the deeper he was marched into the depths of White's. Soon, the rhythmic slap of two pairs of boots on cold stone floors was the only sound, and with it, Kit felt oddly calm. Perhaps the calmness came from knowing a probable death sentence lay ahead, and he was powerless to prevent it. Perhaps this emptiness of mind was common to all men with nothing but the gallows to contemplate, one's body's protective instinct. If so, then Kit was grateful. It saved him from picking over all he was set to lose. Because if he dared let a fraction of that out, a sheer, unstoppable torrent would follow.

Clark's grip on his arm was unnecessarily tight, as were the shackles numbing his hands. The runner waltzed Kit towards the back of the establishment at such a fast lick that, twice, Kit stumbled and almost fell. Older and unfit, Clark's mouth hung open. His breath sawed in and out in quick gasps, and the air in front of Kit's face filled with the rancid stink of a rotten tooth. Unable to cover his nose, Kit focused his mind on Lando's fragrant mouth instead. On their own silent waltz and how light and blissful his lover had felt in Kit's arms. On his lips like ripe cherries, on the joy of his rare, sweet smile. On Kit's short-lived, allotted portion of joy and what could have been.

With a draught of cooler and blessedly fresher air, they reached an unprepossessing rear entrance. Flinging it wide, Clark gave Kit a rough shove. "Off you go. God willing, you smash your head on the ground at the bottom and break your scummy, bastard, thieving neck."

With no time to come up with a suitable riposte and only a second to acknowledge Clark's dark hopes for him had every likelihood of coming to fruition, Kit flew, arse over tit, down a steep flight of stone steps, each one deliberately designed to smack against his hip, his ribs, and his blasted head. He reached the bottom, miraculously still in one piece, whereupon his momentum propelled him headfirst into a waiting carriage, bringing him to rest in a disagreeable heap of battered limbs on the floor, his wrists still locked uselessly behind his back and his legs dangling outside. Two strong hands under his armpits hauled them inside, and then, in the dim recesses of his mind, he heard the carriage door slam shut behind him. With a brisk jerk — doing Kit's abused head and wrenched shoulders no favours whatsoever — they set off.

"Just kill me now," he groaned to a pair of sturdy watchman's boots inches from his face.

The answering low chuckle was his first indicator that all was not as it seemed. And a brutal strike from those boots, which he braced for, never came. Instead, Kit heard a rustle of clothing, followed by the unmistakeable clink of a bunch of keys.

"I've been sorely tempted once or twice, son," grunted a coarse voice. "I took a right kicking in the ballocks for you. But the master will have my guts for garters if I do."

"Jas...Jasper?" Crabby, liverish, one-eyed *Jasper*?

"He wouldn't trust anyone else to come and rescue you, would he? Let's get these off before you do yourself any more mischief."

A searing pain flooded Kit's hands as the shackles fell from his wrists. At his agonised hiss, Jasper chuckled again. Kit didn't care; if he'd been able to wrench himself up, he'd have kissed him. The hard floor, his pains, his annoying saviour; none of it mattered. Somehow, he was free. And freedom meant only one thing — his dear Lando.

"He's done this, hasn't he? Lan — the earl."

"Of course he has, you daft apeth. You think he'd have let the hangman have at you?"

Water leached from Kit's eyes, copious streams of it, as if imprisoned for too long inside a heavy rain cloud. Making no effort to wipe them away, he surrendered to his tears, slumped even more untidily across the dusty carriage floor. A deep-throated half groan, half sob escaped him.

"Never have your dulcet tones and honeyed vowels sounded so bewitching. Keep seducing me, Jasper, so I know you're real."

Jasper snorted. "He'd have my head on a spike if I attempted that." He gave Kit a shove with his foot. "You gonna get up or stay there all day?"

Kit groaned again. Rising to his feet seemed an insurmountable challenge.

He'd never lain on the floor of a carriage before. As the steady rhythm of hooves thundered under his ear and his body lurched to and fro in time, Kit decided it was to his liking. He might make it his permanent home. The noise was strangely soothing, or maybe the wash of relief sweeping through his shattered body was because his beloved, infuriating, beautiful eleventh earl had kept his promises and saved him from his most dreadful fate. *Trust me.*

Eventually, when his breathing returned to normal and he was confident he wouldn't further humiliate himself by bursting into tears again, Kit allowed Jasper to help him up and into the carriage seat. A few more minutes elapsed before he felt able to speak, and when he did, it was not to profess eternal gratitude but to comment on the passing scenery. Which was…increasingly countrified.

"I'm not terribly familiar with this corner of Mayfair," Kit said suspiciously. "And unless we're travelling in circles, we should have arrived at Grosvenor Street by now."

Wordlessly, Jasper handed him a well-worn leather hip flask, and in one ungentlemanly glug, Kit emptied it down his throat.

"You're kidnapping me, aren't you?" he asked.

"The earl is kidnapping you," corrected Jasper. "By way of me. Don't say I didn't give you fair warning, lad."

"So we're bound for Rossingley."

"We are," Jasper confirmed. "Home."

Wiping his mouth, Kit cursed. "It's not my home. Why would I want to go to Rossingley?"

Jasper examined him as if it was the most stupid thing he'd ever heard. "I can always turn us around again and drop us off at Bow Street."

"That...um...won't be necessary," Kit swiftly replied. "But the earl and I have not discussed what...I mean...I don't live there." They had not discussed anything, in fact, beyond the Gartside plan and their increasing fondness, nay, love for each other.

"Well, lad, I've got a feeling you do now."

Kit couldn't stay at Rossingley. Not for more than a short visit, at any rate, until his new set of injuries had healed. Men like them just...didn't. No matter how discreet and loyal Lando's household, word would get out eventually, and Kit had had enough of being arrested to last him a lifetime.

Unless...unless Lando expected to find him employment on the estate, given that Kit had had enough brushes with the law and promised to join the ranks of the honestly employed. But a position working for Lando? Kit would refuse immediately, on principle. He was many things, not all good, but he did have his pride, and he would not be paid by his wealthy lover to be his kept *paramour*.

A pothole tossed his sore backside up off the bench seat and back down again with a hard thump. He swore, unsure if it was directed at the pain, the man, or both. "Bloody Rossingley."

"There're worse homes," said Jasper, not unreasonably. "You got yourself bested outside one of them."

"Yes, there are. But that's hardly the point." Kit began ticking off on his fingers. "In the space of one evening, I have been arrested, humiliated, and handcuffed by a man who has been chasing me for as long as I can recall. Then, with certain death sitting on my shoulder, he lets me go, but only after kicking me down a brutal flight of stairs. And I land in your outstretched arms. To find I'm being kidnapped." He shook his head. "So forgive me if I'm not in the finest of moods."

Jasper's placidity was infuriating. "Just following orders, lad. If the boss wants you at Rossingley, Rossingley is where you'll be."

"The bossy," Kit corrected him childishly. "Not the boss."

His companion cackled. "But you still want in his breeches anyways." And with that startlingly accurate observation, Jasper's lips sealed shut.

Chapter Twenty-Eight

PRITCHARD EMPLOYED SEVERAL methods to communicate *I told you so*. This one, his favourite, centred on tilting his head forward and waggling his expressive eyebrows, rendering words superfluous.

"Yes, all right," Lando said irritably. "No need to be quite so smug. I should have checked he wasn't too put out by the fake arrest before I kidnapped him."

Arriving at Rossingley ready to rush into his youthful lover's embrace, only to discover the man had insisted on being dropped off at the village inn and was not, in fact, freshly bathed and naked in Lando's bed awaiting a thorough ravaging, was a tad aggravating, to say the least.

"According to Jasper, Mr Angel appeared more vexed by the kidnapping part than the fake arrest," Pritchard informed him. "Which can only lead me to deduce that he found being handcuffed perfectly acceptable. Although those cuffs must have chafed, assuming they were the solid iron kind."

"Quite." Lando eyed his valet with interest, having not ever considered the existence of any other type of handcuff material. Pritchard's cheeks were unaccountably flushed.

"For a quiet country soul, you seem awfully knowledgeable about handcuff materials."

"Not at all, my lord," answered Pritchard hastily. "Pure speculation. I am simply reporting Jasper's impression of the whole affair, and he made no mention that chafing handcuffs were vexatious."

As Lando filed away that nugget of information for a rainy day, an extraordinary image popped into his head and refused to budge, of his beloved pearls wrapped around a familiar pair of strong wrists.

"Jasper believes Mr Angel is mostly unhappy about returning to Rossingley to be cast in the role of your doxy. He's had enough of play-acting for the time being. Can't imagine why, poor fellow."

"He's neither to be my doxy, concubine, or courtesan! Why on earth does he think that?"

"Perhaps because you haven't furnished him with your alternative plan, my lord? That tiddly, piddling little plan, the one where he becomes lord of his own estate? All I know is that Jasper says Mr Angel leaped out of the carriage in a blue sulk and stomped off to the inn."

Lando let out a long, needy sigh. "Gadzooks, he's rather lovely when he's sulking. Sulking and stomping combined sound truly marvellous. Did Jasper seem unduly worried?"

"No. He's of the opinion the man is all talk and no trousers. He believes Mr Angel will come out when he's hungry for a fu…for food, my lord."

Lando sighed again. Success was so nearly in his grasp he could stretch out a finger and tickle the edges of it. "I grant you, Pritchard, Jasper is a first-rate bodyguard and soldier. Sadly, however, he possesses the emotional wherewithal of a coal scuttle. God knows Mr Angel is a very capable sulker, but who's to say he isn't, as we speak, marching towards Allenmouth never to be seen again?"

"Because I've ordered that great gobbet of a coal scuttle to watch the inn," retorted Pritchard. "And apprehend him—again—should he attempt to scarper. So my advice to you, my lord, is to have a decent night sleep, pretty yourself up, and allow our hot-headed young friend to stew on his lumpy mattress for a day or two."

*

THE CRAMPED ROOM at the inn served as a constant reminder of the prison cell he'd narrowly escaped. Thanks to the man with whom he was mighty cross. How could one person be so perfectly wonderful yet so damned exasperating?

After an uncomfortable night tossing that conundrum around, Kit embraced the fresh early morning chill and set off for a walk, despite knowing the path he trod and the air he breathed belonged to the man at the root of his poor humour. He needed answers, and his solitary confinement hadn't brought any. Perhaps tramping up a great hill might.

He hated himself for being such an ungrateful bugger, but

now he had his freedom, he wasn't sure what to do with it. He didn't need worry about seeing Clark again. Jasper hadn't furnished him with all the details, but a deal had been struck between Robert and the runner; he knew that much. And apparently, Gartside had slunk off into the beyond with his tail betwixt his legs too. So as far as Kit saw things, he had two options — swallow his pride and stay here at Rossingley with his lover and accept that his lover and his employer were one and the same. But if that scenario griped now, who knew how badly it would chime a few months down the line?

Or Kit could fend for himself back in Kent, alone, miserable, and heartsick.

Two hours later, he concluded that tromping up and down hills, searching for answers, was a fruitless, overrated activity. At the top of the next one, he'd rest awhile, appreciate the view, catch his breath, and then...

Effortlessly poised and completely alone, the eleventh earl was at the highest point already, perched atop Twilight and taking stock of the swathe of ragged fields to his west. Against the skyline, Lando's slender elegance, all sharp lines and crisp angles, had an exacting harshness. He could be an exacting man, and judging by the solemn expression on his haughty face, he didn't care for what he saw.

That was freedom, thought Kit, as he approached. To sit astride a stallion with the wind blowing through one's hair and master of all one surveyed, in every which direction. He wondered how many of Lando's ancestors before him had ridden to this very spot to absorb the ebb and flow of the seasons, of the land, of the birds. Of Rossingley life. The scene held a timeless beauty. In one hundred, maybe two hundred years hence, another Earl of Rossingley, perhaps equally as graceful and aggravating, would undoubtedly be in his place.

The earl didn't turn, though he knew Kit was there. He remained erect and proud and effortlessly in control of the beast pawing the ground underneath him.

"Jasper said you like to come up here."

"My household knows my habits well. After a sojourn in London, I always ride out this way."

"Checking none of your grass has been disturbed in your absence?"

"Something like that."

Panting slightly from his exertion, Kit followed the direction of the earl's gaze. His eyes landed on a ruined cottage, half of its wooden roof beams and part of a clay outer wall in an untidy heap next to it, as though carelessly trampled by a giant's boot.

"Gartside's property?" Kit hazarded. Though unmarked by stones or wooden stumps, the boundary separating the Gartside estate and Rossingley was as clearly drawn as if ribbons festooned the trees. One side thrived, verdant and neat; its forlorn neighbour withered. But it didn't need to. Land was land, and with a firm, knowledgeable hand, there was no reason both sides couldn't match.

"No. Mine now." With an odd expression, Lando's eyes flicked to Kit's. "I bought it from him before leaving London. For a sum less than half of what it's worth."

"A steal," Kit commented, recalling Lando's drunken promise all those weeks ago. "Though I am at a loss to see how you managed it. I left the party a little prematurely, if you recall, with the belief that Clark was rather ruining things. But it was all part of your plan, wasn't it?"

Lando inclined his head. "Yes, Clark quite played into my hands."

Kit felt a flash of irritation. "Feel free to share. Gloat, too, if you like."

"That is not my style." He paused before continuing. "Robert, my brother, discovered a secret your runner would prefer his employers never uncovered. For a modest tenant farmer, he has rather a talent for unearthing such things. But Clark is not a man lacking in pride, and you sorely tested it, as well as his patience. Thus—" Lando gave Kit a hint of a teasing smile. "—Robert permitted him to arrest you in public. To humiliate you. Thereby saving his own face and having the brief satisfaction of putting you in irons."

"And throwing me down a flight of steps." This tale was all well and good, but Kit still failed to see how Gartside was involved.

"My apologies, Kit. He deviated from the script."

"There was a script?" Kit's puzzlement grew even more.

"Yes, can you not recall his words? Robert will be so disappointed. We spent a long while perfecting them."

Wrinkling his brow, Kit replayed his arrest and Clark's accusations in his mind. It had all been a bit of a blur, but one curious part of it he remembered well: *For gross larceny amounting to more than one shilling against Sir Ambrose Gartside, amongst others.*

Two hundred pounds amounted to more than one shilling. But so did a silver snuff box. And a silk pocket square. Along with a hundred other bits and bobs pilfered from well-heeled ladies and gentlemen of the ton. *Sir Ambrose Gartside amongst others.* Why him? Why that particular gentleman?

With a rush of clarity, Clark's words made perfect sense.

"He has no knowledge of the bribe!" Kit crowed. "He arrested me for petty pilfering, didn't he? For pinching snuffboxes and handkerchiefs and thruppenny bits!"

Lando almost beamed. "He knew you as a pocket thief and a card sharp, nothing more."

I'm arresting you for heinous wrongdoings against multiple honest gentlemen of the town. For false representation of yourself. Ye gods, Lando was a genius!

"But he arrested me in such a manner that Gartside and Cobham and Sir Richard were led to believe it was for masquerading as a government officer!"

"Yes." With a modest little toss of his hair, Lando sat even straighter in the saddle, trying not to look smug. "As I said, Clark had a script. He had no idea about the rest of it. It is a pity you missed the moment Gartside confessed to giving you money. The words fairly tumbled from him. Despair leaked from his every pore. And I discovered, as Gartside's jaw can attest, that my shy and retiring cousin is quite the pugilist. You should be proud. Your sister has been well and truly avenged."

Still, Kit was uncertain. "But Clark gave you an arrest warrant. I saw it. You read aloud from it."

"What you saw was an invitation to the esteemed Lady Butterworth's ball. I read out, from memory, the lines my brother Robert and I crafted. After you were carted away, and Clark out of earshot, I read out the supposed remainder of it. That *an arrest warrant has been issued for a Mr Christopher Angel of Sindell Street,*

London, for gross larceny and for masquerading as a senior member of His Majesty's Customs. Thus prompting a petrified Gartside to confess." The corners of Lando's lips gently curved upwards. "The invitation has since been added to my 'burn until there is nothing left but a heap of ash' pile."

Kit's mind raced forward. "So, realising his honour was destroyed, Gartside desperately needed to unload the estate, to pay of his debtors, and you gave him a helping hand."

"Quite." Lando agreed, inclining his head again. "That is the shorter version of events, certainly. Though I shan't own it for long. I intend to give it away."

"Give it away?" Kit scoffed. "To whom?"

"To someone who will care for it, restore it, and become an excellent and close neighbour." Lando allowed himself a small smile. "If my intended owner accepts my gift."

Kit barked a laugh. "Are people queuing up to reject gifts as fine as this one?"

"I hope not." Lando tipped his head to properly look down at Kit for the first time, the hazy sunlight catching the whiteness of his hair and making it shine. "But people are notoriously strange, don't you find?" He looked across to the imaginary line separating his well-tended land from his new acquisition. "You think you know somebody, and yet, they manage to astonish you."

"You'd know all about that," Kit answered. "I have no clue as to what you're conjuring up in that pretty head of yours from one day to the next."

Acknowledging him with a nod, Lando carried on. "One day, I hope I will not be able to discern where my borders begin and this estate's end. The boundary will be in name only. The new owner and I shall be able to wander freely across it whenever we choose."

"Your brother?" Kit guessed. Of course, it must be, and the Rossingley empire would grow even stronger, by-blow or not. Perhaps, Kit thought, with a glimmer of hope, he could find employ with Robert. That would solve some of his problems. "From what you have told me of his talents, he would be an excellent choice."

"No," said Lando, surprising him. "My brother has no desire to become landed gentry. He is perfectly at ease as he is, though I am confident he would relish the opportunity to advise a new owner. His knowledge of barley is unsurpassed, as the new owner will discover at the cost of many a tedious afternoon. No, not Robert. I was...I was actually thinking more along the lines of..."

Lando hesitated, giving Kit that look again, the one which made his belly flip because it was usually followed by a startling announcement. And on this occasion, Lando did not disappoint. "I was actually thinking of you."

For a second, Kit wondered who 'you' was. Rich people had all sorts of silly names for their chums. Sir Brandon had a pal he fondly called Bunny because his surname was Babbit. Gartside had ridiculous chums named Beefy and Poodle, probably both dukes. Perhaps 'you' was another. But the odd look in Lando's glittery eyes gave him pause, a mix of curiosity and...apprehension?

"I think the Angel estate has a rather nice ring to it, don't you agree?"

"The...*what*? *Me*? You're thinking of gifting it to me? I don't know anything about farming! Or cottages or tenants or...or land!"

Lando's gaze returned to the unkempt fields beyond. "Seemingly, nor did Gartside. It appears not to be an impediment to land ownership."

"And look what a sow's ear he made of it."

"Leading me to conclude that anyone else will be a vast improvement," responded Lando drily.

"Well..." Kit stuttered. "Yes. Anyone but me, obviously. I'm no gentleman."

"You're the finest gentleman I know."

"Then you are the most damned deluded."

A second too late, it occurred to Kit that not only was he shouting, but he was also being dreadfully rude to someone he loved who was being dreadfully kind. And who was now dreadfully hurt. Too late, Lando's expression had taken on that glacial look, and he twisted away from Kit.

"Your gratitude is a credit to you, sir," he managed. Then, with barely a click of his tongue, he turned Twilight around, further hiding his face. "Whatever your thoughts on the matter, the land is yours to do with what you will, Kit. The deeds are already being drawn up."

As erect as the Tower of London and just as imposing, he began to trot away. Kit jogged after him.

"Hey, Lando. Wait! I can't simply stroll into an estate and start claiming to be the rightful owner! Gartside might have lost it, but it belongs with a family such as his—nobility, gentry—not to a nobody like me."

The horse continued its sedate trot, its rider staring straight ahead. Ridiculously, Kit found himself trotting, too, to remain alongside. "Say something, Lando. We…we…you and I, we are better than this."

Lando's lips pursed in a thin line. "Gartside's grandfather won that estate at the tip of a sword. From a foolish French duke in a drunken duel, following an even more drunken game of basset. You and I have won it with cunning from a scapegrace unworthy of the grass growing under your feet. It is as rightfully yours as it was his."

"Please stop, Lando. At least dismount before I tumble headfirst into a ditch. I am not your equal with you so high up there and me so lowly."

With a sharp tug on the reins, Lando brought Twilight to a halt. "You have always been and will always be my equal, Kit. Whether I am on horseback or at the top of a mountain and you lying in a valley below. And if you believe my words, then you will discard your pride and accept my offer."

He slipped from the saddle as easily as if stepping down from a low stool, then tossed the reins across a branch of an oak. Folding his arms, he leaned against the broad trunk.

"Please." Kit faced him, this man he loved like no other and yet, now their adventure had come to an end, one he seemed destined to disappoint. "You and I have much to say to each other. But my head is a whirl. I can barely credit that I'm even here — why I'm not being dragged in front of a magistrate. You have won me my freedom and now offer me a fortune beyond anything I could ever dream."

"And yet?"

"And yet, instead of showing gratitude, I find myself cross with you when I should be cross with myself. But can you not see how unequal we are?"

"No," snapped Lando tersely. "All I see is foolish pride and the man I love being an ass."

"Bravo. Like a true earl, you have spoken your mind."

Shaking his head unhappily, Lando's gaze drifted beyond Kit, to the fields stretching into the distance. "You talk of freedom, Kit. A man in my fortunate position can use it wisely and give it others. I offer you the estate not only for selfish reasons, so I may have you by my side, but for good ones too. Where Ambrose Gartside ruled this land and its people with contempt, you could do it with kindness. You know what hardship feels like. You could restore the farmlands back to health. Pay your workers sufficient to afford the doctor. Repair their cottages — stuff them with more thatch than the workers have roofs. Until we find you a trustworthy man of business, Robert and my own man, Will Blandford, will assist." His silvery eyes latched onto Kit's, pleading and full of pain. "And my own knowledge is not too shabby."

Kit groaned. How wonderful the picture he painted. How easy he made it sound. "But Lando. It's too much, even for you. I'm sorry."

Lando inhaled deeply, adjusting his riding gloves. "Then I have no more to say on the matter. I came up here to give Twilight a long canter. Not to beg for your company, your acceptance of my gift, or your love. You will come to me with open arms or not at all. All I ask is that you do not make your decisions in haste. This is not an offer I will make twice."

*

"YOU'RE A BIGGER bleeding idiot than I thought," commented Jasper.

Kit had believed himself alone at the inadequate bar; he was the inn's only guest, after all. But like a guilty conscience he couldn't shift, his footman-soldier-valet-saviour was propped on a stool at the other end, supping on a tankard of ale with an unpleasant smirk on his face.

"Possibly," he conceded.

"His lordship's got a face like thunder. Matching yours, only more handsome-like. Lover's tiff?"

Blushing, Kit took a long pull on his ale. "Something like that."

Jasper shrugged. "My man and me have them all the time. They're good for you. Clears the air."

"Your...you...*what*?" Good lord, was everyone around here a deviant? Seeing his astonishment, Jasper chuckled.

"Been with him nine years. Miserable bugger — he's the second groom. Face like a slapped kipper, worse even than mine, but he gives a man a good t —"

"Does he really? Excellent." Kit buried his face in his tankard.

"It's not too late to say sorry, lad. His lordship's a forgiving sort."

"Me say sorry? I'm the one who was arrested and thrown down the stairs," Kit pointed out. "And kidnapped."

"And you also escaped the stews, the gallows, and are being landed with a huge blooming estate. Not to mention a regular invitation to have your fill of what's hiding under the earl's night-gown. If you know what's good for you, lad, you'll take your stupid pride and shove it up your backside. Pardon my French."

When put like that, the facts were hard to dispute.

"He's too good for me."

"He is that. But without you, he is hardly alive."

Lando's tight, pale face as he stood under the tree, arms folded so Kit wouldn't see his hands shaking flashed through his head. Kit wasn't the only one with a surfeit of pride. But once more, Lando had exposed his soul, and Kit had...trampled over it. *All I see is foolish pride and the man I love.*

"Bloody hell, Jasper, I'm a fool."

Disconcertingly, Jasper rolled his one eye. "Yes, but you're the earl's fool," he corrected. "And if you get yourself up to the big house and do a bit of grovelling, my lad, it's not too late to be his prince."

Chapter Twenty-Nine

"YOU HAVE A visitor, my lord."

Lando tipped his brandy tumbler this way and that, aware Inglis awaited his response but not trusting his voice.

"A Mr Christopher Angel, my lord. The young man says it's important."

"For both of us, I'll wager."

"That is my understanding, my lord."

A low ache tugged at Lando's chest, and the brandy soured on his tongue. The time for farewell had come; at least Kit was affording him that.

"Then you had better show him in," Lando managed eventually. He examined his robe, Kit's favourite grey one, and he allowed himself the smallest of sad smiles. "I'm decent."

He'd never asked Kit why he favoured the gold earring, dangling from its slender hook. He'd admired it aplenty though.

He'd kissed it and fondled it and traced the curve of it with his tongue. Tonight, candlelight glinted off its golden surface, reflecting Lando's dreams and desires back at him, mocking him. The dark velvet ribbon nestling against Kit's strong nape absorbed the shadows, Lando's hopes along with it, and his crushing need for this man.

His vision blurred, and he gulped in a sharp breath. He should stick to port.

"I am here to thank you for your gift," Kit began. "As we both recognised, my gratitude was poorly executed. I have reflected greatly and wish to apologise."

Though the earring brightly shone, Kit's olive skin tones bordered on sallow as if he hadn't slept. Lando's own features were drawn too. Pritchard had entered his master's bedchamber that morning to find him awake, dressed, and staring up at the bleak dawn sky.

"I have…struggled to…" Kit began, then stopped.

"I have too," Lando supplied, and briefly, their eyes met before Kit's gaze dropped to the floor. An aching silence stretched between them. Lando pressed a hand to his tense hollowed-out belly.

"My uncle Charles and you always lived separate lives, did you not?"

Lando started at the sudden swerve. "Yes. By necessity. Charles had his soldiering and his life in Kent. And my sons were younger. At home more often. He visited when he could."

"And you both paid the price. Throughout your time together. Not merely at the end."

"Yes." A sickening pain pulled at Lando's chest with the

memories of dozens of snatched afternoons, secret hurried rendezvous, handwritten notes burned once read. Memories of a love half-lived that he'd stored away since meeting Kit now resurfaced.

"I do not want that for you again, Lando. You are undeserving of it."

As he clutched the brandy glass between his trembling hands, bracing for the agony ahead, a single tear trickled down Lando's cheek. Helpless to stop it, he closed his eyes, letting others join. Perhaps things wouldn't be so bad after all. He'd survived once; he'd survive again. Perhaps the memories of two half-lived loves knitted together made a whole. Fighting the swelling sickness in his heart, Lando wearily rested back against the armchair, heavy thoughts drumming in his head, a familiar melancholia already knocking on the door.

The first he knew that Kit had crossed the room to kneel on the rug before him was when the dry, warm heat of his palm pressed against Lando's hand, teasing it away from the brandy glass.

"Lando, my love," Kit murmured, his voice a honeyed balm. "That is not a future for you and me. We are both undeserving of it."

Bringing Lando's hand up to his mouth, he kissed the knuckles, keeping it there to caress, his breath hot against it. "I want us to live every day to the hilt. Together. I don't want to waste a moment. I want to live freely with you or as freely as two men such as us are able. And…and if gifting me the Gartside estate is the only way that we can always be close to each other, then that's what I shall allow you to do. And I shall accept your gift with pleasure."

Knuckle kisses turned into mouth kisses. Sweet, tender caresses unburdened Lando of his jangling thoughts, turning them instead into pictures of sunny afternoons, the lazy, hazy sort of afternoons. Ones made especially for lovers chasing each other through long grass, for picnics, for sharing dishes of ripe strawberries, for helpless laughter, for seamlessly shifting into the next and the one after that.

Kit's soft kisses bled into one another. Breathlessly, he claimed Lando's mouth, sucking and licking, a little brutal and a little possessive, with his love running bold and strong through each and every one of them as if for the first time. And then his arms came around Lando, and for a long while, he just held him, wrapped up in his undying love. His kisses strayed to Lando's neck, his jaw, and his hair. He licked up the tears from his cheeks, a few of his own mingled with them. He whispered his love, promised his everything, and more.

And then, despite having no music and the drawing room furniture an impediment to gallivanting, when there was a perfectly decent ballroom upstairs, Kit drew Lando up to his feet and performed a deep, ridiculous bow.

"I believe this waltz is ours, my lord," he said.

Epilogue

NESTLED PEACEFULLY IN the foothills of the Kent Downs, there was nothing remarkable about the small village of Burham. Bands of intrepid pilgrims en route to Canterbury would have plodded through it without pause. The modest, stocky church of St Mary, standing on the edge of the village and built of local rag-stone and flint, was of less interest still. Though, as Kit knowledgeably informed Lando, it boasted not one, but two ancient Norman fonts. In addition to an impressive octagonal stair turret.

He couldn't see the sea when he stepped down from the landau, nor hear it. Nonetheless, Lando sensed its presence on the breeze, like a living thing, and he pondered whether it smelled the same wherever one was in the world. Charles would have known—as a military man he was much better travelled than Lando.

Yet another one of the many questions he had not been

afforded the time to ask.

If one overlooked the rows of headstones silently presiding over their tufty, grassy mounds, then the graveyard in the lee of the southwest tower was anything but grave. The spring morning dawned warm and cheery, coaxing sweet birdsong from the oak branches high above their heads, and gave a fresh, verdant shine to mossy grass underfoot. A day for lovers, not death.

Though far from wealthy, Captain Charles Prosser had not been purse-pinched. Thus, his slate tombstone, sheltered under the sweeping boughs of an aged willow, was well-crafted, the florid lines of script and the two wreathes carved above and below etched as sharply as the day they were engraved.

In Loving Memory of Captain Charles Cedric Prosser 1782- 1818
Thou art gone but always remembered.

Oxeye daisies bloomed at the base, their golden centres scattered through the grass like a hundred tiny suns, a splash of joy in a place where none resided. With an ache in his throat, Lando plucked one, bringing it to his nose to inhale the sweet, subtle perfume.

"He was a good man, Lando," Kit observed. He'd watched his lover from a distance at first, finding himself in the delicate position of wanting to pay his respects to a deceased beloved uncle, yet also tupping said uncle's paramour. But now, he drew close.

"The best," Lando agreed. "You have many of his finer qualities."

"He would have approved of me finding love again," Lando continued. "He hated being alone himself; he would not have wished it on me." Stooping, he uprooted a weed from the carpet of grass and daisies at their feet. "I think he would have liked that it was with you."

"Do you?"

"Very much." Lando gave him a watery smile and ran his fingers lightly along the cold slate. "My love once rested with him under this chilled grey stone. There was a time—quite a long time, actually—when I wanted to lie down under it, too, next to my soldier, my hero, my very good friend."

He gave the stone a gentle pat before stepping back. "But not now."

Now love stood at his shoulder. It rested a hand in the small of his back. It ran its strong fingers down his knotty thorns, finding beauty in his troublesome edges as well as in the bloom of his smile. His love smiled back at him, often and easily, with a smile that sometimes brought to mind the memory of another smile, one now lost forever, parted from him too soon.

"We should visit again," said Kit as they turned to go. "Don't you think? We could bring my sister Anne."

"And Sir Richard," added Lando mischievously. "When they are married."

"I'll wager we won't have long to wait."

"The Angel estate will have heirs in no time. And, talking of heirs, it's time you were introduced to the Rossingley ones."

"You want me to meet your sons?"

Lando lightly shrugged. "Of course? Why wouldn't I? They are due home from Eton four days from now."

"Oh. Will they…will they know what you mean to me, and I to you?"

Lando regarded him carefully, cataloguing all of Kit's

attributes. Ascertaining they were alone, Lando leaned in for a kiss.

"No one knows what you mean to me, Kit. Including yourself. But yes, they will. I think it will be hard to conceal it." He gave a naughty little smile, his eyes sparkling. "You are a better lover than an actor."

"And I'm becoming a better landowner than a thief. With your help."

They turned to go, Lando taking a last lingering look at the headstone.

"Thank you," he whispered to his lost love. "For this precious gift. For giving me another portion of joy. For giving me him."

Acknowledgements

I'd like to thank my publisher, NineStar Press, and above all, my editor, Elizabetta, for her endless patience and encouragement.

About the Author

Fearne Hill is a Lambda Literary finalist. She lives deep in the southern British countryside, a stone's throw away from the private country estate providing her inspiration for Rossingley.

When she is not writing queer romantic fiction, Fearne works as an anaesthesiologist.

Email
fearne.hill@fearnehill.com

Facebook
www.facebook.com/fearne.hill.50

Facebook Group Fearne Hill's House
www.facebook.com/groups/1172459269938382

Twitter
@FearneHill

Instagram
www.instagram.com/fearnehill_author

Other NineStar books by this author

The Last of the Moussakas

Coming Soon from Fearne Hill

To Defend a Damaged Duke

Regency Rossingley, Book Two

"It's high time you married."

Benedict Fitzsimmons, the fourteenth Duke of Ashington, regarded his ebullient youngest brother — by five years — over the edge of *The Times*. "Should this betrothal occur before I reach the end of this excellent prediction for Saturday's race at Epsom? Am I permitted to digest my poached kippers first?"

"Oh, all right. I suppose you may." Francis grinned. "But eat up and eat well. I have a dreadful suspicion marriage to a lady of breeding will require courage and fortitude."

"So do I," Benedict agreed drily, adding his lack of both those attributes to his ever-expanding list of reasons never to marry. One of which he kept private, being more pertinent than the rest. He turned a page. "If you don't mind, I'll stick to my four-legged thoroughbreds. At the very least, they will never expect me to endure a week in the country with their parents."

"It's not me that wants you wed," said Francis. "It's Isabella. She has this crazy notion that if you marry, her father will look more favourably on allowing her to be betrothed to me."

Benedict frowned. "I don't follow."

Miss Isabella Knightley and her swooping, dizzy mind were two handfuls of trouble by anyone's standards. Frankly, if Benedict were her father, he'd have offloaded her onto the nearest suitable bachelor—such as Francis, the youngest brother of a wealthy duke—as soon as she came of age. Why Sir Henry insisted her older sisters were suitably wed first, holding off until an earl or higher-ranking noble offered his hand, was unfathomable. Mind you, not the cleverest of chaps, Benedict found much unfathomable these days.

"Nor do I." Francis sounded glum. "And I'm tired of all this waiting." Though he was usually even-tempered, his mouth formed a petulant moue. "Perhaps we could elope? Not to beat about the bush, but old Sir Henry seems to have forgotten that young men in love have certain...urges."

"Eloping won't endear you to him," rebuked Benedict mildly. "Many uncertainties prevail in this life—as this newspaper insists on reminding me—but I can assure you that isn't one of them. And the less I hear about your urges at the breakfast table, the better my digestion."

Francis heaved an enormous sigh, flopping back in his seat. "Don't you ever feel like this, Benedict? As if the...the world is conspiring against you? It's not as if I don't have money. I'm not a gambler, a drunkard, or a rake. And she's the only woman I'll ever love! Whom I've *ever* loved."

The last part came out as a wail of despair, and Benedict threw his brother a commiserative look. *Love.* Never mind the emotion behind it; even the pitiful word had no place at the duke's breakfast table. Not love of the romantic sort with its hooks in his brother, anyhow. Love *for* his brother, yes, Benedict had oodles of that. For Isabella too. Almost rivalling the love lavished on his eighteen thoroughbreds.

"It's quite clear he's keeping you in reserve," Benedict declared as if he knew the first thing about fatherhood, daughters, or, indeed, love. "Isabella might be your childhood sweetheart, but she's a diamond of the first water, and Sir Henry is determined to find the best possible match. Trust me, if Isabella showed the slightest inclination to be falling for undesirable competition, I'd wager he'd accept your offer at the drop of a hat. As things stand, he doesn't need to."

"She doesn't want an undesirable or even a well-mannered, blameless earl! She wants *me*!"

A familiar hopeless tone re-entered his voice. From the library next door, the longcase clock chimed a solemn half hour. Pushing aside his breakfast, Benedict rose to his feet.

"The stables call," he announced. "Care to join me?"

His brother shook his head. "Can't, I'm afraid. I'm meeting some chums later. We're boxing at Jack's, then heading out to that new club on the corner of St James. Tuffy Bannister says its already quite the place to be seen. Even Lyndon's been spotted there, once or twice, losing at piquet. Squire's is the name. Have you heard speak of it?"

Squire's. Benedict frowned. That name had cropped up somewhere else recently. Ah, yes. Plastered in bold lettering above a new betting stand at Newmarket.

"Same chap also owns a brothel or two," added Francis, "according to Tuffy."

Another topic Benedict preferred to avoid at the breakfast table. "Sounds as if this Squire has his snoot in a few businesses.

No wonder his club's thriving if Lyndon's a member." He grimaced. "His coffers are being filled with Ashington money."

"I'm surprised Lyndon has any left to squander."

On that, Benedict agreed. Lord Lyndon Fitzsimmons was a thorn in anyone's side, but the side he needled the most, by far, belonged to his twin brother (by three minutes), Benedict. The duke didn't often wish his pugnacious father back from the grave, but after having all but disinherited Benedict's younger twin, their father had fallen down in a dead heap a day later instead of facing Lyndon's wrath. Which was damned inconsiderate. Reluctantly inheriting the august title nine months ago, Benedict had also inherited the role of human punchbag; overnight, Lyndon had transferred his ire from his father to his brother.

"Funds miraculously appear from somewhere," observed Francis. "We must pray he's not up to something smoky. The 1500 pounds you generously entrust him with per annum doesn't extend that far."

"No." Benedict frowned again. He'd been doing that a lot since taking up his title, ensuring his reputation as serious, aloof, and reserved remained as intact as ever. A useful, if somewhat lonely, shield for hiding his intellectual inadequacies, Francis and his delightful amour were amongst the very few able to penetrate it.

"You should join us," Francis suggested, perhaps witnessing the frown more frequently than he'd like. In a manner which would horrify the very proper Sir Henry Knightley, he crammed a triangle of toast into his mouth, then carried on, spraying crumbs across the table. "At Squire's. Give yourself an afternoon off from all of this."

He indicated the ever-increasing pile of correspondence that inheriting a large dukedom entailed. It cast a long shadow over the breakfast table. Knowing one would someday become the duke was a different beast from taking up the title when one least expected it. Before the old duke's sudden demise, Ashington menfolk had prided themselves on longevity; Benedict had hoped to tread a path of wilful obscurity for at least another decade.

"All of this," he remarked, "Won't miraculously have disappeared on my return." Some mornings Benedict swore it would swallow him whole; a hundred years from now they'd find his body entombed within a pyramid of damned confusing foolscap. "And anyhow, I don't gamble."

"So what? Nor do half the folk in there. Even Rossingley is a member; he doesn't gamble either. Plenty of your White's crowd have joined. Decent scran, excellent port, and uncivilised conversation. Comfortable armchairs, too — and warm fires."

Benedict smiled indulgently, turning to where a footmen held his coat for him. "Comfortable armchairs? You sound older than I."

"I'm simply trying to entice you out of the house once in a while. How will you ever marry if you don't?"

"I'm leaving now! Look! Heading straight through the front door!"

Francis threw a hand up dismissively. "Only to visit the bloody stables!"

*

Benedict was rather fond of the bloody stables. In fact, as he pulled up in his black-liveried phaeton, he'd go so far as to boast (to no one except himself, being far from a boastful sort) that they were the finest in all of London. Eighteen thoroughbreds raced under his ducal colours, the most successful of whom poked his long snowy muzzle over the door of his capacious stall to see what all the fuss was about. Though retired now, after an undefeated career including six St Leger wins, Nimbus's successes continued unabated; last year alone, he'd made Benedict 18 000 pounds from stud fees.

Benedict petted him awhile, largely ignored as the daily routines of the stables clattered on around him. Now and then, he pitched in and helped; more than once, he'd been caught in rolled-up sleeves, shovelling shit. No one ever asked him difficult questions while he was shovelling shit. Some wealthy stud owners turned their visits into a spectacle, parading themselves around, demanding attention. Benedict visited so often that if he behaved in such a fashion there would be no time left for his grooms to attend to anything else. Dressed in the Ashington silks, he'd take his dear Nimbus out for a canter later. Remind him of the good old days.

With a final kiss, a whispered reassurance that he was still Benedict's favourite sugar plum fairy, and an instruction to the stable boy to saddle Nimbus up, Benedict moved on to the next stall. Ten wooden boxes lined this side of the sandy courtyard with another ten facing, some doors hanging open, others closed. Casting his gaze around the peaceable, orderly scene, Benedict breathed in the sour tang of manure mixed with perspiration, festering away under the dusty, sweet scent of hay. Rich, dense smells, combined with the earthy musk of a recent rainfall, wrapped around him like freedom itself.

A sturdy, solitary oak rose from the middle of the yard, sheltering a water pump around which one of Benedict's newer acquisitions, Ganymede, was being slowly walked, his head hanging low. He'd purchased the thoroughbred at Tattersall's six months earlier from a baronet unable to meet his debts. He'd come a respectable second at Newmarket last month, ahead of a fine field, so the groom's troubled countenance perturbed him.

"He's sluggish today, Your Grace." Arthur ran his expert hand down the horse's sleek mahogany withers. "Like he's eaten something that's disagreed with him."

Benedict pressed two fingertips under the animal's jaw, feeling the strong pulse. "Is he excessively warm?"

The groom shook his head. "Nah. He's had a couple of runny shits, but it's back to normal now." He jerked his chin. "Her ladyship over there up the corner was similar last week. After she lost at Heath."

Benedict turned to see an unfamiliar stable boy brushing down Cleopatra, his demanding chestnut mare. Surprisingly, for such a temperamental beast, she was indulging him.

"New lad," explained the groom. "Knows what he's doin'." With a glance up at the leaden sky, he added, "Thought she was just sulking. But mebbe it's the changeable weather."

"Perhaps." Benedict fondled the soft crest between Ganymede's flattened ears. Possibly the skin felt a little hotter than usual. "Keep me abreast of matters."

The horse softly pawed the ground. From a liquid brown eye, Benedict's own image reflected back at him. Tall, dark, forbidding. Diffident. But nothing seemed amiss. "Check over his teeth and hooves and encourage him to drink plenty. He's in the four thirty at Epsom a week Wednesday. Tipped to place."

With yet another niggling anxiety to add to his roster, Benedict walked on alone. Francis accompanied him occasionally. Though a decent horseman and kind master, when his brother swung his foot into the stirrups, it was merely for the purpose of suitable transport from *A* to *B*. Whereas Benedict would ride all day long in circles, just for the hell of it. His thoroughbreds were his best friends, his equals, a means of escape. He rode swiftly, respecting every inch of the muscle, raw power, and sweat between his thighs. With the heart and dedication of a carefree lover.

And God knew those were in very short supply.

CONNECT WITH NINESTAR PRESS

WEBSITE: NINESTARPRESS.COM

FACEBOOK: NINESTARPRESS

X: @NINESTARPRESS

INSTAGRAM: NINESTARPRESS

BLUESKY: NINESTARPRESS

THREADS: @NINESTARPRESS